MW00815590

# THE CAREFUL, QUIET, INVISIBLE

# SERIES

## ISOBELLA JADE

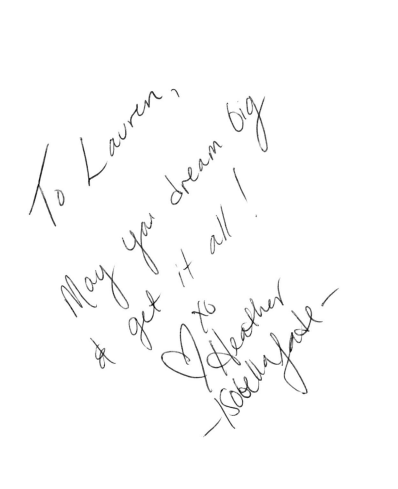

To Lauren,

May you dream big
& get it all!

xo
♡ Heather
— Isabella Jade —

ALSO BY ISOBELLA JADE


ALMOST 5'4"

MODEL LIFE

SHORT STUFF: ON THE JOB WITH AN X-SMALL MODEL

GAMINE PRESS
NEW YORK

Copyright © 2012 by Isobella Jade

All rights reserved.

The characters and events in this book are a work of fiction.
Any similarity or resemblance to real persons,
living or dead, is coincidental and not intended by the author.

ISBN: 978-0-9850-9750-9
eBook ISBN: 978-0-9850-9753-0

Cover photograph by Robert Milazzo
Cover title graphic by Jazmin Ruotolo

FOR MY MOTHER AND SISTER

# Careful

## ISOBELLA JADE

GAMINE PRESS
NEW YORK

## A MOMENT CAN CHANGE EVERYTHING

It hardly matters now because I'll never get to have him, but if he asked me in person, I would have held onto the conversation word by word. But maybe if he had asked me in person it wouldn't have gone so well anyway. I would have probably snorted like I always do and embarrassed myself.

If he asked in writing, on loose-leaf paper, I would have saved it and folded it into a small square and probably kept it safe in my wallet forever.

But no one takes the time to write a note by hand anymore.

Since he asked me in a text message, the best I could do was never ever delete it.

Thinking about that, I wonder how things could stay memorable when in just a moment's slip of the thumb the happiness found in reading someone's words could be deleted by mistake. I always saved his text messages on my phone. It's crazy to think about how much time I spent analyzing the meaning in each word he sent. I'd lie in bed at night, under the sheets, clutching my phone, while reading his text messages over and over, and soon an hour would have passed.

That's what Phoenix Clemens did to me.

I thought about him a lot then, and I still do now.

It was 3:47 p.m. on a Friday when he texted me asking if I wanted to go to prom with him.

Phoenix must have been at Dick's Sporting Goods when he sent me the text message, because in the hallway after school he had told me he was about to go shopping for new lacrosse equipment and asked me if I wanted to come along. I couldn't though. I had told the girls I would meet them for prom dress shopping and didn't want to skip out on them, so I had looked forward to seeing Phoenix on Monday at lunch instead.

He was always the highlight of my day.

He still is.

Because of my track practice commitments, I had only caught a couple of Phoenix's lacrosse games, but when I did, those small hugs he gave me after his game clung to me. I could smell him on my coat for days.

Our quick chats in the hallway by our lockers, our flirty smiles at lunch—they all mesh together now like a silent movie in my memories.

His hand would sometimes brush against mine as we walked down the halls together, and the feeling of even this small touch between us would stay with me throughout the day. He had hugged me hello and goodbye many times during the past year, as friends do, but lately our friendship was becoming something more. Our casual hugs were becoming a little more intimate as my arms went around his torso and as his hands came around me, each time squeezing me a little closer than before. Maybe that was just in my imagination, though.

He was a slow mover, just like I was.

The week before my life changed, he had kissed me straight on the lips. We were in the middle of our ritual goodbyes, and instead of kissing me on the same spot on my cheek where he always did, this time his lips came to mine, with purpose. It was so quick I almost missed it, and it could have been considered just a peck, but his lips had met mine.

I've held onto these little moments that feel huge in my heart now. They are all I have left because he will never look at me again. The last time he did look at me was on that Friday I'll never forget.

Sometimes now I wonder what would or wouldn't have happened if I had told the girls that I couldn't meet up with them for prom dress shopping and had gone with Phoenix instead.

Maybe my life would have been different.

On that Friday I got what I wanted, but only for a short time.

I was in the dressing room at The Palace boutique when I received Phoenix's text message.

Layers of my clothing and sneakers were sprawled on the floor beneath me, while I slipped on the white gown and pulled my curly auburn hair up into a ponytail.

The dressing-room mirrors made my body look more board-shaped than usual, but the strapless padded bra I grabbed from the rack gave me a lot more shape up there. Looking at my reflection, I felt a type of elegance and beauty I hadn't known before.

White could have implied bride, but the beaded one-shoulder strap sold me. I was admiring myself in the mirror and the line of silver daisies that ran across the long white gown while testing out how well I would be able to move and dance in it, when my phone buzzed.

Phoenix's name blinked on the screen, and my heart raced.

Suddenly, this dress shopping excursion with the girls had a lot more purpose. After reading his text message I stared at my reflection again, debating if I liked what I saw.

My shoulders looked huge, especially when I turned to the side. I was skeptical if the white gown really flattered me and whether the strapless padded bra was overdoing it, or if I was prettier with something extra and paying the fifty bucks might be worth it.

My arms were tingling, and my stomach was fluttering and jittery, while I imagined Phoenix in his tux. With his rebellious hair that was always a little out of place and the sexy scar by his eyebrow greeting me at my front door, I would kiss his cheek. His beautiful, dark, almond-shaped eyes, surrounded by eyelashes that are even longer than mine, would be staring at me and my gown with a boiling wonder. He would probably be holding a beautiful white rose corsage that he would fasten on my wrist.

His text message made me feel hopeful for everything else I wanted at that moment. There were so many things I wanted to do, accomplish, see, and be, and it hurts now to think about what could have been.

After some more scrutinizing, I took off the strapless padded bra, settling on my natural self.

I waited a few more seconds before replying back, then sent, *Yeah, it will be fun to go together!* and put my phone on the dressing-room bench.

I would have stared at Phoenix's text for a few moments longer, and now I wish I had, but I heard Zara's sassy voice calling my name, then her fist banging on my dressing-room door, her fingernails tapping in rhythm with her eagerness.

When I opened the dressing-room door, Zara was in a gorgeous pink, beaded gown. She spun around, showing off every detail of the dress; it had thin straps that crossed in the back, and the front had a very low V-cut neckline. I could never have pulled it off, but she had the cleavage for it. She always looked fabulous. The pink silk hugged her body, and the sparkling trails of little beads made her skin glow. Her shiny, long, blond hair fell gracefully against her shoulders and down toward her chest.

Together we spun around in front of the massive full-length mirror, admiring the way our dresses twirled. I pulled my hair out of the ponytail and let it dangle down my back, looking over my shoulder at the pretty way my curly auburn hair and the white dress complemented each other.

As we twirled around, Zara kept saying how toned my arms looked and how thin a waist I had. She also admired the beaded one-shoulder strap and the line of silver daisies. I remember Zara pointing to her chest and worrying if she was showing too much. To let her know that it was nothing to worry about, I grabbed my chest with both hands, trying to push up my small breasts like the strapless padded bra would have done, and said that at least she had something.

It was the first time in my life I had ever grabbed my chest like that, but my body was springing and pulsating like never before. Ripples of warmth surged under my skin, giving me a frisky sensation, tickling at my insides and telling me that I was full of tomorrows.

Eva and Jett were still putting on their dresses, and Zara and I continued to twirl around and admire ourselves in front of the full-length mirror.

Zara was practicing her smile, and I tried to stick out my chest and behind at the same time to create more obvious curves, but I ended up just looking ridiculous.

Then we heard the creak of Eva's dressing-room door opening slowly, and we turned quickly toward her. Over the years Eva had been self-conscious about the chub coming over her jeans, or what happened to her stomach when she sat down. She looked discouraged as the door fully opened, and we could read on Eva's face that she was not totally confident in the dress or how she looked wearing it. Her pretty brown eyes went down toward her stomach.

I thought the dark purple dress against her golden complexion and dark hair looked stunning. And to ease her mind, Zara, who knew fashion, trends, style, and fit better than any of us and always knew the right things to say, explained to Eva that the way the fabric gathered on the side of the dress didn't make her look any bigger; in fact, it gave her a really hot hourglass shape.

Still Eva's facial expression showed us that she wasn't convinced. I told Eva that I wished I had her curves and bumped my hip against hers, trying to get her to smile.

Eva's eyes went down my body; she said something about wishing she had my flat stomach.

It was hard to make her smile sometimes.

We all almost jumped out of our skin when Jett's dressing-room door slammed victoriously against the wall and got our attention. Jett was always putting out a fire or creating one. Her dark black hair whipped back and forth as she pranced out to greet us in her gown.

She was really getting into it, as she strutted toward the full-length mirror and, with full hip action, joined us. When she walked, she always had this hypnotic grace about her. It was hard to look away from her and her flawless, glowing skin. She would probably be a famous supermodel one day, breaking the mold and carving a path for Japanese models all over the world.

The sleek, sequined black dress was a winner. It was as if she was stepping out of a page of Vogue, and I had no doubt she'd be in that magazine one day.

Like me, she didn't have big breasts, but she didn't care—extra padding was the norm for her. She'd become accustomed to stylists molding her during her photo shoots. It was her blemish-free face that mattered to her more.

Willow Ridge isn't a big metropolis like New York City; it's just about twenty minutes outside of Syracuse, New York. Still, I bet that just about every single person in Central New York has seen Jett's face at one time or another. She'd been in the local grocery chain commercials, ads for spas and jewelry stores, and billboards advertising the shopping mall. This past fall she missed school for a beauty editorial photo shoot in New York City with *Teen Vogue*.

As we all laughed at Jett's strut and whipping hair, we stood together, looking at our reflections in the mirror. We didn't care who else was around, watching us or giving us weird looks. We were making different poses, arching our backs, lifting our chins, giving the mirror some attitude, putting our hands on our hips, and leaning against each other. We were laughing like hyenas; our laughter was taking over the store. Even Eva was getting into it.

At that moment I thought about how in a little over a year our lives would really begin and how quickly freshman, sophomore, and now our junior year of high school were flying by.

I wanted to stay young forever in that moment. I wanted to stop time, rewind it, and live it again. I still do.

It crossed my mind that there was a chance we would grow apart when graduation came, while we took on adulthood, but I hoped that no matter where our lives took us we would always be friends.

We were already sold on the dresses; I decided on the white gown but said to hell with the strapless padded bra. While the girls played with their hair, imagining how it should look on prom night, the happiness I felt made me think of Phoenix, and I went to grab my phone from the dressing-room bench.

When I came back out, their eyes hovered around my phone as they read the text message Phoenix had sent me. I'll never forget the sounds of their happiness for me, as their voices became more and more excited. Then Zara reached for my phone, saying how we needed to take a photo together in our dresses, and she clicked the photo icon.

So, we huddled around Zara, her arm stretched out holding my phone, and when the phone clicked it inspired more photos. I can still hear their voices, of each of them wanting to take a photo of us with their phones.

We might not have been the skinniest, prettiest, or richest chicks in Willow Ridge, but Zara was right: "Feeling good is looking good." It was a moment to never forget.

With each of our gorgeous gowns wrapped carefully in plastic trailing behind us, whipping in the wind, we headed for our cars.

It was typical for Central New York to be brutally cold in February, but the cold wasn't on my mind as I headed for my car. I was happy and thinking about how friendship was what mattered and what great friends I had.

Even though it was cold and windy with a little snow on the ground, the sunset was beaming on my red car, making it glisten like new. Ahead of me Jett and Eva were battling the wind as they headed toward Jett's car, and Zara was already hanging her dress neatly on the hook on the backseat door of her car.

I dug for my keys in my purse and found them, but while I dug around I couldn't feel my phone.

You know how people say life can change if you take a right turn or a left—like what would have happened if you caught the train instead of missing it, or if you arrived at your destination sooner rather than later—well, that wasn't on my mind when I asked the girls to wait up because I forgot my phone.

I ran back into the boutique, rushed toward the dressing room door and snatched my phone off the bench—but not before seeing what else was sitting on the bench. There was that strapless padded bra, and the chance to have a fully proportioned silhouette. The minutes slipped away as my coat, sweater and T-shirt flopped to the floor again and I put on the strapless padded bra and admired the sensual and feminine shape that it created again. Then, add to those minutes the time it took to wait in line and buy that strapless padded bra and fork out that extra fifty bucks. Looking back now, those minutes maybe would have changed things. The girls waited in their cars for me, and I can still see Jett's, Eva's, and Zara's smiles, as we all pulled out of the parking lot, honking our horns at each other goodbye.

Some snow flurries had started, but I had grown up around snow and driven in it before and wasn't worried as I headed toward Vine Street.

I was planning to get new running shoes with my father that weekend, Eva had to help her mother at the bakery, Zara was looking forward to trying out her new webcam and making some new fashion tip videos for her blog, and Jett had a modeling casting for a local jewelry designer that she really wanted to book. Sunday we usually never saw each other because we spent it sleeping in past noon or lately studying for the SAT, but we were all going to meet at Lilly's Café for breakfast that Monday morning, like usual.

And I'd see Phoenix at lunch, like usual…

After leaving the dress boutique I remember driving toward home, glancing toward the backseat at my prom dress and the amazing strapless padded bra, and feeling that something was in the air, something good was going to come of us. We would all become more than what this small town offered, and no matter where life took us we'd always be friends.

What I didn't know was…that day at the dress boutique would be the last memory of us all together. It would all be over in just a few minutes.

A few miles down the road, my track teammate Heidi Mazza was gliding down Vine Street in her white SUV. Heidi was the top 100-meter hurdler on our team and, like me, she was always featured in the newspaper. She had lucked out big-time. She could have easily gone down a wrong path in life, but something was on her side. Something saved her from destruction. Heidi's mother had abandoned her; she spent time in foster care in elementary school and wasn't happy about it. It was obvious to all of us that she was an angry, short-tempered girl who got a thrill out of pushing, kicking, and being argumentative with other students. Some students let her win; others fought back until they regretted it, with swells on the back of their legs or a handful less hair on their head. Heidi's guardian's names were always different than her own until fourth grade, when she was adopted by a wealthy family, the Mazzas. They owned one of the leading chiropractor offices in Central New York.

Basically, I think, they had enough money to straighten her out—or at least distract her mean streak with new things and horse lessons until freshman year, when she found the perfect stress relief for her inner anger by putting it toward competition and running the 100-meter hurdles—she really got your attention when she flew over those ten hurdles with wicked speed, her dark blond hair in a ponytail, bobbing up and down, and her signature perfectly straight bangs just above her eyebrows that always went right back in place after her race. It was impressive how she never knocked down a hurdle when she was competing. The whole track team knew Heidi was destined for big things.

The Mazzas had adopted two other girls, but they were more than ten years older than Heidi and were in college or busy with their careers when Heidi joined the family, so she really got the princess treatment.

Right after the Mazzas adopted her, we all recognized the change in Heidi when she brought cupcakes in on her birthday, not just for her homeroom class but for the whole fourth grade. Pink frosting, with your choice of vanilla or chocolate inside.

Over the following years, she came off a bit stuck-up, but maybe it was because she had survived the doubt of teachers and the Department of Social Services and had risen beyond expectations.

With my teammates, I had cheered for Heidi many times while she raced, and usually won, in the 100-meter hurdles. And she had yelled, "Come on Estella!" while I ran the 400 dash—the team supported one another. Aside from seeing each other at practice and congratulating each other on track meet days, Heidi wasn't someone I spent a lot of time with off the track, although of course we knew each other's social circles. This year we had the same honors English literature class, but I never thought our worlds would collide like they did on Vine Street that Friday.

Vine Street was the main drag through town. It wasn't a particularly dangerous street, and although it had started to snow a little more heavily and the street was getting slippery, Heidi felt safe driving a little above the speed limit. She pushed on the accelerator, and went a little faster down the road.

As Heidi glided down Vine Street, her phone buzzed three times.

Her right hand let go of the steering wheel as she reached for her handbag on the passenger seat. Her hand went inside the bag, scrabbling for her phone.

She looked at the text message; it was from her boyfriend, Jackson.

Heidi prided herself on her skill of not having to look at her phone when she was texting; she only needed to look down at it for a second to make sure she used the right buttons. She was about to hit send when our lives collided. She pounded on the brakes of her SUV as she flew through a red light and into the intersection—into the side of my car.

If only I hadn't forgotten my phone in the dressing room at The Palace boutique and then bought that stupid strapless padded bra after the girls and I were prom dress shopping. I would have been through the intersection minutes before; I wouldn't have been there to be struck by Heidi's SUV.

Tom Petty's "Free Fallin'" had just come on the radio. I hadn't heard the song in a really long time and I was singing to it. I had just turned the volume up, but the chorus never came.

I'm glad the crash happened fast; I didn't even feel it. I didn't even hear the sound of the metal crunching.

Heidi's jaw was bruised badly and she was bleeding all over her sweater. She was coming from the mall, and when her car hit mine shopping bags from her backseat thrust forward, bursting a confetti of mascara, lip gloss, shirts, and shoes. She was conscious but the whiplash was so intense and she was in too much pain to move.

Then there was my car. Or what was left of it.

The silver ladybug charm that always hung from my rearview mirror, where it would spin round and round, was gone. My white gown and the strapless padded bra had gotten disheveled among my laptop, notebooks, and track bag.

The center of my car looked as if someone had taken a piece of red construction paper and scrunched it in their hand. My door had been pushed inward very deeply; it created a jagged cave from the outside with all its guts hanging out, and I was behind the caved hollow. The force of Heidi's SUV slamming into my door had crushed my chest, broken my shoulder and arm, and shattered my collarbone. My head and my face looked like a rotted pumpkin with red spiraling hair.

My text message to Phoenix wouldn't matter now. It was too late. Even though I sent him a "yes" an hour before, we wouldn't be going to prom. There wasn't even a chance that I could be saved. It was February 12th, and I was dead.

# Careful

## BECAUSE YOU CAN'T REWIND TIME

It's hard to accept *that's life*, but it is. You can receive a text message that warms your heart at 3:47 p.m. while trying on a prom dress with your best friends, and be dead an hour later. That's the precious unexpected part of life that I hate.

My time as a runner and a visible human being who could feel things—like the burn in my calves and the dryness in my throat as I pushed my body a little more toward the finish of my race—was over. But it didn't take long to realize what had happened and discover that I was not alive any longer.

My soul escaped my body quickly after the crash. I zapped up and joined a fresh, cool breeze. I stayed there whirling around, drifting in a heavenly dream,  relaxing in the wholesomeness and enjoying the ride, just letting it take me wherever—but the gentle feeling didn't last.

Just as I was feeling wispy and serene up there, a harsh wind propelled me back to earth and jolted me out of my tranquility. Everything sizzled around me. The sky started to spit out pellets of sleet as a burning fevered through me. Then I heard the wail of the sirens, saw bright red lights flashing, and heard frantic shouts coming from men in yellow-and-black uniforms. A shuffle of paramedics hurried to my car.

There was a loud cranking and clattering as the door of my car was seared off to reveal my lifeless body lying in the driver's seat. I wish it turned out to be a terrible dream and I'd wake up, but it wasn't. When I reached for the arm of a policeman, he only considered me another chill in the air. When I spoke, nothing but dead silence came out of me. I could only watch as time betrayed me and left me throbbing hopelessly for answers, enduring the anticipation of not knowing why my body was being placed in a body bag…on a gurney.

I was dizzy with panic, whisking around my car, searching desperately for a reason. I wanted to go back to the way it was; I wanted this not to be real. Anxiety and the fear of the truth ran through me as the air got heavy and colder. I reached for my arms but couldn't feel them or my legs. My neck, my stomach, my chest — they weren't mine anymore.

I didn't know what was left of me. I wasn't even the shape of a human being anymore. I was shapeless, useless, not even a creature. Now I was just another chill in the air.

I found myself unable to decide where I should go next. I could feel a pull of light calling my name, encouraging me to follow it. But I wasn't done with earth and I wasn't ready to say goodbye to my friends and family. My time here wasn't over, it couldn't be, and I needed to see my mother.

ᕫ

Like always she smelled of rosemary. I could sense only emptiness around her, a dark hole that seemed to swallow her — she already knew.

Amazingly my purse, wallet, and, yes, my phone were still intact after the collision. The police found my purse down in the footrest, and that made it easy for them to track down my parents, since their numbers were in my phone. Also on a little piece of paper in my wallet there was a list of emergency phone numbers that, of course, included Mom and Dad.

My father was still at work when his cell phone rang. It was the police chief asking if he was my father; obviously he was.

My mother had just gotten home from a long day of teaching when her cell phone rang. It was my father telling her, "There was an accident with Estella," and that he'd be home immediately.

The police chief had waited to call my parents until the medical examiner was finished collecting any evidence at the scene and after my body was hauled off.

Over the phone my mother and father told the police chief and the medical examiner's office what I looked like, what clothes I might have been wearing, the color of my hair, and the "e" charm necklace I always wore.

I watched the shock build. It didn't seem real to them that their daughter had died. It was so unbelievable that their minds hadn't allowed them to feel the truth. At first they were just like two reporters trying to get the facts of how it happened. When? Where? How? My father wrote every single thing the police chief had told him about the crash on a notepad, and asked over and over for more details. Could anything else be shared? Was I wearing a seatbelt? How was my body found? How was I positioned in the driver's seat? Were my eyes opened or closed?

The police chief had been there and had seen my battered face, but he didn't want to share too many of the gruesome details with my parents. He did the best he could to explain the circumstances without scaring them.

Dental records and a fingerprint were needed to help identify me because my face wasn't in great shape. Also the police chief said it would be best if an immediate family member would come to the morgue as soon as possible.

There really was no question that it was me, but my parents clung to the hope it wasn't. It all added up, though. It was the description of my car, my track bag, my running shoes, my "e" charm necklace around my neck, and my curly auburn hair.

My parents went to the morgue to see for themselves. Well, actually, my mother waited in the car, and my father went in to see me after my mother said nervously, "James, you go."

I didn't like the heartbroken look on my father's face while he nodded his head that, yes, it was his daughter, his dead daughter.

"She doesn't look like our little girl anymore. But it's her," my father said when he got back in the car, shaking his head in disbelief from seeing my disfigured face and body. His stern glance at my mother said everything she needed to know. Gently he reached for my mother's hand to soothe her, but she became stiff and unexpressive. They didn't say a word in the car. My father thought about how he would carefully share with her that it was going to be difficult to have an open casket.

The medical examiner's office would call tomorrow with the full autopsy. The stress of waiting congested the air around my parents as I followed them back inside our house.

They were now standing at opposite ends of the living room, looking lost in our own home. Slowly I went toward my mother. She was still in her work clothes, standing there frozen with her arms folded, gazing out the window directly into the setting sun. Her hair looked redder when the sun hit it, and I thought she looked beautiful squinting her eyes against its glare. She chewed on her fingernails like she always did when she was nervous, and she didn't notice when I reached out to hug her.

She was aching, deeply worried that I had been in extreme pain before I died. Thinking of what the police chief shared haunted her. The image of Heidi's massive SUV crushing me wouldn't leave her mind. Thoughts of my frightened green eyes, my pale face now red with blood, my curly hair flung back in shock, my body now crushed filled her mind. While anticipating the autopsy results tomorrow, her imagination went wild thinking about how bad it had been for me.

At first the local news station didn't release my name, just the description of a sixteen-year-old girl with curly auburn hair, driving a red vehicle struck by an SUV, but it was enough to make my friends wonder if it was me. It made me sad when Zara, Eva, and Jett each texted my phone, asking if I was okay. But of course they never got a reply.

I wondered if Phoenix knew.

I wished I could have had one last conversation with him, one last hug and maybe even one last little kiss and said goodbye to him, instead of being pulled into this new state of being that made me feel distant from everything I had known.

The weekend would only consist of traumatizing grief. That first evening our home started to feel unfamiliar, and each room felt strangely colder as the night wore on. Within the quiet house there were whispers between my parents of how unfair life was and how it wasn't right that bad things happened to good people; how they wished they were the ones who had died.

My father spent the evening on the couch in front of the fireplace mantel, where a shrine of my track medals and my trophies was always displayed. He called my older brother, Evan, a sophomore at Le Moyne College, and told him to come home. Then he spent the next hours calling our close relatives to tell them what had happened before more news broke with my name and the horrifying details.

This weekend my father and I had originally planned to shop for a new pair of training shoes. My pink and white ones were pretty worn out. Also before each track season I got a new pair of racing flats; I always thought of it as a new beginning. Wearing new shoes inspired me to set new goals for the season. I wouldn't be getting those shoes now, I guess.

He seemed to forget about shopping for my running shoes and what we were supposed to do that weekend, but he was thinking about the last time he saw me run. This coming outdoor track season was going to be the big one; the one in which college coaches would be eyeing me or were supposed to be. My father's eyes stared at the track trophies that represented all I had accomplished—and the end of it. There would be no other races for me to run or train for, and there wasn't a future to come. He could only look back. The thought was killing him.

I wanted to say, "It will be okay, Daddy," because it was all I could think to say as the night dragged on. I was just pretending, though, because it wasn't okay that my life had been cut short.

I think my mother pretended I was staying out later than I should have that night, because she kept looking toward the door, waiting up for me to walk through it. But I wasn't going to be coming home, kicking off my sneakers and bag and asking what was for dinner.

I was telling her all night, "I'm not going to open that door. I'm already home, I'm right here with you already."

Finally, around three a.m., she went upstairs and tried to get some sleep.

It was hard to watch the optimism that always radiated from my mother's face be yanked out of its socket. And the way my father's face suddenly went numb and his usual high-strung energy became sluggish, like an old man. He wanted to cry, I know he did, but he knew he had to be strong in front of my mother. She started to shake and cry uncontrollably while lying in bed, unable to sleep. He wanted to be her rock, but she pushed away his soft rub to her shoulders. He didn't want her to feel more agony, so he'd take care of the difficult details in the next days; he'd gather his strength, push aside his own pain to plan my funeral. I really don't know how he did it, but I was proud of him.

In the morning I watched my mother clutch her cell phone and quickly answer it on the first ring. Then the medical examiner consoled her by sharing that I had died instantly. Actually, I remember now gasping and losing my breath for a split second, as if the wind was being knocked out of me from being punched in the chest. I felt a rush of heat on my face and then died instantly.

That evening a follow-up news segment, which included my name, aired. My mother and father were interviewed, and they said heartfelt words about how much they loved me. Everyone could see unimaginable pain in their faces. The interview only made things worse and more real for my parents.

To really stab my heart, Heidi's mother and father were interviewed also. They were in disbelief that their daughter had totally caused the crash by looking at her cell phone for a split second while driving; they blamed the crash and my death on the dangerous intersection that everyone in Willow Ridge knew wasn't really that dangerous. Sure, their eyes were full of shock and remorse for my family's loss, but they were also dealing with their own type of loss, I suppose.

Over the weekend Heidi had a nervous breakdown, and her mental state was deteriorating. She had gotten two speeding tickets within the last eighteen months, in addition to a ticket for talking on her phone while driving. Now she threatened to kill herself with an overdose of aspirin or whatever else she could get her hands on. She had told her parents she didn't want to go back to Willow Ridge High School. She suddenly didn't care about her track hurdling success or racing anymore—she wanted to get out of Willow Ridge altogether.

Heidi's wish would be granted. Her parents were very concerned about her mental health, and their family dignity and the family chiropractor business were in mind. Heidi would be getting counseling at a psychiatric center in a nearby city and staying in seclusion for the first weeks of treatment. Her parents hadn't told any of this to the news network, but I saw it all happen. From my new perspective, I could now see things I didn't even want to see.

⌒

My mother created a long list of the things that I would never get to do. She repeated the long list over and over to my father, and soon I wanted to tell her to stop.

I couldn't help but think about what it would be like if someone else in my family had died in the collision instead of me, and I was almost glad I had died while I watched my father. If he had died, my world would have stopped. Losing him would have been like dying myself anyway, along with all my dreams.

Of course I had a terrific track coach and trainers over the years, who had influenced and shaped my craft on the track and been sources of encouragement, but it was my father who really guided and steered my running success the most. The trophies and ribbons on the living room mantel and the newspaper clippings with the results of races I had won over the years, some framed on the wall — they all had celebrated the hours, the training, the hard work, and we had never forgotten where it started.

Track wasn't just running around in circles to me, it was my religion; it was everything I woke up for.

Before my father's marketing company took off, back when we lived with less in the village of Willow Ridge and barely survived on my mother's teaching salary; fun was created with imagination and improvisation. The biggest treat when I was five was going to Zogg Field and learning from my father the basic techniques of how to crouch down and position my feet and hands before a sprint. He would say, "Ready. Set. GO!" And he'd time me as I ran around the old gravel track.

My father was a big smoker, but he promised to quit when my mother got pregnant with me. He gave up smoking completely the winter before I was born and soon took up running. He said he could feel the same type of burn in his throat and lungs that a cigarette gave him when he pushed himself to improve his endurance each time he ran.

I didn't even have a good pair of running shoes back then—we couldn't afford brand-new ones—but it didn't matter; sometimes we could find decent running shoes at thrift stores around town. Some were really busted, with worn-out rubber soles, ratty laces, and a bad smell inside, but they were still useable.

Wearing shoes with a professional running logo on them, even if it wasn't a brand-new pair, made me feel faster. Our block was almost 400 meters around, it felt like a very long way and a little scary to run around by myself as a five-year-old, so my father would run with me and time me as I sprinted around it, taking breaks. But soon I didn't need to take breaks anymore.

It became our Saturday morning routine, and during every run he'd share with me something new about running, racing, and training. Once he explained how improving one tenth of a second was still a big improvement for a sprinter.

When April 26th came around, and my sixth birthday, I got what I wanted most. It was astonishing unwrapping the beautiful, brand-new yellow running shoes with matching yellow laces—and for sugar on top, yellow and green running pants and a hoodie. It was perfect.

That following summer our stability emerged, we moved to a bigger house in a new development, and my father signed me up for the McClure Bowerman Youth Track & Field Summer Club, which I ran until I started high school. Throughout the summers we'd travel to other school districts and nearby cities to compete at regional youth track and field meets.

I remembered how disappointed I was when Coach Berlet thought I was going into ninth grade but I was really going into eighth grade. He wanted me to run for the varsity track team, and I was invited to attend a summer training practice at Willow Ridge High School, where I was going to train with all these older girls who I could still keep up with. But then Coach Berlet told me that he was sorry, I was actually too young and I had to wait a year. I was ready and anxiously waiting, while that year was taking its time to go by.

My freshman year of high school I was deeply dedicated to becoming the fastest freshman on the team, and while running varsity I did just that. During the indoor and outdoor season I ran all the sprints, the 100-meter dash, the 200, the 400, the 600, you name it.

At first glance I wasn't that intimidating. I wasn't as buff as most sprinters, and I was younger than most of my competitors, but my father always told me that my smaller body was my best weapon, because I'd surprise them all when gun went off. He said that even though I was kind of short I had a long stride length and I had inner strength and that was what mattered. He was right—I had the trophies and ribbons to prove it. Looks could be deceiving.

I found my groove running the 400-meter dash my sophomore year. Willow Ridge High School finally got a new track and stadium put in, and I'll never forget the day I broke 60 seconds in the 400-meter dash on it. That was the greatest day of my life. There's nothing like the feeling of your lungs burning while cruising down the homestretch. The last 100 meters are the most painful, but as you push your body it's a feeling of power that makes you feel so alive, even though your legs feel like jelly, just knowing that if you push yourself a little bit more, until you really feel like you're going to die, you'll accomplish what you wanted to.

At least I took with me all the good memories of my life.

I always searched the stands with my eyes to find my father in the audience before I hit the track on race day, and he usually wore a bright green windbreaker so he was easy to find. His eyes would follow my hot pink racing flats all the way around the track. He usually timed me too, which meant one time my father got into a huge argument with an official because my father clocked me in at 59.9, but I was put down at 60 seconds even. At the time it was embarrassing how intense my father could be about setting the record straight, but now it seems funny and I'm glad he stood up for me and believed in my potential as a runner.

This year Willow Ridge High School was holding the outdoor New York State Meet. I had planned to qualify again for it; I had no doubt I would.

But I wouldn't.

My father was thinking about that too.

I could remember every pair of running shoes he had bought for me, and I wanted to hug him and thank him for his support.

The phone rang nonstop. He didn't have to call the recruiters to let them know about my death. The way things spread on the Internet, all of the college recruiters had heard about it and many had already sent their condolences before my father had a chance to call them.

After I came in third place at the Class A state championship for the 400 dash last year during the outdoor track season, the phone started ringing like crazy and the letters came. I was catching the eye of coaches at Clemson University, Texas A&M, Louisiana State University, The University of Southern California, and Villanova so far.

To hell with keeping my dreams small.

Now I looked back on every race I had run and wished I ran better, even when I had won.

It was so irritating, I died just one month short of when the outdoor track season started. I had been so close to getting everything I was aiming for—but I guess my dream was over now. I wished I ran harder, pushed my lungs more intensely and really strained myself with effort, even when I had an amazing race, because I'd never get the chance to reach my new goals now. The end had come, and whatever hadn't been done had lost its chance.

A lot that hadn't been said also had lost its chance too.

Seeing Evan sit on the couch in our home as the only child now made me feel even more distant from him. There were a lot of things my brother and I hadn't said to each other.

He was four years older, which would be a good reason for us not being extremely close, but we had grown distant for a reason I still didn't know.

I had no idea what Evan was doing up at Le Moyne College, and he hardly seemed interested in what I was doing; we never spoke anymore. He had often come home on the weekends, although he never stayed around long and just went out with his buddies, practically ignoring me. Now my mother never wanted him to leave. She wanted him by her side at all times, or running errands for her, or making calls for her. I could tell my father was proud of Evan's strength and maturity to be a messenger of my death. Before each call Evan cleared his throat, and like an actor who had memorized the lines to a play, with great composure he repeated once again to another neighbor, coworker, or family member the news—the when, the how, the where—each time perfecting his tone, the order in which he told the events, and then being careful to not rush his exit.

He was more than a messenger, though. He eased the news to each person by saying with a sorrowful tone, "It was fast. She didn't suffer," making my death easier on them. He nodded his head, saying, "Thank you, she was an amazing sister." Or, "Thank you;

she will be missed a lot." It was truly the first time I heard Evan say anything nice about me, but to be honest, I don't think he meant it.

He carried through on the program of action with a sense of duty and respect. While researching on the Internet price comparisons between one limo company and the next, there were times his eyes would narrow and creases would appear on his forehead, and I wasn't sure if he was annoyed helping with the responsibilities that came with a sibling dying or if he was sad for me.

Watching my father and Evan prepare all the details and arrangements for the funeral was not only sad but surreal. Death made people do strange things. My mother showered up to three times a day, and I could tell she liked the pressure of the water hitting her bare back, because it helped to calm her. After each shower she paced the living room while crying, coughing, and gagging. When she had used all the tissues, she took to carrying a small washcloth around with her; she would cry hard into it—so hard that she'd lose her breath like an asthmatic. She even threw up a couple of times. It was like she was pregnant and having morning sickness while she mourned the daughter she had lost.

It was hard for her to sit still, and she tired herself pacing. She listened intently over each phone call made by Evan and my father to the funeral home. She often rudely yelled her suggestions at them or bashed their idea of being sentimental.

She screamed with tears in her eyes that I would never have liked the flower arrangements Evan and my father were choosing. She had tormented herself for hours over the type of gravestone they should buy.

When my father called the funeral home again to confirm the details he kept halting while giving his credit card information, hesitating, hoping it was all a mistake or a bad dream, but it wasn't.

Paying for my funeral arrangements put everything into perspective for him and brought a dreadful clarity to the fact that it would be the last thing ever bought for me. I could tell he had anger inside and a feeling that God had let his family down.

On my bed my mother slept. She cried hard into one of my track hoodies that she pulled from a pile of my dirty laundry—I used to wear it all the time. I listened as she talked to me about how much she missed me, needed me. She called my name over and over, asking me why, why did this happen?

I was speechless as she was sobbing. Her face looked so pale and dispirited; she did not look like the mother I knew. I wanted to let her know I was there, right next to her.

She lay there with her eyes swollen with dark bags under them, her lips dry, her wrinkles unmasked and undisguised, looking as if she had aged ten years.

She wore the same sweater and sweatpants as yesterday and had curled up on her side like a baby in a womb while having a hard time catching her breath in between her cries.

I crawled to her softly to lie with her, hovering at the curve of her back, which shook each time she inhaled.

I rested there. Nestling against her and burrowing into the strands of her wavy red hair, which she now dyed on a monthly basis, made me feel closer to her. She felt cold and trembled uncontrollably with chills that wouldn't subside; as much as I tried to give her a sense of my warmth, I couldn't warm her. I wanted to tell her I loved her. It had been awhile since I had told her I did. Lately it had seemed that all she wanted to do was pry into my life, and I had begun to push her away, but now I wanted to be close again. While listening to her bawl thick tears into my pillow, I moved a little closer to her shoulder. Together we stayed huddled like that and watched the darkness become dawn.

My father would ask about a hundred times a day, "Gracie, are you okay?" And it would make my mother crazy and emotional. She would snap at him, "No I am NOT OKAY! My daughter is dead!"

It was difficult to watch my father struggle to console my mother's grief and see her push his embrace away. Although our next-door neighbor was a therapist and dealt with a lot of depressed people, it was too awkward for my mother to knock on the door and ask for help. I knew she needed some, though.

The song "Songbird" from the Fleetwood Mac album *Rumours* played over and over while she wrote the first draft of my obituary. My father would later edit and add to it the details of my track accomplishments, the meets I had recently run, and how

I was looking forward to being an assistant coach this summer at the McClure Bowerman Youth Track & Field Summer Club.

When they looked for photographs to accompany the obituary, I watched as my mother abruptly snatched a photo out of my father's hand and hollered, "No, not that one!" She flung open another photo album and flipped wildly through the pages, hunting with a high and mighty attitude to find the perfect photo for the newspaper, as well as ones to display for the funeral.

Although my name would soon stop appearing on the news, now news segments were being based on teens and safe driving. It was like a trend had started, and the networks went wild with it. It was annoying and painful for my parents to hear the words "cars," "accident," and "death," anytime they turned on the TV.

The list of things I would never do was placed in my desk drawer. There were a few watermarks on the paper now, from when she cried into it.

She decided to take a sleeping pill and snuggled against my pillow. My father didn't stay up with her or tell her to come to their bed. He didn't know how to help her and she hardly noticed his comforting words. The what ifs would start, and I could tell he thought it was best to just let her be, but I wished he wouldn't just leave her alone.

Obviously my mother wouldn't be going to work that Monday. She had been a third-grade teacher at my elementary school since I was in kindergarten, but she told my father she might never go back and didn't want to be around other people's children.

## SAY IT NOW BEFORE IT'S TOO LATE

Phoenix had seen the news segments and newspaper articles about the crash; he read them over quietly and put the newspapers inside the chest in his bedroom. I wasn't sure what he was feeling but he seemed in a daze while spending the weekend touring the Cornell University campus with his new lacrosse equipment and preparing for his future.

Zara, Eva, and Jett didn't sleep a wink over the weekend. Eva got out of helping her mother at the bakery, and Zara could not have cared less about her fashion videos. Jett didn't go to the jewelry casting; she spent the weekend in bed. They texted each other, but I could sense they were all scared and thinking about why this happened. I understood because I wasn't sure either.

That Monday morning my body was in a dark ice-cold room at the funeral home with a cloth draped over me.

31

The funeral director was a very kind man, although I wouldn't want his job; it takes a certain kind of person to wake up each morning to prepare funerals.

Together my parents went to see him.

The funeral director suggested a closed casket. Before she made up her mind, my mother thought perhaps seeing me would be something she could handle; she wanted to just hug me goodbye. My father kept telling her she shouldn't do it, and after opening the door just a little bit to get a glance of me she shut it quickly.

She hoped the mortician could put my face back together again. She'd see me when I looked normal again, but there was deep worry in her eyes, as she wondered how much of a challenge it would be to actually make my face look normal again.

The blood had been cleaned off my face, but I didn't look the same aside from my curly auburn hair. My face was lopsided, like my cheeks had been punched upward towards my eye sockets, my lips were uneven and jerky, frozen in time, as if I had been yelling before Heidi's SUV smashed into me.

The funeral director gave my father the items that medical examiner had retrieved from my car. My father shook his head with disbelief when handed my track bag. He unzipped it and saw my pink and white training shoes inside. That was the breaker. His stomach dropped. He broke down, leaving tears on the funeral director's suit.

A clear plastic baggy with my "e" charm necklace inside was placed in my mother's hand. She gripped it tight, closed her eyes, and brought it to her chest—it was all she had left of me.

⌒

The girls and I were supposed to be having breakfast at Lilly's Café, but that obviously didn't happen.

I was actually shocked when they tried to go to school. Just as I figured, driving would make them all nervous.

Eva didn't have her driver's license, so she usually got a ride with Jett, since they lived near each other. Zara lived on the other side of town, but she was nervous to drive herself. It wasn't like she couldn't ask her parents for a ride, but she didn't want to answer a thousand questions from them about whether she could handle driving anymore.

She texted Jett, asking if she would pick her up for school.

The color had faded from their faces; their sparkle had dimmed way down. Zara didn't even have any lipstick on and had skipped brushing her hair and had thrown it in a messy ponytail; without her natural cheerful glow she looked pasty and sickly, and she wore a bulky sweater that she'd never normally choose. Jett wasn't wearing her dark eyeliner. She hadn't cared to notice that there was a huge rip in her gray tights and her turtleneck was on backwards with the inner tag itching her neck. Eva looked frumpy, like she rolled out of bed and put on whatever had a dark hue; and didn't dress up her eyes with heavy mascara and hardly wore any bronzer.

In the car Jett turned down the radio like Zara requested and went slower than usual like Eva suggested. They drove in silence, all of their eyes focusing intently on the road and each car that sped past them.

They thought that being together would make it easier to mourn and face the first week without me, but it was hard to ignore the whispers down the halls.

As mortician started to examine my facial features at the funeral home, the girls were leaving their first class.

At lunch it was hard for them to look at my seat; I wouldn't be sitting in it anymore.

The school felt different, quieter; there were many eyes looking at them. Rumors were spreading, and many believed they wouldn't see

Heidi ever again. They definitely would not see her until the class had graduated over a year from now, and who knew after that. Since Heidi had made her mark as one of the fastest 100-meter hurdlers in the history of Willow Ridge High School and also as one of the most popular girls in school, it was like two people had died. Sure, there were fashion models, celebrities, and plenty of singers and actresses to admire, but Heidi was the girl that many others in school had looked up to or wanted to be seen with. Now she wasn't in the halls, in the cafeteria, or available to be adored. Many of the faces looking at Zara, Eva, and Jett were angry and confused about who to mourn for—their idol, who was now in a psychiatric center, or me, who they hadn't admired in the same way but had died tragically.

And yet despite this emotional confusion from Heidi's fan club, Zara, Eva, and Jett received a great outpouring of sympathetic smiles and consoling hugs throughout the course of the day. There was even a nice morning announcement about my death and a moment of silence.

It wasn't all kindhearted for them, though.

I never was against Heidi before I died, but now a rivalry was igniting between us.

Heidi's loyal sidekicks Sonia and Gwen were unable to believe that she had caused my death, and they didn't see it that way. Despite what the newspaper and police reported about the crash— that Heidi's SUV ran the red light and smashed into me—Sonia and Gwen refused to believe Heidi had been the one at fault, and firmly told anyone who asked about Heidi that I had actually been the careless driver who caused the accident.

Of course Zara, Eva, and Jett defended me and were just as dutiful to my innocence, as students were deciding what to believe.

I didn't think of Phoenix as the fighting kind, but Heidi's boyfriend, Jackson, and his friends started spreading a rumor that I had been flirting with Jackson and that the accident had actually been caused by Heidi's purposeful road rage towards me, not by her careless driving. I'm sure Jackson wasn't happy that his girlfriend was now in a psychiatric institution. He could still visit Heidi on the weekends for an hour or so, but that wasn't much—she obviously couldn't be his prom date anymore.

A lot of girls had crushes on Jackson—of course they did, and they had no problem eyeing him more often now since Heidi wasn't around. He had those pretty blue eyes and a seductive smile, his shirt was always ironed or new; he came from a well-off family. It wouldn't have been hard for him to get a new girlfriend. I didn't know if he was seriously scouting out the available girls, but he sure acted like he was the main attraction.

I couldn't stand how he walked down the halls with a hotshot you know you want to be with me type of swagger, and would sigh loudly and say "Come on!" or "Let's go!" whenever someone walked too slowly in front of him. He may have been a little taller than Phoenix, with more facial hair and a bigger build than Phoenix too, but I didn't care that Jackson would probably grow up to be one those suave and polished guys in GQ magazine. I liked Phoenix's scar by his eyebrow and wrinkled shirt and how he wasn't in such a rush to huff at the slowpokes to get out of his way.

The grub of the day was pulled pork, a favorite among the lacrosse boys, but Jackson wouldn't get to enjoy it. He wasn't at his seat with his tray before Phoenix was in front of his face. Phoenix was furious. Something had come over him, and he had thrashed through the cafeteria, pushing aside chairs, even other students.

The way he fiercely demanded that Jackson stop with the lies made me believe that this wasn't random, and that Phoenix had planned this tell-off. He wasn't kidding around, and he smacked Jackson's tray to the ground. Pulled pork exploded with a thud and flew in every direction. Obviously embarrassed, Jackson pushed Phoenix away from him while dishing out a cruel comeback line, which only added fuel to the fire. Phoenix was uncontrollable as he pounded his fist against Jackson's face.

I couldn't believe Phoenix would punch someone because of me. But there was Jackson, on the floor in the cafeteria, almost unconscious. After the knockout, I couldn't help but feel powerful, like I was being boosted on top of a pedestal. I soared up high, high over the school and zipped through the halls, rattling and spreading my energy against all the lockers, and then flittered back into the cafeteria.

In a strange way their fight made me feel alive again, and I fluttered around Phoenix and brushed against his arms until one of the teachers on cafeteria duty grabbed his arm and took him to Principal Falcon's office.

Because of the fight, Phoenix would be suspended from two weeks of lacrosse once practices started in March, but he didn't seem to care. Phoenix's buddies, Brett and Caleb, told him that they were willing to miss a few lacrosse practices as well if someone wanted to start some more ruckuses.

Even after the fight, Jackson didn't act like he felt guilty; I mean his text to Heidi had in a way killed me.

It was a terrible first three days back at school for the girls.

On Wednesday afternoon Zara, Eva, and Jett were encouraged by Principal Falcon to take a couple days off from school, even though that was a lot to miss during junior year.

That same day my obituary came out in the newspaper.

The girls had each bought a dozen copies for themselves; it was sweet but also kind of ridiculous—like I was a celebrity or something.

By late afternoon the tension at school had simmered down a little. But as the week wore on and my funeral approached that Saturday, the school had become divided. Blame brewed as rumors spread about Heidi's involvement with my death. I didn't really know how to feel about Heidi, about dying, about anything yet. But I was certain about one thing—my body may have died, but I was still here and I didn't want to go anywhere else, even though I could have.

# *Careful*

## GIVE AS MUCH AS YOU TAKE

It was a closed casket; it would be embarrassing to share so bluntly how bad the damage had been to my face. Instead there were other things to look at, since my mother had gone overboard on the flowers, with beautiful wreaths of fresh hydrangeas and lilies and huge vases of pink roses, deep pink orchids, and ivy. It didn't feel like I had been dead a week, it just felt impossible and unreal.

I was impressed by the thousands of dollars my family put into my funeral—the flower arrangements were so beautiful, my photos blown up to poster size and framed, my track ribbons and trophies displayed.

The shoulder-to-shoulder crowd—it was all very overwhelming to watch, and it looked like everyone from Willow Ridge High School was there too. I stayed in the back, swaying slowly.

It made me skittish being there, invisible to everyone yet able to watch and listen to everything around me. From a distance I admired my life accomplishments on display near my casket, but started to feel restless and tense while observing everyone else appreciating my memories and the artifacts that summed up my life.

I sent a sensation of gratitude to everyone who was there. It spread out over the room and hailed throughout the air.

When I was alive I had thought about how every person had a soul, but now I knew that it was true, because it was all I had left.

When I had tried to reach for the police officer or hug my mother after the crash it didn't work—I couldn't feel others in that way, or be felt in that way, like wrapping my arms around them. But I could feel the energy of the room, the warmth it held from the people who were there and their thoughts of me. I felt that it was possible to give out a certain amount of the energy and love I felt inside. I just wasn't sure if anyone could feel it. I wanted to be in sync with the people around me and their hearts and lives. I just wanted to let everyone know that I was okay.

My mother, father, and Evan sat in the front row. I felt inclined to walk forward and sit by my father, but I stayed put.

My mother held her favorite silk scarf in her hands and cried into it, her mascara running a little. She looked pretty in her black lace dress, even though she hated it. A few days before, she got angry as she stared at her closet of bright colors. Then her car screeched out of the driveway and out of our neighborhood. She had to get to the mall. She didn't like lace or black, and tried to smile as the saleslady kept bringing her different black dresses to try on. She forked over a large sum for the dress that she planned to never wear again after today. Now at my funeral she was staring at my coffin.

She didn't want to pick out my coffin, so my father did it.

I had walked with him as he looked over wood choices and metal caskets; there were even bamboo coffins. He started to get emotional going over all the choices, the shapes, materials, colors, as he touched a few with his hand.

I actually got tired listening to the funeral director talk about the new innovations in coffins, like eco-coffins for natural burials, and I noticed how comfy they looked, like little beds.

Then my father said, "Do you have anything that could be written on?" He remembered how much I enjoyed looking through my old yearbooks and reading what my classmates had written inside at the end of the year. At first my mother was appalled at the thought of it, but then she agreed with my father that maybe it would be nice if at the funeral my classmates could sign my coffin like they would a yearbook—one last time. So that is how my coffin became white. With a Sharpie pen, people could write a message on it—a message to me.

Soon my body was lying inside the shiny white casket, wearing the white prom dress I had picked out at the boutique the day I died. At least I got to wear it—sort of.

That dumb padded strapless bra had ended up in my room, in my underwear drawer, the tags still on it.

Even with the casket closed, and despite the fact that no one could see my face, the morticians had done a nice job of putting a pretty white veil over my face. "Using makeup and foundation would only make it look worse," my mother had declared. She didn't dare look at my face before the casket closed. She assumed that even a surgeon or professional from a movie set couldn't put my face back together. Even when the morticians were done prepping me, and it was okay for my family to see me, my mother wouldn't get too close; she stood by the doorway and only from a distance saw me. My curly auburn hair looked even redder against the white satin pillow—prettier than it did on a normal day—and it wasn't bouncing in a million directions.

My legs were covered with a satin white blanket, and although my ears were pierced I didn't wear any earrings. My silver "e" charm necklace was now in my mother's purse.

The necklace wouldn't go into the ground with my body. My mother would hang onto it; she wanted to keep it with her.

⌒

Only a few feet away from the casket among the many, many beautiful flowers was a huge bouquet of long-stemmed white roses. There wasn't a card signed with a name of the sender, but it wasn't hard for me to figure out who sent them. I studied each rose.

I could feel his energy before I saw him. The service was about to start when he came in discreetly, like a whisper in my ear.

Phoenix. His heart was racing as he looked toward the front pews and saw my family. He had never met my family, and he felt a rush of sadness in his chest, knowing it would be too awkward to introduce himself now. He stayed in the back of the room, with his head down, not wanting anyone to approach him, not even Brett or Caleb.

Phoenix kept his hands in the pockets of his suit; he was so handsome in a black suit, and I couldn't help it, the sight of him reminded me of prom—it reminded me of our lost chance to be together.

From my new vantage point I could see things in more detail now, or maybe I just noticed details more carefully. He couldn't see me, but I could stare at him without him noticing. I could hear things more clearly too—like the sound of his breath going in and out of his chest, his heart beating inside of him.

His eyelashes looked longer than ever, and his lips looked so soft, it made me ache. I wanted to go over to him and put my head against his shoulder and tell him I was here. I slowly slid closer to him. I wanted to be near him and work up the nerve to kiss him right there in front of everyone. But I couldn't. Maybe he knew I was there, somehow, as he leaned gently against the wall and listened as the service began.

It was actually Coach Berlet who opened the service. I wanted to pay attention, but when Phoenix heard my name, he thought back to the last time he saw me and what I looked like on that day. My hair was down, a bit frizzy, not in its usual ponytail.

I was heading toward the parking lot after school, and he had called my name. He remembered my smile as I looked back over my shoulder and told him to have a great weekend before I went to the dress boutique to meet the girls.

As much as it angered me that my life was over and that I could never run again, I wasn't listening to my coach talking proudly to the crowd about my achievements. I was too busy focusing on the warm sensation I felt all around me, and I hoped Phoenix could feel it too.

He was thinking about the day he gave me that silver ladybug car charm, and now had a peaceful expression on his face that told me he could feel the love for me bubbling in the room.

The girls didn't need an introduction; everyone there knew that they were my closest friends. Everyone saw the grief on their faces. They looked nervous and scared, as if they were about to walk the plank.

Zara stood in the middle, Eva on her right, and Jett on her left. When Zara's eyes scanned the room she noticed Phoenix standing in the back of the room. On the side wall stood Brett and Caleb.

Zara made several glances at Brett; his dark hair was slicked back like a badass as usual, but in a suit and tie he looked more grown-up. I could tell Zara felt deeply drawn to him; there was a magnetic current between their glances at one another.

When Brett whispered to Caleb, asking if he should go talk to Zara afterwards, Caleb gave him a *what-the-hell-are-you-thinking* look.

Caleb had on a serious expression, and his thick dark eyebrows narrowed as he ran his hands nervously through his hair and sideburns. He seemed a bit antsy as his eyes looked toward the girls.

He noticed Eva's black knee-length skirt and took a deep swallow, itching at his neck as if his tie was too tight. Just like in school, he looked paranoid, like he didn't want to get yelled at by an elder for talking at the wrong time, because he always did.

I stayed by the doorway and watched the girls. They each held a piece of paper in their hands.

Zara cleared her throat again, looked down at her paper, and began, "There's no way to even begin to express how much we miss Estella, so we wrote a poem to share our love for her. It's called Close at Heart."

Her eyes scanned the room again, making sure she had everyone's complete attention. She cleared her throat and continued.

"A calm breeze awakes the day. As we gaze at the bright blue sky and pray…"

Then one by one in rotation they each read a line of the poem. Each one of my friends had highlighted in yellow their lines on the paper.

Jett: "Hoping that you are coupled with protection and embrace, to know this would give us faith…"

Before even saying one line, Eva broke down, choking on her words, "As…you…look down to all of us…shedding warmth and love upon us…"

Zara: "Letting nothing bring you strife, you were once so full of life. That's how we will remember you…"

Jett: "Secure on life you stood determined with your dreams…"

Zara gave a comforting smile to Eva before she read, "And now every time the wind blows and wraps its path around us we will feel your arms near…"

Jett: "We will never let your smile leave us, as angels call you to join their flight…"

Eva: "For with every spread of your wings light is shown from behind the clouds…"

43

Zara was about to lose it as well and reached for Jett and Eva's hands, as she ended the poem with, "Which inspires little flowers to grow, sending beauty throughout the world."

It might have appeared to the crowd at the funeral home that Zara wrote the poem herself since she led the reading, but poetry and writing was Eva's passion, and it was a big deal for Jett to read aloud, as she hated public speaking.

The night before my funeral they had sat on Zara's dark purple carpet, like we did over the years when we all hung out, and they wrote the poem together. That evening, the truth that I was gone sank in deeper with each line of the poem. They really didn't want to write it. They all seemed unsatisfied with it, as if something was missing. They felt a disturbance behind each line of the poem. Writing it had made them sink into themselves and dive into thoughts and feelings they didn't want to explore. Crafting and rehearsing the poem had made Zara weary, Jett exhausted, and Eva impatient, and they struggled, stuttered, and stumbled over their lines while reading the poem out loud together over and over again.

That night the girls had also created a memorial page for me on The Annex, the popular social media site we were always on. They titled the memorial page, In Loving Memory of Estella Montclair. It was decorated with photos of me and our memories over the years. The girls made it clear that only positive comments were allowed on the comment wall of the page and anything in bad taste would be removed.

Immediately the word spread about my memorial page, and similarly to how I could feel the energies, warmth, and love in the room at my funeral, I could also feel the sympathies each time someone commented on my memorial page, which the girls checked on daily.

My parents had access to my original profile page on The Annex, and they left it as is. The last thing I had written on my page was on the Thursday before I died. It read, "Can't wait to go prom dress shopping tomorrow after school with my besties!!!"

It made me sad to see that now.

The girls also checked my profile page daily, and it was covered in comments that read, "Rest in peace, Estella," and other words of condolence.

Phoenix had posted on both the memorial page and on my original profile page, "I'll miss seeing your beautiful smile. Rest in peace, Estella."

I loved that he thought my smile was beautiful.

I was very touched by the poem and watched each of the girls hug my mother and father and Evan, and go back to their seats. Sitting there together the girls didn't look at each other during the rest of the service, and I could sense that their mourning was something they each would do alone and in their own way.

A shadow fell over me. As if a window in the funeral home had broken and a chill of the wind busted in and sadness plowed over the day.

The eulogies had been spoken, my accomplishments had been mentioned, and the celebration of my short life was over now. The visitors started to exit the funeral home.

But wasn't I more than just the list of accomplishments or things I had the potential to become? Why didn't anyone talk about how nice or how thoughtful a person I was? Maybe it was because I hadn't been that person.

Maybe I would not be remembered after all for anything good. How long can people repeat your could-haves, would-haves, and should-haves? The things I thought defined me really had no meaning at all.

Eva had always envied my body, but my body was gone now — my flat stomach didn't matter anymore. Neither did my strength and ability to run and break another personal best record time. I couldn't see my toned stomach and calves; I couldn't hold or smell the white roses sitting by my casket that were from Phoenix. I didn't have my skin or my little boobs or face at all anymore. It didn't matter how frizzy my hair was today.

It hit me that all I really had left were the thoughts that people had for me. If they stopped thinking of me, maybe it would be like I had never been alive.

I wanted to plead to everyone and say, "Wait! Wait! Don't forget me." I felt the urgency to nudge against their elbows and squeeze their hands while visitors were leaving, begging them to please keep me on their minds after today was gone…and then Phoenix slipped out too.

I was also scared that I couldn't seriously count on anyone to do that. No one could carry me constantly in their mind with them. I worried I would end up being a weight on my friends' and family's shoulders, perhaps draining their own dreams with thoughts of my would-haves and could-haves. I didn't want to dampen the glimmer of their future, as I followed my family and the girls to the cemetery for my burial.

There was a hole already waiting. The ground was ice cold with a thin layer of snow, and it crunched as my family and friends gathered around the plot.

The headstone was ruby red, like the color my hair had been. I could see the breath in the air of my loved ones, their warmth inside hitting the cold air, while they were thinking about me. I didn't want my body to go into that cold dark hole in the ground; I didn't want to be left behind. I wanted to scream "Nooo…wait!" as my casket was lowered into the ground.

My mother held her hands to her mouth and closed her eyes, unable to watch, but my father, with tears in his eyes, watched me go down into that cold deep place.

This couldn't be happening. I started to wonder if this was just a dream, and I wasn't really dead. On Monday I would walk the halls of Willow Ridge High School, I would see Phoenix, I would meet the girls for lunch, I would be there for the outdoor track season, I would go to practice every day and improve with each race and I'd qualify for the New York State Meet, I would go to prom with Phoenix, I'd get that track scholarship, I would go to college, I would get married and have kids one day, I would succeed in all the ways I wanted to succeed.

Life would continue.

But while huddling together and looking at the ground, the faces of Zara, Eva, and Jett told me I was wrong. So did the headstone that bore my name.

### Estella Marie Montclair

You know how they say nothing is set in stone. Well, when you see your name set in stone on a grave, you know that's not true. Some things are set in stone.

⌒

As close as my friends appeared to be with one another, after my body was put into the ground, their mourning started to eat at their friendship. I could feel it, a distance between them. I watched, and I worried.

They stood together in the cemetery in front of the mound of dirt that covered my coffin for a while. Long after everyone else had left, they still stood, staring down at the white and pink roses on the mound of dirt. They were quiet, in their own thoughts, trying to find some meaning in why I died.

I tried to hear what they were thinking, feel what they were feeling, but the only thing I could feel was the cold chill from the sun going down as the orange and pink sunset grazed upon the silhouette of my friends standing there together.

I could sense that they were all anxious to leave, but none of them wanted to make the first move. None of them wanted to leave my body alone. I watched them each hug their bodies tightly, freezing. Zara's eyes were all red and puffy, and her body ached from crying. She kept rubbing at a knot that was building up in her shoulders. Jett reached for her neck; it was sore from staring at the mound of dirt and all the roses. Apart from breaking down during the poem, Eva hadn't cried much, and now she wondered why. She worried it meant she was a bad friend. She was filled with a thick void in in her chest. Her eyes didn't leave the ground.

After some time, the girls finally zigzagged through the graves, following each other single file but not saying a word to each other. They hardly waved goodbye to each other when they met each of their parents by their cars. After the funeral, there was no way they were going to drive themselves home.

While watching my friends get in their parents' cars and drive slowly through the cemetery, I had mixed thoughts. I was glad I had been there for it. It was so great to see everyone and watch them grab a Sharpie marker and sign my casket. I didn't feel like I was dead. Was I? Maybe my body was laid to rest and I was supposedly flying with the angels now, but it seemed like that was something said just to comfort the minds of my friends and family. It all sort of seemed like a scam or a joke. I was here. I was still here, why didn't they seem to consider that. Just because my body was laid to rest didn't mean my soul was going to sit still.

I had never thought about death at all before this happened, and I was curious about what would happen to my body. The thought that my body was in the ground bothered me.

The ruby-colored gravestone with my name on it seemed unreal. It was kind of overwhelming to think about—I mean, I was not really there in the ground anyway. When my friends thought of me,

I hoped I could somehow show them that I was not below them, or above them, but actually right there, beside them.

As the cars of my friends' parents disappeared through the cemetery gate, Phoenix appeared on my mind. He had written on my casket:

*You're unforgettable xo Phoenix.*

I sure hoped so.

# *Careful*

## NOT TO LEAVE STRINGS UNTIED

A few months before I died my mother had told me she was "on the verge of menopause," but she still got her period. Go figure she would feel cramps on the Sunday after my funeral. She was out of tampons, so it was a perfect excuse that morning to drive to the store, where she could escape the clutter that formed in her mind as she sat frozen in the house.

No matter which way she drove, it was hard to avoid the sight of the crash. My mother tried to avoid it by going through the different neighborhoods, but when she exited to the main road, all she had to do was look to the right, and there it was. Small pieces of metal were still on the side of the road. Tiny pieces of evidence of my death crunched under the tires of cars that whizzed by.

Unable to avoid seeing the sacred scene of the crash, my mother decided to face her fears. I went with her to a craft store as she bought a Christian wooden cross, meant to be hung on a wall, red ribbon, and some artificial flowers.

When she pulled over by the side of the road where I had died she kicked aside a few scraps of metal and studied the ground carefully. As cars sped by, she looked up to the sky. I could feel her soul saying a prayer that I would be okay, and with some force she stuck the wooden cross into the snow and soil at the side of the road, jabbing at it a few times to make sure it was secure, so it wouldn't blow away.

That afternoon my family had to relive my funeral, sort of, at a quick memorial presentation at Willow Ridge High School with the director of athletics, Principal Falcon, and Willow Ridge High School's whole administration team, who shared with my family a huge and beautiful memorial plaque that hung on the wall near the gym. Engraved on it were my athletic achievements and academic efforts. It would be hanging up there for the whole school to see on Monday. It was kind of them to create a memorial for me, but even I felt it was a bit too much death for one weekend.

My funeral weekend ended with my mother curled up on the couch, trying to write thank-you cards to the police chief and investigators, the medics, and the funeral director. She even went overboard and called the hair salon I went to and the bagel shop we'd stop at on the way toward Interstate 90 when I had track meets near Albany. She called all over, asking for the manager, telling him or her how I recently passed away and how much I had enjoyed their bagels or haircuts or whatever. I think it helped her to talk about the things I liked. After calling every place she could possibly think of, she went back to writing cards, but she couldn't get through even one letter. She kept messing up, unable to write at all. She wasted three cards on the police chief.

Heidi didn't attend my funeral. She couldn't. She probably wouldn't have wanted to come anyways. By then, she was an hour away, settling in at the psychiatric center. Sonia and Gwen didn't show up either.

However, soon Heidi was moving into a correctional institute for juveniles. After only a few days at the psychiatric center, she got into a bad verbal and physical fight with another patient that involved hair ripping and blood.

A part of me liked knowing where Heidi would be sent, but it wasn't like I planned to visit her.

$\backsim$

A new Monday was here. I guess I'd have to create a new routine for myself.

Jett picked the girls up for school. Zara had brought Eva and Jett a copy of the photo we had taken together at the dress boutique that fateful day I died. She had printed the photos from her cell phone, and put them in pretty matching frames that said "Best Friends" on it. I wanted one, and it was the first of many things I wanted to be a part of.

It had been a better day until lunch came. The girls checked out my memorial plaque on the wall near the gym, and there were flowers underneath it in vases from other students and faculty. Now they were on their way to the cafeteria, but Sonia and Gwen were walking behind them, staring them down.

Without Heidi around them, they didn't appear as intimating, but it was still annoying to feel their stares. Jett waved her hand for Eva and Zara to follow her, and they decided to bail.

It wasn't typical to totally go off school grounds for lunch, and as we all piled into Jett's car the same expression was across their faces: Where would we go now? It was a windy but sunny afternoon, and Zara had an idea and asked softly, "Do you want to go see Estella?"

It was funny because I was already in the car with them.

On the way to visit my grave they had to pass Vine Street and the site of the crash. They were all quiet, having a moment of silence for me until Eva said, "Look! A wood cross is there!" Their eyes were on the cross with the pretty red ribbon and the artificial flowers.

It made me smile when Jett wondered out loud, "Maybe her mom put it there?"

The pile of dirt in front of my grave still looked fresh but now the colorful roses sprawled about were wilting from the harsh February wind and blowing snow. The girls held hands as they walked up the small hill. When they reached my grave, Eva said, "I can't wait for it to warm up so we can plant flowers." Zara smiled, "That would be nice." Jett's cell phone buzzed, but she turned it on mute; her eyes were fixated on the pretty quote on my headstone. Below the date I had died, it read, "Let peace meet you there."

Then something surprising happened. With her eyes on my grave Jett started humming softly. Zara and Eva listened; it was unlike Jett to hum like that. Then the humming became a song, and Jett started singing quietly.

Jett didn't have the best singing voice, but Zara and Eva followed her lead, joining in together.

They stood there united by the memory of us singing "Bridge Over Troubled Water." Not long ago we had sung it together at the karaoke café near the mall, and we all had a laugh over the singers' names, Simon and Garfunkel. I had liked saying "Garfunkel"—it came off the tongue in a fun way.

The wind was blowing the girls' hair all over the place, but they continued quietly singing, not caring about the strands whipping them in the face.

I knew they were cold standing there, but I didn't feel anything cold at all. Warmth rushed over me.

It was a very genuine moment for them, and for me. Like a breath of life, their faint singing wrapped around me and vibrated off my yearning to be with them, soothed my broken wish, and penetrated into the core of me. I truly felt loved.

After the song, they left and went back to school and their next class and I rotated my time between each of them. Maybe it sounds creepy or weird, but I wanted to be near them, everywhere they went. I wanted to hang out where they were, I wanted to give them my full attention. Most of all, I needed them. We were supposed to always be friends.

# *Careful*

## TO NOTICE THE LOVE THAT'S AROUND YOU

That night I went to visit Eva. She was sitting on her bed, adjusting the laptop into a new position on her thighs as she pulled up her chemistry e-book. Glancing at it for just a few seconds, she closed the laptop altogether and let out a huge sigh. I could tell she wanted to think about something else but me, even chemistry. It was no use. I wished she would call or send a text message to Zara and Jett, but she didn't.

The smell of *arroz con pollo* and sounds of salsa music drifted into her room from downstairs. In a few minutes her mother would yell her name, but she didn't seem to care.

Without getting off the bed, she reached for her journal from her side table and then fluffed her pillows, shaping them with her fist and placing them all on top of each other so she could sit upright in bed against them. With the journal against her thighs she looked ready to write something important.

I waited for her to write.

Her chin started to tremble, her mouth and lips became pudding, and tears appeared in her eyes.

She closed her journal; pen tucked inside and curled up to her pillow, hugging it tight. She wasn't sleeping, just lying there.

Then she started talking to me.

Over the next days the girls would each talk to me, and continue to do so. It was really strange to be talked to when I wasn't able to speak back.

Eva was holding her hands together like in a prayer when she started to cry. Her mascara running, she said, "Thank you. Thank you for always being there for me. I wish I told you how much it meant to me that we were friends."

She was quiet for a few minutes, and then said, "Remember when you told off those assholes in seventh grade?"

She smiled with a little laugh. I did too.

I had saved her from humiliation in the hallways of our middle school. There had been a phase in middle school when certain groups proudly flaunted their ethnicity by wearing flags like capes around their shoulders and shouting nicknames for each other between classes.

"Are you white, black, Hispanic, Puerto Rican, Brazilian, Mexican? Iranian?" She got asked it all over the years. With a narrow nose like her mother's, she had a white girl's appeal, but her complexion was called beige, olive, or tan; it always looked sun-kissed, as if she just come back from a Caribbean cruise. She had obvious hips and a round booty like her grandmother on her father's side, who she mentioned lived in Puerto Rico.

It might have been considered a social gesture for students to give each other ethnically inspired nicknames, but Eva didn't want a nickname. In seventh grade, while we were walking down the hall with Eva, a pubescent jerk and his sidekicks taunted her about her skin tone, which seemed too light for her hair texture. They had the nerve to ask her what color her hair was down there. I remember that I had turned back and snapped back at them that they'd never get the privilege of knowing because they were disgusting pigs and soon after their remarks did stop.

I now realized that I had been one of the only people in her life who ever complimented or stood up for her.


Throughout our friendship, I noticed how Eva seemed distant from her mother and never talked about her father, but I didn't press her about it. Whenever we hung out we talked about everything but her family, but I got the impression she didn't get along with her mother—who owned a small bakery in the village of Willow Ridge, which was often struggling to survive—and her father wasn't around anymore to help out.

I caught little pieces of his story over the years. I had felt uncomfortable asking more about him, but now I wished I had.

I could see now how sometimes when someone acts like they don't want to talk about something, they actually do. Sometimes the things we keep to ourselves are the things we most want to share with someone.

I never told Eva that I knew her father was in jail for crystal meth. She had never told me, but I knew, we all knew, because it had been in the newspaper. He had been arrested. I didn't even know what crystal meth was. I had to Google it.

It was awkward when my mother asked me about Eva's father while pointing to the article. "Isn't this Eva's dad, Mr. Moreno?"

For a while my mother didn't want me to go to Eva's house.

Our parents only knew each other in passing—when they would drop us off at each other's house as kids and stand in the kitchen for a moment, talking about the smells of dinner on the stove or mainly about us kids. Our parents didn't have a close-knit friendship with one another.

Honestly, I think my mother was worried about the language barrier, but Eva's mother spoke English just fine. Remembering this moment made me feel frustrated that my mother didn't call Eva's mother and be there if she needed her. Toward bad news, my mother always said, "That's too bad," or "What a shame." Then she would bite her lip and debate over what she could do about it, then usually decided there was nothing she could do.

But I think the kindness and the sympathy cards she received from strangers after my death showed her that you don't have to know someone well to comfort them with a moment of your time when they needed it most.

The last time I had seen Eva's mother she hardly said hello. As I headed up the stairs to Eva's room, she looked like she lost her smile permanently in her lonesomeness. I wondered how Eva lived with such a sad mother.

Her father's arrest came and went in the newspaper, but it was like the topic was banned. None of us brought it up to Eva when we saw her; we just acted cool, the same. We were at the outlet mall and we acted like everything was fine when we all knew it wasn't. I regret that now.

Her father won't get out of prison for four more years. Eva will have already graduated from high school by then—who knows, she might not even be in the this area and away at college.

She opened her journal again.

Without her knowing I was there, among the quiet sound of her pen hitting the paper, I could see more clearly how strong Eva was. She had been through a lot, and she was so much stronger than she gave herself credit for.

My funeral was the first she ever attended; I remember she had mentioned that since she was born, no one in her family had died. She wrote in her journal that she felt lucky on one hand, but experiencing what death meant for the first time, how can you be here one second and then gone the next, scared her. She asked her journal if it would be better to know when she was going to die ahead of time, or if not knowing was better after all? Was it better to go quickly or deteriorate over time from a long sickness?

Although I had gone quickly, I wasn't sure if it was the better way, because being torn away didn't leave time for last hugs or words.

Watching Eva with the pen in her hand, it reminded me of how she helped me so many times prepare inspirational pep talks and speeches that I would share with the track team before race day. She always knew just the right words to truly express how I felt about not giving up on our goals, facing the competition, or overcoming the odds.

I had come up with the slogan, "Run with your heart." She thought it was perfect to inspire the team and encouraged me to end all my pep talks with it. I wished I could have written something inspirational with her again.

I watched each word appear on the page of her journal as she wrote a poem tonight.

*If only you could see me cry*
*Or feel the tension in my spine*
*If you were able to feel my affection*
*And all I have to give*
*If only you could see these tears*
*I'm trying to hide under dark dripping eyes*
*If you could rescue me from my fears*
*If only you could see me when I cry*
*Maybe then you'd shelter me and a true angel would be by my side*

It wasn't me she was writing about.

She was writing about Caleb; he was still playing those games of not letting her fully see how he felt about her. Eva had six journals full of poems tucked inside one of her desk drawers, and her latest journal was full of her thoughts about Caleb.

Once Caleb's mother found a poem in his school bag that Eva had given him about how he made her feel inside; she confronted Eva discreetly about it, telling her that some feelings are best not put on paper. Ever since, Eva felt very uncomfortable being around his parents. At their house Eva would say hi very quickly to them—they were usually reading in the den and hardly noticed her—and then she'd hang out in Caleb's room, or they'd watch movies in the basement. Their careless silence toward her made her feel like a whore. Eva usually left before dinnertime because it was so awkward, plus she didn't know their Jewish prayers before meals.

Caleb never made it easier for Eva or tried to get his parents to warm up to her. They had their hopes of the type of girl Caleb would be with one day, and it wasn't a girl like Eva. The girl they had in mind for their son was less ethnic.

It was as if his father wanted Caleb to enjoy Eva as a treat to his youth or something, and even let Caleb buy her two pairs of luxurious earrings with his credit card this past Christmas. It was easy to see now how misleading the whole thing was to Eva, who deeply cared for Caleb and wore the earrings almost every day.

I wanted Eva to have a good guy in her life. She needed one, and I didn't think it was Caleb.

In school and around us, Caleb always acted a little distant to her, as if we didn't know they had something going on.

Unlike other guys who would brag about their moves and what they received from or did with a girl, Caleb kept quiet about the time he spent with Eva in his bedroom or the basement when his parents weren't home. Eva played along, like it didn't bother her that they could be close one day and then totally detached the next day—but I knew it was just an act.

She had bluntly shared with us that his mouth spent hours down there and how good he was at it. She called the way he did things erotic.

Down in his basement I saw them kiss recently, on the couch. His tongue was rapidly moving around in her mouth. I would have choked. His hands squeezed her body affectionately but then could be aggressive. He even yanked at Eva's hair while they were kissing, and she didn't seem to mind, which surprised me.

He kept saying how much he liked what she was doing. I hated seeing her please him; for some reason I felt like he didn't deserve what she was giving him, though it looked like she had a knack for knowing what to do while giving it to him. I was appalled at him smiling, arrogantly, and looking down at her and pulling at her hair like he was the one really in control. She really wanted him to like what she gave him and went overboard, constantly asking him if he liked it. I felt like telling her she was a dumb-ass.

When they were just lying there, he pinched her stomach chub in a teasing way, and she pushed his hand away embarrassed—I could tell she wished he wouldn't poke her belly like that.

We'd always feel bad for her, wishing Caleb would call her back or reply to her text message sooner, or show up and be without an excuse, but Eva had a habit of rolling her eyes like it didn't matter, as if she had become accustomed to being treated like shit, and would just say she'd talk to him about it later.

It all made sense after Eva wrote her poem tonight, though; I knew she hadn't been honest to us or herself, but she had a hard time pulling away or getting fully fed up with him.

He looked like a hairy ape.

Caleb had thick wavy hair and these really long sideburns; they went to his jawbone practically, and he'd scratch at them intentionally as often as possible so you'd notice them. It would make me roll my eyes. He trimmed them so carefully.

Besides his sideburns the first thing you'd notice about him was that he never shut up. He loved to share how much he knew about whatever you were talking about, like he was a professor or something.

I knew she wanted to believe he'd come around one day and want her more seriously, and she'd wait. Things were clearer now; I could easily pick up on Caleb misleading her. To me it seemed more like she was being used.

I wanted to tell finally Eva so many things that I couldn't: that she had so much life to live still, that she would meet someone else who appreciated her and one day have the love she wanted. But really, who was I to know? I was still dreaming of a barely-there kiss from a boy who would probably forget my name by next month, but I wanted to tell her that everything would be okay, especially because she was crying.

Eva had tears in her eyes as she continued to write in her journal, *I don't want to go to prom. He hasn't even asked me.*

I hated that I couldn't hand her a tissue. My body was in the cold ground, ants and worms were probably starting to build homes around my coffin, and my body and arms were stuck like superglue in a place I didn't want them to be. That night, I started to build anger for Heidi and all she took away.

# *Careful*

## NOT TO COUNT YOUR CHICKENS BEFORE THEY HATCH

After visiting Eva, I needed a pick-me-up. Phoenix had just gotten out of the shower, and his lower half was wrapped in a towel. Part of me felt like a stalker, but I had to see him.

I had gone swimming with him in his pool last summer with the girls and Brett and Caleb, but being in his room, alone with him now, was different. Little droplets of water were on his chest, and a huge part of me wanted to wrap my arms around his torso and say hello, but I knew I couldn't. Instead, I stayed near his desk and watched him pack up his school bag for the next day. When he put his gray lacrosse hoodie near his bag, I wanted it; *Clemens* was embroidered across the back of the hoodie. I wished I could have owned something with his last name on the back of it, something that he had worn and smelled like him. Not that the hoodie could have come with me after I died anyway, but I was enjoying smearing myself against it now.

Then he dropped his towel.

He wasn't even going to put on any sweatpants or shorts, and I realized he slept naked. Would I have ever seen him this naked if I hadn't died? I didn't know. Maybe not. I felt lucky and guilty at the same time.

I tried not to stare.

It was hard not to. I'm sure if he was the invisible one, able to silently be in my bedroom, he would have watched me get ready for bed too.

He hadn't turned the light out yet and grabbed his phone off the charger. He slipped under his navy blue sheets and navy comforter, and he looked so comfortable and relaxed against his pillows. I wanted to touch his damp light brown hair and the side of his cheek. I wondered what it would be like to nuzzle my head against his chest and lie next to him.

He didn't look like he was thinking about anything that involved missing me. Maybe he didn't miss seeing me at school anymore. His eyes were on an Angry Birds game he was playing on his cell phone. I kept wedging myself between his hands and the game, but nothing budged.

If I had hands, I would have thrown that stupid phone out of his hands and grabbed his face and told him to tell me what he missed about me.

Each second made me more upset. I was burning up, enraged by all I could and could not touch, by all I could and could not say, and I was getting sick and tired of being unable to be seen, heard, or felt.

His eyes went from hopeful to deflated when he failed to pass to the next screen of the ridiculous game involving flying birds that soared then crashed into cement blocks to reach the golden victory inside the blockade.

I stayed there until he finished the stupid game. Finally he turned off the light and put his phone back on the charger. The room became dark, and when he got back into bed he rolled over facing the wall.

But of course, it was ridiculous to think that someone who was so reclusive with his true feelings about me when I was alive could become more open with them now that I wasn't. I probably wouldn't have been able to tell when he was thinking of me, if he actually was thinking of me, anyway.

# *Careful*

## NOT TO FORGET WHERE YOU COME FROM

The next morning on my way to Zara's there was a strange aggressiveness in the air, the wind was even colder than usual, and now it was knocking me off my course, making my normal glide rough and uncomfortable. I also felt icky and frail while turning through the neighborhoods, like something was contaminating the air around me, but I tried to ignore it and thought of the lyrics of "Free Fallin'" by Tom Petty, to distract myself from the nauseating feeling during the last blocks before entering Zara's bedroom.

Zara was already awake and in her bathroom. Her hair always looked like it had been styled by a professional, and now I knew what it took to make her voluminous blond hair look so shiny and alive. She woke up so much earlier than I did, just to maintain her hair routine.

I leaned against the bathroom counter. Being still for a moment made me feel better, while I listened to the soothing sound of the hairdryer blowing against Zara's hair.

Ever since she had come to Willow Ridge in sixth grade, Zara's thick and silky blond hair had made everyone notice her. Along with her hair and straight teeth, she had full breasts, even back then. Eva and I had met in our kindergarten class, and Jett soon made us a trio when we met on the playground and collected acorns together and became friends. By sixth grade, sure we had other friends from our classes, but the three of us were always together. We passed notes to each other in the hallways; we folded our notes in a special way, in an origami pinwheel shape.

The day Zara came to the school, we figured the preppy clan had already snatched her up by the time we saw her at recess, so we did our typical thing: we went to the swings.

Moving to a new school during sixth grade and starting over would have been a terrible and frightening experience for most kids, but not for Zara. She had moxie. She had an aura about her that made people want to know who she was and where she came from. Classmates wanted to know how the town she came from in Connecticut was different from Willow Ridge. Even then she seemed ahead of everyone when it came to her sense of style.

Since she seemed to have it all, she was in demand. She had a lot of options for creating her core group of friends. Everyone hovered over her, asking if she needed help with anything, if she was getting the hang of her locker and catching up on the class assignments okay.

While Jett, Eva, and I were swinging on the playground, higher and higher and pumping our legs hard, Zara was walking around the playground with a few other girls. They were introducing Zara to all the boys they had crushes on as an excuse to say hi and flirt with them. We figured she found her clan.

That was until Zara and those girls walked by our swings a little too closely, and I came down from a very high swing and my foot smacked right across Zara's face and chin. The other girls screamed when Zara's nose started bleeding down her shirt, and they ran to get a teacher.

As Zara stood there covering her bloody face with her hands, I tried to drag my feet to slow down my swing. Jett and Eva were also trying to slow down, yelling, "Are you okay, are you okay?"

Zara was trying not to cry, and now other students were coming over to see what was wrong. I knew Zara didn't need a crowd and said, "You guys, she's fine, she's fine, go away." I pushed my hand out to shield Zara.

It looked worse than it was, and the teacher, Eva, Jett and I all walked her to the nurse.

So honestly if I hadn't kicked Zara in the face we might not have become a foursome. That day in the nurse's office was almost five years ago. Sometimes the best friendships are built in the most interesting ways.

〜

Zara was an expert texter. She always sent us these long detailed text messages, like novels. Now, though, she was really short with her messages to Eva and Jett, and I wondered if it was because texting reminded her of how I had died.

In classes, Zara usually had a colorful personality, but now she was quieter than usual.

Something was building inside of her, a silent rage. Between classes the girls would talk about how they wanted to kill Heidi and smash Heidi's face to shreds like she had done to my car and my life. I knew they weren't really going to hurt Heidi, but I noticed how the thought of hurting her made Zara smile.

Whenever Zara needed to think, she drew in her sketch book. Mostly she drew with colored pencils or pens her own original fashion illustrations, sometimes using fashion magazine ads as reference for product designs and sketching out how she'd have made the design better. She had even drawn an illustration of me standing in a fashion pose in my prom dress and wrote my name under it.

Drawing was her format for letting out her frustrations and thoughts, or her grief.

During the days that followed, I'd discover what really was at the pit of Zara's anger and quietness. It had been there for some time.

Also I'd find out what was in the air, causing me to feel so off balance and nauseous while making my rounds around town.

On Thursday evening Zara sat in front of her computer and took a deep breath as she prepared to send an email. It was to the producer at the local news station. This coming weekend she was supposed to be featured in a prom dress fashion segment for the local news channel, sharing the latest trends for gowns and shoes. It would be great exposure, great for her resume, and she could plug her fashion blog. I was excited for her. But now the thought of standing up and speaking enthusiastically about prom dresses was a depressing thought to her.

In the email she wrote that she couldn't do it and had to attend some last-minute fashion event outside of town, but it was a lie.

After she sent the email, she checked on the In Loving Memory of Estella Montclair memorial page and smiled at the comments that were still flowing from other students and my track teammates of how I was missed. I wondered if there would be a day when the comments stopped.

Then Zara checked her phone and texted Brett, who had already texted her twice, once to tell her something she didn't want to know:

*Jackson told me Heidi is coming home to visit the second week of March*

The second week of March would be around March 12th—one month after I had died.

And right when outdoor track season started.

We both wouldn't be on the team.

I wondered who would now be the captain on the team since I was gone, and who would now be the top hurdler since she was gone.

Perhaps mistakes happen, perhaps timing is everything and death was my fate, but I couldn't accept that—Heidi played a big role in ruining my life.

Suddenly I was being punched in the stomach fifteen times in a row and I heaved over, sailing low to the floor—the icky feeling I had felt in the air was Heidi's soul preparing to visit and moving closer. Or that's what it felt like.

Even if it was just for a weekend, I just knew that when Heidi arrived it would be terrible—and not just for me.

Zara drooped back against her chair after reading Brett's text.

Brett also asked if they could ever have their Valentine's Day dinner. I had died before Valentine's Day, and Zara hadn't been in the mood; she forgot about it altogether.

*I don't know. Xoxo*, she texted back.

A few seconds later, Brett texted back with too many *xoxos* to count.

I wished someone would comfort me.

Zara didn't text him back anything about Heidi. And by not doing so, it was like she was brushing off her visit. But I could tell when she scrunched her lips in an irritated way while reading his text again that Heidi was on her mind.

When her eyebrows narrowed and she looked off at her calendar she didn't want to care, but like me, she did. She texted Eva and Jett the news, but to keep from making it sound like a big deal she included the words *Not like I care* at the end of the text.

Eva texted back, *She's a stupid bitch. If I could drive I'd run her over.* Which I thought was kind of hilarious coming from Eva, knowing how nervous she'd been about getting her license. When Jett's text read, *We should egg her house. LOL!* I imagined Heidi's house covered with eggshells and yolk. I'd be lying if I said it didn't make me feel better, but I wondered if Eva and Jett were serious—causing pain and messes might bring temporary satisfaction, but it wouldn't bring me back.

Sputtering toward Zara's bed I sort of stumbled onto it and spread myself out wide and felt flatter than ever in anticipation for the month to come and the second week of March.

I slumped around Zara's room some more as she started looking through old photo galleries on her computer, which put me in a better mood. I looked at them with her. Some of the photos were years old. There were photos from birthday parties at bowling alleys, or at roller-skating rinks, shots of the four of us on the first days of school from each new school year, all of us hanging at her house and sunbathing by the pool in the summertime. Then there were our crazy Halloween costumes.

We really had been a quartet. Looking at the pictures made me remember that we even had gotten our periods for the first time only a few weeks apart at the start of seventh grade. That's also around the time I started getting really good with my running and was already traveling to races on the weekends.

Zara and the girls had caught a bunch of my races, and they would scream and yell in excitement, but usually afterward they left. None of my friends were into running for the fun of it; they didn't exactly understand where my passion for racing came from, but Zara understood the work ethic that was involved with having a goal and gaining success. She understood it well.

She wanted her own fame and success. She already had it in a way, with the following she had gained through her fashion blog. During freshman year she had set up the blog. She was always a wiz at self-promotion.

By now everyone knew about her style blog and that she was the go-to girl for fashion advice, tips, and forecasting trends for all sizes and budgets. She had a strong social media platform which included over a hundred fashion tip videos. Sometimes before she went to bed she would answer IMs and emails from students, like an emergency question about whether a pair of shoes looked okay with a certain skirt or dress. Zara often asked her readers to submit their own style photos, and she would offer prizes and discounts to local nail or hair salons. She would hold product giveaways and walk into local clothing boutiques to ask if they would offer her readers a gift certificate. Her blog had become a small business and even had a few local brands advertising on it, although for her it wasn't about making money and getting rich off the blog…yet. It was about being a voice, sharing her opinion, being able to be counted on, connecting, and making something of herself, by herself. Or, that's what she told us.

In this suburban town, she was the only teen riding a social-media wave and building a noticeable following through her blog.

Publicity was the only thing she needed more of. Zara wanted the press coverage I had gained through my track accomplishments. Zara had saved just about every single one of my features or mentions in the newspaper and on the Internet (it was sweet that in the weeks following my death, many high school track stats websites posted memorials that shared my obituary and aspects of my running career).

I sat on the edge of Zara's bed and watched her click the mouse, over and over, and scroll through photos of the four of us over the years. I was sad wishing there had been even more memories, but there weren't because I was training or out of town so often at a track meet.

However, Zara didn't complain about how I wasn't always around on the weekends and after school. She liked that I was active and doing what I wanted. Ambition was something that had made us even closer recently.

Zara always confided in me that her parents thought her fashion blog was a waste of time and were not impressed with "hits" and "downloads."

All Zara wanted was more "hits" and "downloads" to keep building a brand around herself as a fashion expert. It would help her later to pursue a career as a stylist or fashion journalist, perhaps.

I had confided in her about the pressures of being a competitive runner, the draining hours and drills, the focus it took to strive, and how hard it was sometimes to come back on the track pumped up after an off day and encourage yourself and your team at the same time.

I hadn't mentioned how lonely it was sometimes, but I wish I had, after now seeing how lonely Zara actually was.

Before moving to Willow Ridge, when Zara was a child in Connecticut, she took special speech therapy classes and tried to hide the truth from the other students, saying she was a part of a "special reading and writing group" and also a "special math group."

After moving to Willow Ridge and being friends for a couple years Zara admitted to us that she couldn't solve simple multiplication problems until fourth grade. Her parents had spent a fortune on weekend tutors and summer-school programs to get her up to speed.

I can't be certain, but maybe something related to her birth was to blame.

When she was eight or nine she had overheard her mother talking on the phone to one of her friends about what the process was like for her fertility treatments. To Zara's young ears the words "in vitro fertilization" sounded like being a part of a new superhero film. When she asked about it, her mother had just said sweetly, "It's the special process that helped you become born."

It seemed special, like she was a part of something almost magical.

Later, after she moved to Willow Ridge, in middle school during one of those corny sex-education classes, fertility treatments didn't come up. The class was just about where the guy put it and him wearing a condom. So, Zara started Googling for more information on what fertility treatments were, but it was in a medical language she didn't really understand.

Her parents didn't originally want to have a child, and later when they decided to try, her mother was older. Her mother's eggs were not fertile, and her father, five years older than her mother, was not exactly at his prime for creating a baby.

From what Zara gathered over the years and from what she Googled and assumed, eggs were removed from her mother's ovaries, then her father's sperm was mixed in, and they blended together, like the ingredients for making a cake. The mixture was then injected into her mother's uterus, and there could have been some sort of hormone-enhanced ovulation going on as well. It was kind of gross and weird to think about.

Through nosing around her mother's filing cabinet, Zara discovered paperwork about how her parents got the girl they wanted with something called selective reduction.

"We could have had two babies, but we just wanted you," her mother had said sweetly, but it sounded fishy. They just wanted one baby, but the odds of using just one embryo in her forty-four-year-old womb to make it happen were slim.

Selecting her didn't mean her parents were now always involved and caring. Her father, a business lawyer, had his own firm, Kensie & Associates, and now was in his mid-sixties. Her mother, a homemaker, whose face had been pulled back so tight over the years that it had lost all expression, was sixty. It would be fine to have older parents if they were more interested in her.

Years ago this type of baby making was something families kept to themselves, but lately it seemed that every week Barnes & Noble had a new book on infertility treatments, sharing the immense joy it brought to people who really wanted to be parents and also the controversy about how multiple births pose the risk of the baby or babies having brain damage or physical disabilities because they are squished together inside the mother's womb, or something like that.

I thought it was incredible that one of my friends was made like that. The discoveries Zara shared with us showed that a lot of life's learning happened outside the classroom, from your own hunting.

Health class had scared us with frightening slideshow images of diseases on private parts and made us squirmy with a bloody film about birth, but had skipped that part about how actual sex wasn't even needed to have a baby these days.

It made me think about how I died a virgin.

I wondered what it would be like to do it. Romantic movies had given me plenty of ideas, making me feel tingly inside sometimes, but I would never know how it really felt. I would never know if it was true that it hurts a little the first time, or try out the different ways to pleasure each other.

I would stay behind. Untouched and unknown, unable to give or receive. Everyone else would gain experience, but not me. Those wonders would never be unlocked. I would be stuck in girlhood. And now something I had saved so carefully, I almost wished I had rushed. Sadness fell down over me, as I realized that later I wouldn't be experiencing those next acts of life that involved creating the miracle of what life was all about.

Soon Zara's eyelids got heavy, and she closed the folder of our memories on her computer and started to peel off the layers of the day's clothing. I turned away to give her privacy while she tugged open the middle drawer of her dresser and pulled an oversize T-shirt over her head.

After turning off the light, she dashed back to the bed like I had done on nights I was afraid of the dark.

She was grateful for all she had, but with more money and stability than Eva and Jett ever had, I could see why Zara felt like she'd be a whiner if she vented about not feeling understood by her parents.

Still, I wished she would let Eva and Jett see what I could see, the side of her that wasn't always so peppy and full of life.

Under the covers with her eyes peeking out and focusing on the nothingness of the dark ceiling, she said, "I miss you, Estella. I hope you're at peace."

She kept glancing up, thinking I was up there, but I was sitting right beside her hoping she too would find a sense of peace tonight.

# Careful

## WHO YOU GIVE YOUR HEART TO

I didn't sleep anymore; I simply lost the need to sleep. So, when the world around me was sleeping, sometimes I would travel through Willow Ridge and let the night air carry me until I could feel the first light of dawn.

Some nights I went to the track at school, even though there was snow on it. Like when I was alive, I would swish around and around for hours with the moon glowing down on me and reenact certain races I'd won or redo the ones I hadn't.

Other nights, I'd take a trip through my favorite course. I'd swoop through the neighborhoods, making quick cuts through backyards and over fences, sometimes sliding down the snow piles at the side of the streets, and head towards Willow Lake Park. If I wasn't too tired I'd run the three-mile loop on the trails at the lake, or I'd stroll out to the center of the iced-over lake and admire the blue-gray shadows dancing atop the crystalline ice on the slender branches of the weeping willow trees. From a distance the shadows of the iced branches looked like a pack of mammoths.

Then usually I'd skim over the frigid water and graze against the lake's edge until I got to Maple Point. The numerous picnic tables and grills were blanketed in snow, like an isolated winter wonderland; it looked magical in the moonlight. Once I reached the large wooden playground, I'd start sprinting to my favorite Maple tree, the biggest one. Its figure made an upside-down rounded heart shape.

I'd start climbing up the ridges of the trunk of the Maple tree, brushing up against the bark and shaking a little snow off the branches as I zoomed up, gaining speed until I reached the top. From there, I would burst out of the tree like a cannon ball. I'd rocket higher and higher and higher until the porch lights from all the houses in Willow Ridge looked like tiny specks of glitter. In the darkness up there, there seemed to be no boundaries, just a great magnitude of sky that was endless and open. Cruising the vastness of the sky was exhilarating and a little frightening.

I could have gone to another town if I wanted to explore the Central New York area. I could have traveled to another state, visited Yellowstone National Park in Wyoming, or gone to California, or soared along the Alaskan tundra, maybe even traveled to another country like Italy or France or somewhere in Asia. Maybe I could have even visited another planet.

I stayed right where I came from, though. I stayed as close as possible to the people I loved, and swayed about the sky and wind that now formed the landscape of my new home—I had more freedom than I knew what to do with.

There was enough here to keep me busy, though.

When I didn't keep myself busy enough hovering around the people I loved in Willow Ridge, observing how life went on without me, I would sink low to the ground and float discombobulated, full of regret and self-pity—I didn't want to be that.

Knowing Heidi was planning to visit our town soon, I found myself pacing the earth a lot more. I couldn't stop thinking of her and the crash. Staying busy and wandering around was the best thing to do; I didn't want to sulk. I didn't want to fall into the loneliness and despair that came from not being able to change my circumstances and fate.

There was always somewhere to go and someone to visit. I could easily dash from one place to another, whizzing from one location to the next in seconds.

Each day I was discovering things about my new dimension and how the energies around me all worked together.

I would ride the air like a current.

Following the energy that radiated off people's bodies was enchanting, sort of like following the scent of perfume or cologne that drifts in the air. Sometimes I didn't choose where I would end up at all, and I wandered around and waited for someone's or something's energy to find me, guide me. Other times the vibrations of a sound would grab my attention, and I'd gravitate to where it came from.

The pull of energy could come from the feeling of being needed, or a spark would run through me alerting my senses of what way to go or not go, like reins that control a horse's direction.

It became clear to me a little more each day that there was an invisible pulse of life that streamed through all people and things. I hadn't considered these energies during my life on earth, but now these invisible pulses were a part of my new existence.

At first I thought these pulls and yanks were the best way to stay in tune with my loved ones, but soon I discovered I could connect in an even more personal and powerful way.

After Zara started to drift to sleep, I went to see what Jett was up to, even though it was getting late. But when I headed toward her house, something pulled me in another direction, telling me that she was not at home.

I found her parked car sitting in an apartment complex. Rain was softly hitting her car window as she talked on the phone to her mother. Sitting in the passenger seat I listened to her tell her mother she was spending the night at Zara's. I knew it was a lie because I had just seen Zara sleeping, and we didn't typically have sleepovers on a school night.

She really wanted to get her way and stretched her lie more by saying she had to hurry and get off the phone because she and Zara needed to finish up their homework.

I noticed the shape of a guy in the window of the apartment in front of us; he was glancing out the window at Jett's car.

He felt a strong attraction to her.

She must have been parked in front of Kyle's apartment.

Watching Jett lie to the mother she didn't respect about where she was going to spend the night, and thinking about Eva's father in jail and Zara's parents ignoring her, it hit me how lucky I was to have parents who were still married, who had supported my running and dreams, and had been there for me.

My parents always put Evan and me first. I missed my mother's lasagna and my father waiting in the car, honking the horn and waking up the whole neighborhood some weekend mornings when we'd drive to Beaver Lake for a run together. I regretted rolling my eyes so much at my mother and, one time, telling her I hated her. That was something I thought about a lot now, how I didn't ever tell them I appreciated all they had done for me and the time they had dedicated to my happiness—not because they were supposed to but because they wanted to support me and be a part of my experiences.

I could see some guilt in Jett's eyes as she bit her fingernail while talking to her mother. Her mother believed Jett's lie, saying, "Okay, that's fine," with a tired but agreeable voice that convinced Jett that her mother wasn't going to call Zara's house to see if she was telling the truth about where she was sleeping tonight. In a few minutes Ms. Kuro would collapse on the couch and fall asleep, happy that her daughter could be trusted. She was too tired to question that Jett was anything but honest.

Jett's mother had reason to be tired.

Like Eva's, Jett's father wasn't around, only he wasn't in jail; Jett had no idea where he was. When she was a child and constantly asked her mother where he was, the reply was basically the same time and time again: he wanted another life.

In kindergarten when Eva and I met Jett, her mother legally changed her last name. She started the school year writing her last name as Shimizu, but by the end of the year she was Jett Kuro. The teacher always had the students line up alphabetically by last name, and Jett moved from the back of the line to the middle of it.

It was eleven years since kindergarten. Eleven years of Jett realizing her father had left them and was never coming back, and eleven years of blaming her mother.

Jett had shared with us how much she had wanted a sibling, but her mother could hardly afford her. They ate mostly soba noodles, stretching tofu and soy sauce for a week, not wasting a drop.

The economy had done damage to her mother's dreams of owning her own real-estate company, and she was struggling to make a better life for her daughter and herself. When Jett was young, she and her mom shared a single bed in a small studio apartment near the gritty south side of Willow Ridge.

No matter how gritty it got, Jett took pride in her long, thick black hair just as Zara treasured her long, thick blonde hair. Jett squeezed bottles of shampoo and conditioner until they made grunting, farting noises and at last spit out their final drops of luxury. Sometimes she'd jab the plastic bottle with scissors or a knife, cutting it open, just to get the last of what was inside.

Even when she was still a child there were so many compliments from random shoppers in the canned-food aisle at the grocery store and from mothers at the public pool about Jett's hair and beautiful skin, that Jett's mother decided to take some photos of her and mail them to modeling agencies in Central New York and New York City. Ms. Kuro soon grew tired of all the running around and waiting that was involved with model castings, though. She grew disenchanted with putting so much hope into a potential booking when time and time again the bookings ended up being given to another girl.

Without her mother as her taxi, shuttling her to one part of town and then another, Jett had no way of pursuing her modeling career on her own. Mila, the founder of Mila's Model Management in Willow Ridge, saw potential in her, though. She encouraged Jett to come back to the modeling agency when she had her license and could drive herself.

When Jett reached high school, her mother started working at an established real-estate company. At last they were able to upgrade to a small two-bedroom house in the better part of town, which was good, but with her mother working long hours, Jett was often left to her own devices.

She went back to Mila's Model Management as soon as she got her own car last summer, and this past year the agency had been booking her consistently for local print work for regional stores. This past fall, the agency had even submitted her to that contest that flew her to New York City for the beauty editorial in *Teen Vogue*. It was so exciting to see one of my best friends in a national magazine. It had been weeks now, though, since she had booked a job. I wondered if this worried her.

When Jett hung up with her mother, she sat in the car for a moment listening to the rain. I listened to the rain with her. It tapped harder now, in a rhythm like a tap dancer doing a shuffle ball change on the windows, windshield, and roof.

Jett checked her voice mails. There weren't any new messages, so she listened to the saved ones. One was from her modeling agent; Jett hadn't booked the print campaign for Kodak. Jett rolled her eyes and deleted the message.

One was from Kyle asking if she was staying the night. She smiled and re-saved that one.

Suddenly I heard my voice.

It was from a message I left her the week before the crash. She must have been saving the message over and over so that it would still be there.

It had almost been two full weeks since I died, and it felt like I hadn't heard my voice in a very long time.

In the message I talked about almost hitting a squirrel while driving home from hanging out with Phoenix at the Arcade.

"I almost hit that sucker," I said on the voice mail.

I sounded so giddy and high-strung—I sounded so alive.

My message made Jett laugh as she held the phone to her ear and closed her eyes for a moment. Then she re-saved the message again. When she scrolled through her phone list, my number was still there.

I was glad that she kept my phone number still in her phone and had saved that message. It made me wonder if Phoenix still had my number in his phone as well, and if the last text messages I sent him were still preserved.

Jett grabbed an oversize handbag that was probably full of clothing for the next day and ran to Kyle's door.

Kyle had been gazing at Jett the whole time through his apartment window, and she hardly had to knock before he answered the door and welcomed her with a long, nurturing hug.

In his apartment I got a strong sense of security. It felt to me like the walls were pillars, holding up something genuine.

I had never met Kyle. He hadn't been at my funeral, but I could sense Jett had told Kyle about my death. He hugged her gently, like she was fragile and sensitive.

When he slowly released from Jett's embrace, I noticed he wore two small silver hoop earrings and had some scruff on his chin, which I hadn't noticed when I saw him in the window watching Jett approach. He was also older. The stress faded from Jett's face when she entered the apartment, as if Kyle's home was a land of peacefulness. After hugging Kyle, she dropped her bag immediately on the floor, kicked off her shoes, and went to the couch, like it was her place of tranquility.

Being with them now was like seeing the pieces of the puzzle come together to reveal the truth of Jett's love life.

This past October Jett shot a local print campaign for a new spa opening up in Willow Ridge, and Kyle had been the photographer at the shoot.

She was not the legal age of eighteen to pose half naked with just a towel wrapped around her, but the spa was offering a nice chunk of money for the gig, and her agent didn't want to pass it up. Mila told Jett to just be quiet about how old she actually was, and if they asked her to show identification for proof of her age to say she forgot it.

Seven years older than Jett, Kyle had graduated from Syracuse University with a bachelor of fine arts degree with a focus in photography. A couple of years ago he had started his own photography business, and he'd made a name for himself already among the boutique advertising agencies in the area as a quality photographer whose rates wouldn't break the bank.

The first time they met was the day of the spa shoot, and Jett was lying on a massage table, wrapped in a towel, ready for the photo shoot. Kyle had admired her exotic beauty, soft complexion, long, dark hair, and the pretty curve of her bare back and shoulders.

The day at the photo shoot appeared in front of me, like a vivid dream or memory of my own, and I caught up quickly on the details and passion of their secret relationship.

I remember she had mentioned to us that she had met this cute photographer at her shoot, but then said she could never be with a photographer. She said she didn't want to date someone who was too close to her own career path. It had been a cover-up; she had been with him all along.

She told us that during the photo shoot, the cute photographer had made small talk about how no one ever shot with film anymore and how much that bothered him.

She had liked that he was gentle and kind about how she should position her arms and body to look longer for the shot.

After the photo shoot, he told her to keep in touch and gave her his email, which she jotted down in her notebook. At first they had an email relationship; Kyle would tell her about an exhibit he was doing and his trips to Philadelphia and Boston for photography gigs.

When she admitted her real age to him, he didn't seem to care about their age difference or that she was a minor. Their little email conversations continued after the New Year.

And then Kyle appeared in our lives—not in person, but through the text messages that Jett was always reading and rereading.

To be honest I had no idea that Jett had such an attachment to Kyle and his apartment. None of the other girls or I had ever met him. She always said he was busy, out of town, or too tired from a job to meet up with us. She only shared with us little details: a dinner they had or that she couldn't hang out sometimes because she was with him. I wasn't sure what his background was, but now as I looked on, the intimate relationship was becoming clear to me.

Of all of us, Jett was the most sexually experienced.

It looked routine as she leaned back against the couch, put her feet up on his coffee table, and then rested her head against his shoulder. They were like a two puzzle pieces fitting together, and it was obvious she felt truly at home with him.

While I was getting a thrill out of a tenth-of-a-second kiss from Phoenix, hoping it meant something to him too, Jett had outgrown those little flutters of flirtatious wondering. As she curled up beside Kyle on his couch, she had a seductive, knowing allure about her.

The living room was only lit by the television, and they didn't say a word as his fingers slowly combed through Jett's long, dark hair. There was a connection between them that didn't happen through talking or even looking at each other. They were melting into the comfort of just being next to each other. It was the type of comfort I had only recently begun to understand, when deep feelings are present but no words can express it and the action, or touch, says it all.

Compared to the other guys Jett had been with, there was a sturdiness about Kyle that came with being years older. Kyle seemed self-assured, as if he already had weeded through the insecurities that come with trying to figure one's life out and now recognized his skills and how to best use them.

I could sense that was something romantic about him—or maybe it was simply that he looked directly in Jett's eyes when she spoke and gave her his attention in a way that no other guy had.

Among the rustic scenery of his apartment, he looked as mellow and relaxed as the jeans he was wearing.

Sitting on a decorative hardwood stand was a beautiful globe of the earth; it looked like a precious heirloom. Kyle's photographs were showcased on the walls of the apartment, matted and framed. They showed off his travels to China, Australia and South America.

As Kyle stretched his legs across the couch, with Jett now lying on top of him, her head on his chest, I counted more than twenty frames in the living room alone.

And a nude sculpture of a goddess on one of the shelves of the floor-to-ceiling bookshelf. There were also a few framed black-and-white nude photography prints hanging in the dark hallway near the bathroom. The model's face couldn't be seen; it was just the back of a girl lying nude on a bed. She had dark, long hair that reminded me of Jett's. Maybe it was.

His apartment reminded me of a little museum.

My tour was interrupted when Jett asked Kyle, "Do you think I'm pretty?"

Kyle's fingers swayed up and down Jett's back while he said to her, "I think you're beautiful." He pulled her body up toward his lips and kissed her forehead, and she giggled when he kissed her nose.

I couldn't help but be in awe of them. Then she asked him, "So, you think I have a chance in New York City? What if I can't get an agency?"

I froze, as he said, "You're going to be great. Stop worrying."

I knew Jett wasn't planning to go to college right after graduation—but moving to New York City?

It was the first time I had heard Jett discuss her future with a somewhat serious tone, and I started to get the idea that maybe she was silently plotting her escape to the big time or something. These weren't plans Jett had shared with us. Part of me felt like she was rushing into things with Kyle—they hadn't known each other that long, and making plans to move to a whole other city seemed like a huge risk that could become a disaster. Where would they live? How would they survive? Kyle was gaining success with his photography, but his freelance lifestyle seemed like it could easily become unstable.

What if Jett couldn't get an agency?

What if their plans didn't work out?

Snuggling against Kyle, Jett didn't look nervous at all, like I would have been. She looked content in their thoughts of possibility and adventure. Her face was blissful and dreamy and comfortable against Kyle's shirt.

Maybe next to Kyle she didn't care about the risk.

I started to wonder if maybe taking a risk was what making it big was all about? My future had been organized like a straight line with bullet points of goals to hit, and hers looked more like a swivel, with the next turns unofficially planned and inspired by the unknown. But she liked it that way, perhaps. If things didn't work out, at least Jett and Kyle could always come back to Willow Ridge.

Where was the wrong in trying?

I knew she wouldn't find real modeling success in Willow Ridge, and it would be great for Jett to try to make something of herself.

It would be cool to have a friend in New York City; I could visit her and experience new things in the city.

Just as I was becoming curious about what New York City would be like, she suddenly started ranting to Kyle with my similar concerns.

"I don't know, maybe this is crazy. Maybe we shouldn't do this. I haven't booked any work in weeks. My phone never rings anymore. No one books girls that look like me. It's just the way it is. The other models are going to be so much prettier. I'm going to show up with three stupid tear sheets, and the agency is going to laugh at my face. Everyone else is going to be living in a college dorm with prepaid lunch plans, and we are going to be in a shack with rats!"

She was talking a mile a minute, but Kyle didn't seem concerned. "Chill," he said and rubbed her back. "I'll scare all the rats. We'll be fine. We've got a year to plan it. We'll visit the city this summer, and you can get a feel for it. Willow Ridge is nothing compared to the type of gigs you're going to get in the city. You're going to take over New York. Relax, babe."

Kyle didn't say that modeling was competitive and cutthroat or that it was a crazy idea. He didn't rag her about the risk of failure, and how living paycheck to paycheck was not fun. He seemed fearless.

Jett quieted down and put her head back on his chest and pressed her body close to his while they stared at the TV. After about twenty minutes they moved from the couch and headed down the dark hallway. I followed them into Kyle's bedroom.

I wondered when she was going to break the news to the girls of how serious her relationship with Kyle was, and that she was planning to move to New York City with him to pursue modeling next year after graduation.

The light flicked on in the bedroom. It almost blinded me, and it took a moment before I noticed the glow of his aquarium with tropical fish. Kyle shut the bedroom door even though—to his eyes—there was no one else in the apartment watching them.

Jett rushed to the bed, her hair flying by me, and flopped on to the mattress with an ease that suggested she had known it many times before. The bed was huge, probably queen-size, with a pine-green comforter, big fluffy pillows, and a dark wooden headboard.

On the bed they shared a few short kisses that soon became long sensual kisses.

I moved closer and studied Jett's mouth, how she angled her head slightly, and how their tongues swirled around in each other's mouth.

Kyle held Jett close to him, and Jett's socked feet massaged against his socked feet as if it was a sign for something that only they understood.

I anticipated their next move.

As one of Kyle's hands rubbed Jett's thighs through her jeans, his other glided up the front of her shirt, and I got the idea that Jett didn't mind where his hands went.

They knew each other's bodies so well, like they had known each other a lot longer than they had. I stared, spellbound, as Kyle unhooked her bra while kissing her intensely.

Jett ran her hands over Kyle's back, scratching him lightly with her fingernails.

They had a rhythm to each movement of their hands and lips, unspoken but orchestrated so perfectly. They made it look so easy, but I knew I wouldn't have known how to touch a guy the way Jett was now touching Kyle.

I stayed back by the bedroom doorway and watched. Jett didn't hold back or tell him to slow down when he unzipped her pants and she pulled her shirt over her head. She yanked at him to be nearer and even closer.

As I watched them, the air around me started to feel humid. A trickle of heat slithered through me.

Their socks came off. Their jeans were thrown on the floor. Kyle's shirt and Jett's bra, already unhooked, soon followed. She was only wearing her thong now, as Kyle kissed each of her breasts softly. He kissed down her stomach to her belly button. The thong was getting in the way of what they really wanted to do, and it was flung across the room, along with Kyle's briefs.

If I had ever seen Phoenix's underwear fly across the room, it probably would have made me laugh, but Jett only looked seductively into Kyle's eyes, wanting and needing him, and wrapped her arms around him, pressing her bare chest against his, tighter and tighter.

His hands fondled her again with interest, care, and intensity in each touch.

Their bodies moved around like nude wrestlers. He moved around every part of her body, and she grabbed at his hair and lightly sucked at his earlobe and his small silver hoop earrings.

While they indulged in each other's bodies with caressing and breathy kisses, the comforter was pushed off to the floor and the sheets were kicked and scrunched to the bottom of the bed in a flurry. Then Jett grabbed for his waist and pulled him closer to her.

He rushed to put on the Trojan condom. Watching Kyle lying on top of Jett, I wondered what the weight of a man would feel like. It was a type of pressure my now shapeless body wouldn't get to ever understand. Once he put the condom on, Jett's coy expression became flushed and sensuous. She fell into a state of a pleasure I would never know, and I couldn't help but feel jealous.

I could hear Kyle's breathing, Jett's breathing, Kyle's hum of enjoyment, Jett's aroused pant. Her breath became short and quick. They were gasping together, louder and louder, as they changed their position and started again.

Soon all I could see was Jett's behind moving back and forth. She was on top of Kyle, who was obviously enjoying every moment of it.

Suddenly a strange loneliness came over me, telling me I was watching something I wasn't supposed to see. I started to feel awkward watching them as they continued thrusting their bodies together, so I left.

Unsure of where to go I went to my house.

It was past midnight, and the lights were all off. It was strange how the house always creaked a little when I entered now. The wood floors seemed to notice me. They hadn't creaked like that when I was alive.

My father's running shoes weren't in their spot by the door, like always; instead they had been thrown in the closet — put away in a box on the top shelf.

Like an intruder I crept around.

The house was very quiet.

Evan had gone back to Le Moyne earlier that week; he couldn't miss any more school. His bedroom at home was dark and his bed was made.

I panned around his room.

I had loved his vintage wooden chess set, which now sat on top of his bookshelf. He had taught me to play when I was younger. I had always lost, but I liked how he would notice every movement of my eyes as he tried to figure out my next move. He was proud of me when my move worked out, but he always seemed to be one step ahead of me. Back then he'd always chosen to play the black set, but we hadn't played in years, and now dust collected on each piece. I noticed that the black knights were missing from the chessboard and searched the floor but couldn't find them.

I wondered whether I should visit him at Le Moyne, where he rented a room in a house with other juniors. He was probably really busy, but it was kind of fishy that he hadn't talked about any internships or plans he had for after college. He'd probably figure it out—it was his life, not mine.

In his childhood bedroom I also noticed his old comic books, although now they were in a cardboard box in the back of his closet. I remembered the day Evan stopped caring if I snuck into his chest of comic books and even gave me a couple that he had read over so many times that some of the pages were torn or missing.

That was back when we still hung out.

He changed when he started smoking pot; he stopped asking me how my track meet went and instead asked my mother for the update. For a while I could feel a gap growing between us, and I wasn't sure why. I can't remember the last real conversation we had before I died. He just wasn't the brother I wish he had been. I would have liked it if he had more of an interest in me and wanted to be that big brother who looked out for me. At my funeral he just sat there, probably stoned, and felt nothing, just zoned out, not saying a word. I wished he had stood up in front of everyone at my funeral and told them how he missed me and how sorry he was for not being there for me. I wanted to hear it from his heart. I wanted to hear his apology.

Maybe he was still in disbelief I died — or maybe he wasn't sorry.

I hated how he constantly rolled his eyes at whatever I said, as if he thought I was spoiled or stupid or immature.

Alone in his room and inconspicuous, I wished I could have tumbled his chessboard to the floor with a huge crash. I wanted to see all the pieces sprawled about in a big mess.

Maybe he was a little jealous of the attention I had been getting from college coaches recently. I mean, he had always wanted to play baseball for the Miami Hurricanes at the University of Miami and could have gone there, but he decided to stay around the Syracuse area instead. I wondered if he had regrets about not going away and if he ever wondered about the life he could have had there. He had been playing really well at Le Moyne, and it was a good fit for him — so my father told me.

This past Christmas, I hardly knew what to get him as a gift because we'd grown so far apart. I ended up getting him one of those preppy sweaters he wore. He hardly said he liked it. He now had a short tolerance for family functions. He didn't even try to pretend he wanted to be with us. After opening presents, he rushed out to meet up with his college buddies.

While imaging his chess set cluttered on the floor in his bedroom, I could see how little I actually knew about him. My fingers strummed past a few books about space and the cosmos. I didn't know he liked books by Carl Sagan. I guess you could live with someone your whole life and never really know them.

I really wished he wasn't my brother; I deserved a different type of brother.

I couldn't stand being in his room and gracing it with my presence. I slipped under the door, wishing I could slam it shut and shake the room.

I traveled into my parents' room. My mother was getting agitated while tossing and turning and adjusting her pillow in bed. My father was snoring next to her. I stayed by her vanity table and, even in the dark, the gold finish on the metal handle of her old handheld vintage mirror glowed. The mirror had a mysterious, ancient beauty. It was engraved on the back with two owls facing each other. When I was younger, I had asked where my mother had gotten it; she found it at an antique fair in Paris when she traveled there with some of her friends after college. I remembered the curious feeling of realizing that my mother had a life before I was born.

She had told me that I could have the handheld mirror when I graduated high school. Seeing the mirror now reminded me that it would have been passed down to me had my life gone according to plan.

Downstairs I snooped over some mail sitting on the kitchen counter. There were opened envelopes from an insurance company and a car donation organization. There was also the outrageous receipt from the funeral home.

I slouched across the living room couch, looking at our family portraits on the wall. There was a picture of me smiling, wearing some ugly outfit my mother had suggested. After a while I slowly went toward the main portrait of us together. I softly brushed myself against my hair in the photo, and I stayed against my hair for a long time, wondering if every single time my parents saw someone else with curly red hair they would think me.

Memories ran through me. I remembered how every Christmas Eve my mother made candy-cane cookies, sometimes making the fire alarm go off. There was also the memory of how when I was little we had a big garden and I helped pick the juicy tomatoes. Sometimes without even washing them, I'd just take a huge bite and let the juice dribble down my chin. My mother loved to remind me that I was such a chunker as a baby. I would get so embarrassed when she brought it up in front of my friends, but now it was funny.

My father had trusted that I would behave, and most of the time I did, except that time I bridge jumped into the Seneca River with

Evan and his neighborhood friends. He yelled at Evan for letting me tag along with him. Then he gave me such a hard time and wouldn't shut up about how I could have been killed and how I had a brain and needed to use it. He went on and on about it for a week. I was so annoyed—but he was right. It was a pretty stupid thing to do.

I remembered the first time my running stats were posted in the newspaper. Proudly he bought a stack of about forty copies of the newspaper, telling me I'd want them when I was older, to remember this moment.

He was right. He was right all the time. The stack of newspapers was still in a box in my closet. It sat next to all the scrapbooks I made during my scrapbooking phase and the many board games I hadn't played in years. I wondered how long people kept things after someone dies.

That night I decided to sleep in my bedroom. My mother had washed my pile of dirty clothing and now each shirt, pair of jeans, and even my underwear sat folded, neatly stacked on my bed. I didn't see the point in folding something that wouldn't ever get unfolded.

Although only two weeks had gone by, there was a light coat of dust on the computer keyboard and bookshelf. As I looked out my window, waiting for a sign or a vibration to pull me towards my next destination, I noticed there was dust on the windowsill too.

I listened to the rain and thought about Jett, wondering when she'd share with the girls her secret New York City plans. I didn't understand why my friends didn't share things with each other that they obviously wanted to share. It made me wonder if we really were as close as I thought.

I thought about her sleeping next to Kyle. I wanted to still have a glimmer of hope that one day I'd wake up in Phoenix's arms, but it seemed like that hope was totally gone.

While I thought about what I was hopeful about now that my life had been taken away morning quickly came but it appeared gray and grim, it was like the sun never came up.

The first sound I heard was my father moving off the bed and stepping on the cold floor. After a great yawn, he stumbled to the bathroom and took a long piss. I wished I couldn't hear the vibrations of everything around me so clearly. He thumped down the stairs and clamored with the coffee machine. I stayed in my room; I was still upset he stashed his running shoes away in the closet and just didn't feel like rushing downstairs to watch him eating a bagel. He wouldn't be there long anyway. Before long, he'd tie his tie, kiss my mother's forehead and shut the door, and who knew when he'd be home from the office. It made me sad that he left my mother isolated in bed for the rest of the day, but he didn't want to be in our quiet, cold, sad house. I didn't either.

Thankfully, from afar I heard the hum of Jett's car's engine starting, and was pulled to my next destination.

# *Careful*

## WATCH WHO YOU TRUST

It was still raining as Jett zipped out of Kyle's driveway to pick up the girls for school. At least the weekend was almost here, and I flung myself into the passenger seat.

Sitting there I could see Jett's two worlds come together. One involved growing up, being adventurous and making plans to move after graduation to a different city with her older boyfriend and go after her dream, while the other involved the current landscape of cafeteria food, the catty, sneering eyes of other girls noticing what she wore today, and being among the confusing high-school boys she couldn't stand but that Eva, Zara, and I loved.

When she reached Eva's street it was littered with trash, making the block look even more ghetto. There had probably been some neighborhood scoundrel pushing down the trashcans in the night. I would have hated to live there and felt bad that Eva had to face her neighbors' garbage—a week's worth of waste, discarded food, liquids, and scraps that had been mixed with rain and were in the slushy, mucky snow.

Jett honked three quick *beep, beep, beeps*, like she always did, even though Eva was already waiting near the door. It was funny how the beeps embarrassed Eva and reminded me how silly Jett could be sometimes. I jumped to the backseat as Eva struggled to tame her umbrella, which had flipped inside out. She flopped into the passenger seat, totally unhappy.

Jett drove cautiously, and I could sense she was a little scared as she dodged the beer and soda bottles and cardboard pizza boxes scattered across the street.

As they reached the main road to Zara's house, Eva's face was painted with her usual recent panic of being in a moving vehicle, and now the rain added to her paranoia. She could hardly see out the windshield and kept asking Jett if her windshield wipers could go any faster.

Unlike them, I didn't have to wait for lights or traffic to move, so I left the backseat and beat them to Zara's.

The wind struck Zara's face fiercely, and hard pellets of rain zapped her smile away. Zara stepped back inside her house, shivering as she stood by the window and waited for Jett's car to arrive.

The wind slapped against the window. It was a soggy and depressing mess of a morning. Mother Nature was having a hissy fit.

While getting ready for school, Zara hadn't checked the weather forecast and hadn't even glanced out of her window as she focused on shining and shaping her blond hair. Now the extra time she had spent perfecting herself was pointless.

She wrapped the blue silk scarf that had been around her neck into a cute bandana to help protect her hair from the rain when Jett arrived. The scarf looked pretty around her head, and I wished I had been able to ask her how to tie a scarf like that.

Zara reached inside her tote bag and pulled out her makeup bag. Pulling out a powder compact, she checked her face again. I also studied her face, trying to imagine what she'd look like when she was older, as I often wondered now about my friends, since I would never experience my own face changing with age. I tried to picture myself a few years older, when I might eventually become more comfortable with the real me, my frizzy hair and small breasts.

She closed the powder compact with a loud snap and stared out at the gray day unenthused. Her red trench coat made her look more sophisticated and confident today, but her expression wasn't as hopeful. I wouldn't have wanted to go to school on a day like this either. At least it was Friday.

I thought about the last time I had felt rain. Although the wicked winds, the rain, the sleet, and the snow of Central New York were all things I had been annoyed living with, I missed being able to feel them on my skin.

When Jett's car pulled in the driveway, Zara seemed to have decided it was foolish to open her umbrella for such a short distance. Careful not to fall on her butt from the slippery slush, she focused on keeping her balance while she ran to the car. She let out a sigh of relief as she slumped into the backseat.

They drove through the downpour, Jett with both hands on the wheel, Eva's eyes pinned on the road, and Zara sighing over and over, wishing the day was already done. I sat quietly in the back with Zara. Even though her tote bag took up most of the other seat, it was easy for me to find room since, being formless, I could easily adjust how much I spread out or squished myself together.

Their shoes squeaked down the hallway, as they headed toward their homeroom classes. Whispers about my death, about Heidi, about our alleged rivalry, still echoed throughout the school whenever the girls walked by. It was hard for them not to notice, but they carried on through each class period, met up with each other between classes, and focused on their own conversations with each other, complimenting each other's shoes, necklace, or earrings, or rolling their eyes at the thought of a certain class assignment. Sometimes they walked in silence and just looked tired. Sometimes Zara would be talking fast and breathless about something relating to her fashion blog or a comment she received. Sometimes Jett would make a sassy remark about the looks she got from a group of horny sophomore boys, and Eva would burst out laughing. I ached to not have a voice anymore to contribute to the conversation. Sometimes after talking about the things we all used to talk about, they would notice themselves, their words, the three of them, and my absence; the glow in their eyes would fade a little, remembering that they were mourning still.

〜

The cafeteria was always an uncomfortable place, with the sounds of forks scraping against plates, food crunching loudly in unmannered mouths, and everyone noticing who was sitting with whom and who was eating what. We always carried our lunches in their tote bags; cafeteria food was unpredictable. We only bought drinks in the cafeteria.

The girls nonchalantly scanned the cafeteria, not giving the gawkers even a glance, and headed to our usual table. Each year we had arranged our schedules with our counselors so we would be able to have lunch together, since usually our class schedules didn't match up. This year, my schedule and Eva's actually had aligned for honors English literature class—Heidi had been in that class with us. Before the crash, Eva and I would walk together after lunch; now Eva would have to walk to the class alone, without me.

Brett and Caleb didn't have the same lunch period we did, so Zara met up with Brett at her locker at various times throughout the day. Eva usually spent time by Zara's locker often as well, in case Caleb was with Brett, which he always was.

Phoenix, Caleb, and Brett were friends before any of us became close to them. They hadn't known each other since childhood, the way we girls had known each other. They'd met though lacrosse in high school. They'd managed to keep their own childhood friends while also gaining new friends from the lacrosse field. To me, the lacrosse team seemed like a fraternity or something. The teammates would joke with each other, smacking each other's shoulders and helmets; they talked about girls in a sexually offensive way, bragging about all the things they could get from them if they wanted, while they made statements about their "sticks"—it gave me a bad vibe.

So even though I could now watch Phoenix's lacrosse practices and games anytime I wanted when the spring season started, I didn't look forward to it. How I imagined Phoenix to be was very different from how he acted with his lacrosse buddies, and I wasn't sure I wanted to see that side of him.

But like always, I still hoped to see him in the cafeteria.

This year lunch had been the main time during school day that I saw him, since we didn't have any classes together.

And there he was. Phoenix's energy could unzip me. I knew his energy like I knew no other. I could always feel it before he arrived. His trusting and soothing ambience filled the air, covering the room and me like a warm blanket. It was hard to miss.

At lunch Phoenix had usually sat with some of the lacrosse guys. I never felt comfortable hanging out at the lacrosse table, but he'd always walk by our table and chat with me for a few minutes. It had made my whole body radiate when he would squeeze my shoulder before he left. It was one of those little moments in the day I looked forward to most. But now those shoulder squeezes were only a memory.

Phoenix shoved his hands into the front pockets of his gray, zip-up hoodie. The hood drooped over his head, making him look slightly rugged and grungy.

He was standing by the beverage cooler, deciding on a juice or sports drink. He smiled and nodded his head toward my friends when they walked by and mouthed "Hey" to Zara.

When she waved back my heart fell. I wanted that, I wanted him to mouth "Hey" to me, and I envied Zara as she told Jett and Eva she'd be right back and walked over to Phoenix.

Zara could feel the whole cafeteria looking at her as she walked and gave him a quick hug. I wondered if she was thinking of me, or thinking of how he and I were supposed to go to prom together, and I wondered if seeing Zara had made Phoenix think of me, since she was one of my best friends.

He offered her the soda that clanked to the bottom of the vending machine after they hugged, and then they went their separate ways to different sides of the cafeteria.

But before Zara got back to our table and joined the girls, she noticed what I had noticed.

It seemed like Phoenix and Jackson were on better terms, and Phoenix was walking over to sit with Jackson.

I understood they had made up, but it just felt wrong. Especially with Zara, Eva, and Jett sitting across the cafeteria, watching as Phoenix patted Jackson on the back and sat down next to him while talking to him about something that made them both laugh. I had a bad feeling about the way they laughed together.

Zara was quiet, and pursed her lips. Under clenched teeth she whispered to the girls to discreetly look near the wall clock, at who Phoenix was sitting with, when they went to get their food trays.

That stung. Phoenix should have come over to sit with them, at least for a few minutes.

The girls went to get some drinks. Eva was about to say something about Phoenix when Zara gave her a look, shook her head, and rolled her eyes.

When Phoenix did glance toward the girls for a moment, his lips created a small frown and he had an apologetic expression on his face. But trying to act sincere now didn't matter to them.

They had been insulted in more than one way. Across the table from Phoenix and Jackson sat Sonia and Gwen.

I had always noticed Sonia's changing hairstyles because we both had red hair, although hers was straight and shorter; it was never frizzy or tangled like mine could be.

Sonia's red hair was cut at a crisp, even line just below her chin and now had perfectly straight and blunt bangs just above her eyebrows. Her short bob made her pale neck look very long, like a giraffe's, and with her V-neck sweater today it was hard to miss her protruding collarbone.

Gwen had gotten some bangs too. She had a large forehead, so the choppy bangs framing her face looked good. Her dark shoulder-length hair was pin-straight, and she constantly ran her hands through it. Gwen was the only other Japanese girl besides Jett in the cafeteria that lunch period; Asians were sparse at Willow Ridge. Gwen and Jett had always stood out as the prettiest Asians around.

Jett was known as the taller Asian, and the one with the longer and shinier hair. Gwen and Jett might have had similar facial features, but that's all they had in common these days. They had a few laughs together during gym class just a month ago when the gym teacher confused them during a volleyball game. They both agreed the sport was not meant for their manicures. But since Heidi had been sent away, Gwen now always acted sick and never wanted to be on the court with Jett. Gwen watched Jett, who remained on the court, complain about the pain of the volleyball smacking her arm and rolled her eyes. She suddenly thought Jett was prissy and full of herself, a stupid model wannabe whose bones could easily break.

Back at our cafeteria table the tension between them was obvious to me, as Gwen smirked in our direction while she ran her fingers through her hair and panned the cafeteria. She knew she had something at her table that was supposed to be ours—but really he had been only mine.

I wanted to rip her face off. Back when I was alive, dealing with Gwen would have meant dealing with her older sister Olivia. Olivia could probably break your arms in two like it was nothing. Olivia was one tough bitch—a smart one too. She was the senior class president, and she could also kick the shit out of you.

Jett tried to ignore Gwen's smirks. She clenched her teeth as she shook her head. Throwing eggs at Heidi's house was probably on Jett's mind. She was getting heated and her heart was racing. The only thing holding her back from erupting was how thankful she was to have Kyle and a plan for a new life in New York City. Eva and Zara didn't know about that yet, though, so they kept telling her to calm down and ignore Gwen. To distract herself from wanting to look over there, Jett took out her powder compact and touched up her makeup, checking whether her eyebrows needed a tweeze while discreetly looking at the reflection of Sonia and Gwen in the mirror.

I kept dwelling on their bangs. Maybe Sonia and Gwen had gotten their hair cut together and decided on the bangs as something to unite them with Heidi, who was now absent but returning for a visit.

A musty and groggy feeling came over me.

Heidi wasn't going to be visiting Willow Ridge High School, but I was sure she would somehow still make her appearance in town a spectacle, and that was enough to make me feel deader than ever.

At the correctional institute for juveniles Heidi wasn't allowed to use her phone—it was taken away—and she was allowed to use the computer only for an hour a day and only with supervision. She would sign onto the Annex and usually she wrote on her profile about the boredom she was experiencing there or how much it upset her that she couldn't take a shower for longer than ten minutes, and how lonely she felt.

I couldn't feel bad for her. She was still alive.

Heidi's online profile had a constant flow of encouraging comments from her parents and friends, reminding her that she would get through her time there and to stay positive. She was very missed and she was such a beautiful person, or so they said, despite having killed me. That wasn't all. Sonia and Gwen had created a supportive fan page for her on The Annex, calling it We Miss You Heidi, and it was based on her innocence and the great friend and hurdler she was.

Maybe she hadn't killed me on purpose, but she had run a red light while texting Jackson, and her SUV had smashed into my body and face and taken everything away from me. She wasn't innocent.

I wanted to jerk Sonia and Gwen's shoulders each time they giggled with Phoenix.

There was the *We Miss You* card for Heidi going around Sonia and Gwen's table for everyone to sign.

When the card got to Phoenix he scribbled his name nonchalantly in between bites of a sandwich. He wrote his signature purposely sloppy. You could hardly tell it said Phoenix, but his hand held the pen, which hit the card, and he signed it.

I couldn't believe it.

The hurt of it blazed through me like a wildfire.

Zara, Eva, and Jett didn't know—they were not looking—but I saw him.

The liveliness in their eyes killed me all over again, Sonia's and Gwen's squeals, and the sound of their hands smacking the table were like bolts of lightning that could be heard all through Willow Ridge.

It was as if they were shrieking with laughter on purpose so everyone would turn and see that Phoenix had chosen to sit with them. He seemed a little embarrassed with their obnoxious, hyena-like laughter, but he stayed put.

Although Zara, Eva, and Jett hadn't seen Phoenix sign the card, the girls couldn't ignore the screeches of Sonia's and Gwen's laughter—it was worse than the howls of the bad witch in *The Wizard of Oz*. They all rolled their eyes.

Jackson could only visit Heidi once every other weekend, he planned to keep dating her and sent her letters updating her on what she was missing. I felt even more squeamish thinking about how Jackson and Heidi were still dating.

Every time Jackson spoke to Phoenix I felt bitter, decayed, and small, moseying around the ankles of my friends.

Even with Phoenix's presence the air in the cafeteria still felt stuffy, and the aroma of bean chili was suffocating. Zara cleared her throat and said loudly exactly what I wanted to say: "I FUCKING hate this place." She practically spit out the "F," as her front teeth scraped against her bottom lip. Perhaps she was hoping Phoenix would hear her, because he had glanced towards them, and it seemed like he had.

"This place is bullshit!" Jett agreed with a sigh. Eva just stared at her plate of food, swiveling her fork around and not actually eating anything. The minutes until the bell rang could not have gone more slowly.

～

For once Jett actually waited with Zara and Eva for Brett and Caleb after lunch. When Brett asked Zara how lunch was and squeezed her hand, Jett cut in before Zara could answer, saying,

"Lunch involved bullshit and immaturity with two sides of bitch." It was perfect and true, and we all laughed.

Caleb asked Eva what she was doing this weekend but also looked at Zara and Jett as if the question was for all of us. Jett talked about a casting for a dental commercial, and Zara mentioned the Youth Technology Conference she was attending; I could tell Eva wished they had just said they were doing nothing because she wanted Caleb only to care about what she was doing. With an unenthusiastic tone, she said she was just going to be helping her mother bake a cake at the bakery. She wanted him to know she wasn't too busy for him. Caleb said something about wanting her to give him something sweet, and his tone implied he wasn't talking about cake batter and frosting, but then said he was kidding and stepped away from her, creating a little distance between himself and Eva. I wished Eva could grasp the insincerity that shed off him, but of course she'd have to see that for herself.

As I perched on the backrest of Zara's chair in her chemistry class, Sonia was only a couple of rows away, and every few minutes she would glance over toward us.

The class was learning about the earth's physical and chemical behavior. I thought it was all pointless and boring when I was alive, but now science meant more to me than lab experiments and chemical equations that I never really understood.

Each day in my new existence, I felt closer to the rays of light touching down upon Willow Lake, and when the sun warmed the earth it was like our energy now connected in some obscure way.

When Zara was asked to the teacher's desk, a sneering smile appeared on Sonia's face, and then a small gust of air came out of her nose as if she was having a hard time keeping a rude comment to herself. But I thought Zara was gracious and sweet to do the teacher the favor of being partners with Aubrey, who was a little unusual and unsocial. Between classes Aubrey always raced to her next one, not even noticing any of the other students or interacting with them at all, looking straight ahead, like her mission was strictly getting from point A to B. I remembered a rumor once that when Aubrey had her period, no one told her that her pants were period stained all day, and the thought of that made me feel bad for her. I should have told her about her pants and kindly whisked her to the bathroom or to the nurse so she could get cleaned up.

I was proud of Zara, and I knew why the teacher had asked her. Zara was the only one in the class who had the decency to handle scooting her desk closer to Aubrey's. But of course the other students stared. When they started working on the first lab exercise, I could tell Zara was a little embarrassed being her partner, especially with Sonia eyeing them, but she'd probably rather have been Aubrey's partner than Sonia's.

It was fun now sitting in on my friend's classes, but sometimes it made me uncomfortable too.

Honors English literature class was normally Eva's favorite, but not anymore. Heidi's seat remained empty next to Gwen, and the whole class was unusually quiet, knowing why my seat next to Eva's was also empty. As Eva sat down, Gwen had anger in her eyes. She stared at Eva's back like a wolf hunting down its prey.

Eva didn't look behind her once; we both could sense Gwen's piercing eyes on her.

Heidi had often been called on to read aloud, and absent-mindedly Mrs. Davis looked in the direction of Heidi's chair, and also looked at my chair briefly, but then redirected her glance to Eva, which made Gwen puff a sigh.

When Eva was asked to read out loud to the class, I felt like a little girl listening intently for her to start. There were many books I would now never read, and there were stories left unfinished. It wasn't like I could pick up a book and flip through it. Writing didn't just appear across the sky for me, so when people on earth opened a newspaper, researched on the Internet, or read a book, that's how I still got to enjoy those things.

Eva always put emotion into what she read, like a performance — it was the poet in her, but today she looked unenthused. As she cleared her throat and started reading *The Crucible* by Arthur Miller, I was immediately distracted. Gwen purposely started having a coughing attack, and under each violent cough the words "ugly," "bitch," "fat," "slob," went into Eva's ear.

Eva's voice was shaking a little. When she stumbled on an easy word and Mrs. Davis corrected her, I knew she was embarrassed. Of course Gwen enjoyed Eva's mistake and rattled her more.

If I could have, I would have smacked my hand against Gwen's desk and reminded her that her friend might have been sent away, but Eva's had died, and wasn't that worse? I did what I could do instead. I spread myself out in front of Eva's neck and across her throat, hoping that if I focused on letting out some warm energy I might be able to shield Eva's vocal cords and warm them up so her pronunciation would be beautiful and she would stop stuttering, and she wouldn't be bothered by Gwen.

This wasn't the first time Gwen had been disrespectful towards Eva.

⌒

Years ago, in art class in middle school, while collecting her sculpture tools, Gwen had struck up a conversation with Eva about her shirt, asking her where she bought it.

Eva had responded confidently, "JFK's."

But Gwen looked puzzled and asked with a sly, patronizing tone, "Like the president's initials, JFK?"

Eva's effort to abbreviate the name of where she bought her clothing, to make it sound trendier, had failed. She had to admit, "No, it's called *Just for Kids*."

"Oh yeah, next to Chucky Cheese," Gwen giggled. "What's it like inside there? Is everything really under $20?" Gwen would not let it go.

Eva, ashamed, wouldn't have gone into the store at all, but that day her mother had a tired look in her eye that said take it or get nothing at all.

Desperate to keep her dignity and get through this art class, a small smile appeared on Eva's face, distancing herself from Gwen's pretentious comments.

At her desk in front of her blob of clay Eva got busy again, holding a stainless steel carving knife. She acted like she was really amused with her creation.

Chunks of clay landed on the table as she tried to pretend the conversation never happened, but all day long, through every class, Eva rewound the conversation in her mind again and again. Eva knew that Gwen would tell anyone she could, perhaps the whole seventh grade, about her stupid *Just for Kids* shirt—and of course she had.

By midday Eva's mind was racing. She felt desperate to change her shirt.

Unfortunately in her gym locker there was nothing even partially fashionable and appropriate besides a smelly orange tank top that she wore under her bulky gym T-shirt. She had stopped showing her bare upper arms and thought that changing into a little tank top would be too showy and gross.

So there was nothing she could do. She wore that irritating JFK shirt all day, and then never wore it ever again.

Ironically, a year or so later, Eva and her mother moved into the junky townhouse development right behind the *Just for Kids* store. That terrible store that always reminded her of the day she admitted she was a loser, or at least felt like one, was always nearby. It was one of the worst memories of her life. She could still visualize Gwen's stupid face when she'd said, "Just for Kids."

Seventh grade felt like centuries ago, but time hadn't killed the memory, and even if Gwen might have forgotten about the art class incident, Eva steered clear of her most of the time.

When the bell rang, signaling the end of honors English literature class, Eva grabbed her bag and rushed for the door. She was breathless when she reached her calculus class.

After seeing Phoenix in the cafeteria sitting with Sonia and Gwen, then Sonia's sneering smile toward Zara in chemistry class, and then Eva's struggle to read while Gwen hassled her, I had an eerie feeling that something threatening was only just beginning—especially when the girls reached the student parking lot after school.

When they pushed through the side doors leading to the parking lot, it was foggy with rain, but they could still easily spot the disaster all over Jett's car.

Jett started swearing and shouting like a madwoman.

Her black hair was whipping back and forth, wet and straggly, as she ran past the rows and rows of other cars to get to her own car. She didn't even think to open her umbrella. She was completely freaking out, belting out every cuss word she knew.

Dripping down the sides of Jett's car were illegible words spelled out in yellow and red goo.

Because of the rain, we couldn't make out what the words said, but it was most likely nothing kind.

With her finger, Jett touched a tiny amount of the red stuff. It was icky and clumpy. She smelled it; it was ketchup. The contents of five large bottles had exploded all over the windshield, windows, hood, roof, and trunk. Add to that mustard, relish, salt, and sugar, all of which were dripping down the car windows to create a massive disgusting and embarrassing mess. The saucy liquids had mixed together and were seeping deep into the crevices of the hood, trunk, and doors of Jett's car; it would take weeks for it to finally come clean.

Jett would have to drive out of the parking lot with her car looking like that, or they'd have to clean it up fast. Other students were rushing out of the school and would notice soon.

With a small rag that she kept in her trunk, Jett started to frantically wipe the condiments off her car, while Zara and Eva sprinted as fast as they could to get paper towels from the nearest bathroom inside the school.

I watched the girls hurrying to swipe the smeared gunk off Jett's car. They had worried looks on their faces, and I paced around the car with discomfort. A growing vengefulness within me wanted to get even for the ridicule that my friends were receiving lately. It wasn't right, and I had a feeling that Sonia and Gwen were not done expressing themselves with their cafeteria laughter, vulgar coughing, sneering smiles, and condiment graffiti.

Eva was holding back tears, fearing that it was her fault somehow for causing this mess. Zara kept swearing along with Jett and mumbling that they were going to show them and hurt them.

The paper towels weren't thick enough to pick up a good amount of the runny splatter all over Jett's car, so they used the paper towels to push the goop off the side of the car until it sludged onto the pavement. Working fast, they did their best not to get any of the condiment combination on the other cars parked close by, which wasn't easy.

As the girls moved spastically fast around the car, flinging the slap-in-the-face slime to the ground with a whoosh and flop, the dark feeling of desperation that I was coming to know so well was making me feel weak. I knew I was partially the reason for the mess. I was responsible for my friends being targets of assault. Because of my death they had to cover up the embarrassment of harassment.

If Heidi and I hadn't collided, if our cars hadn't created the separations that came afterward, if I hadn't been in the wrong place at the wrong time, my friends wouldn't be wiping shit off Jett's car. Well, that's how I felt. I wished I could have changed Sonia and Gwen's minds somehow before they got to Jett's car. I wanted to make them see that they were idiots, that nothing good was going to come from wasting a life supply of condiments on Jett's car.

As the girls were swooping up the last of the nasty glop, I huddled around them. They looked defeated and fed up.

While guilt and irritation weighed on me, I wanted to tell them not to get crazy. I wished there was a way to let them know that there was more to life than what happened in the parking lot at Willow Ridge High School, and that they had to carry on. I wanted to give the girls a sense of strength and patience as I brushed against their hands, but they didn't seem to notice.

After discarding the paper towels and rags in the nearest trash can, they zoomed out of the parking lot.

Alone, I stayed in the middle of the pavement, where a clumpy red and yellow oval of condiments marked where Jett's car had been parked.

Watching the other students observe the gross red and yellow oval curiously, I felt empty and lost.

Just watching things happen to others, especially the ones I really cared about, was torture. Being untouchable and unrecognized was stressful and agonizing. I was watching without speaking, listening without being heard, feeling but not being felt, there but unknown. It was pointless to be here if I couldn't be a part of it. I felt absolutely useless.

## DON'T BE CARELESS

It was amazing how life went on and the days and weeks just went by, the third week without a voice, without a future, would be here in no time. The girls had started a Friday movie night at Zara's. I had died on a Friday, and perhaps they didn't want to be alone on Fridays, when their minds might wander to the whys.

Of course I watched the movie with them for a little while. It wasn't like I had my own TV and could watch movies. I could no longer pick up a book on my own either and had enjoyed listening to Eva read *The Crucible* aloud in class, so whatever the living were reading I got to read, whatever they were watching was what I watched, and whatever music they played I listened to. Sometimes while Jett was driving in her car while playing her favorite songs she would say out loud, "Estella, this one's for you." It was usually an old song I liked by Stevie Nicks, Michelle Branch, Jewel, Vanessa Carlton, Sheryl Crow, or whatever reminded her of me. It always made me feel special to still be present in the minds of my friends.

Before putting the movie on, as they were standing in front of the microwave, waiting for the popcorn to pop, Zara blurted out, "Do you think she can see us? Like, do you think she's here?"

I was buzzing around the kitchen, knowing they were talking about me.

"I don't know, maybe. But I hope she's in heaven," Eva said, with full belief.

"I think she is here," Jett said with some conviction. "Maybe she's up there, sometimes... but I think she is right here eating popcorn with us and laughing at us for watching one of Eva's corny movies...again."

I wasn't laughing too hard at them. I too liked the classic chick-flicks, like *When Harry Met Sally, Thelma & Louise, Breakfast at Tiffany's,* and *Pretty Woman.*

And not to disappoint Eva, I wasn't in heaven, and I didn't plan to go there anytime soon. I was finally getting used to my new form and new ways of moving around.

"When my Grandma died I wondered if that meant she could now see me naked," Zara shared bluntly, though she was pretty sure her grandma would turn her eyes away.

"Oh my God!" Jett was appalled with the thought of it.

Eva suggested, "Well, maybe she only sees what we want her to see." She seemed worried at the idea that I could suddenly see all types of things.

It was the first time they had talked about me still being with them in a way, and I really loved it. They were saying all the things I wanted to know if they wondered about me. Maybe they understood what I *really* was now, a spirit, an energy, who was still their friend. But I wasn't sure what the new me was supposed to be doing now that I couldn't laugh with them or eat popcorn. I wanted to be a part of their memories still, and I needed to think about this more.

That night the clouds looked grayish purple as I glided toward Willow Lake and rested under the first willow tree I saw. The willow tree's branches were droopy from the snow and rain, and ice dangled off of them like half-frozen snakes. I spent the rest of the night there among the rain, earth, and wind, pondering if I was using my energy fully and in the right ways, and trying to understand exactly what I was.

At first, it was difficult for me to come up with a clear resolve as to what I had left to offer the living. Maybe it was too early for me to fully know. In the cold of the night air surrounding me I focused on the liveliness I felt, the energy running through me. I considered what was keeping me going and what I might have gained in death.

I was still able to feel emotions about the things I saw and the people I knew. The feelings charged through me intensely. I still had my ability to care; it was always with me, as if it never left me, even after death.

What did it mean?

It had to mean something.

I could feel that there was more to do and give, but without an instinct as to how. I hadn't thought much about my purpose when I was alive, and I wasn't sure what my purpose was now, but I decided in that moment of emptiness and loneliness under the willow tree to give finding my soul's purpose a try.

When I was alive, it seemed that my purpose had been based around maintaining my body and keeping it toned and lean, keeping my stomach muscles tight and legs strong in preparation for the next track meet.

Now, absent of an earthly body, I had to discover myself beyond my verbal and physical attributes.

I had tried to brush up against, curl up next to, and be close to my friends and family, but my warmth obviously wasn't something that skin could feel so easily. There was a barrier of muscle, vessels, glands, and bone between us. Their nerve endings hadn't felt the pressure of my touch or registered that I was near them. I realized I had been expecting the wrong things, trying to be what I wasn't, and not noticing the right path.

Somewhere deeper within them, in a place that I could relate to better, was where they'd feel and hear me.

When my soul did interact with another's soul, I wondered if I could speak to it and be heard. Maybe I could send a vibe of my compassion outward, like an electron traveling through a circuit, and it could reach them. I wanted my aura to have a positive effect on others.

Was it possible to somehow speak to the soul of others and give them a sign of hope? Could I influence others to listen to what their inner self was saying?

I wasn't sure, but maybe there was a chance I could now be that tingling sensation of reasoning for others, and be that concerned voice within that I had felt in my stomach when faced with a decision when I was alive.

Maybe I was now that springing affection of warmth that I had felt inside my gut for Phoenix and the caring reminiscence I held for my friends.

But maybe their souls wouldn't listen anyway; I knew how easy it was to ignore the inner self when it mattered most.

It was an epiphany gained too late. Maybe my indecisiveness about the strapless padded bra at the dress boutique had actually been a sign, something speaking to me and my inner self, warning me that I shouldn't have spent those extra minutes worrying about the shape of my silhouette but appreciated what I naturally had instead.

I wanted desperately to attach like a comforting hug to the souls of those around me, so that I could put my goodness to use. I hoped I could remind my friends to find value in what they might consider imperfection. I could perhaps spread concern to be careful and wise with the uncertain amount of time they had on earth. I needed to have a relationship with their inner voices to tell them not to forget their love inside that was waiting to be acknowledged and expressed. This was my new beginning.

At least I could try to connect in this way.

A surge of sunlight began to sparkle against the ripples on the lake, which was no longer completely frozen. I might have found my new purpose. Now I just had to use it.

# *Careful*

## DON'T SPREAD YOURSELF TOO THIN

Filled with liveliness and enthusiasm for the new day, I did the three-mile loop on the trails by Willow Lake by myself that Saturday morning. I had loved running that loop with my father, but oh well.

Over the weekend the girls were all busy doing their own things. Jett was on her way to the casting for the dental office commercial. She would have to put on fake braces for the before and after shots if she booked it. It wouldn't be a glamorous job with a makeup artist or anything, but it was a gig. Eva asked Jett to find out if they could get a discount on braces, and Zara wanted to know about getting a free teeth whiting or cleaning if she booked it.

Eva's mother's bakery had gotten a big order for a Quinceañera party, and Eva was being an assistant pastry chef to her stressed-out mother for the day. Eva often helped her mother on the weekends when there was nothing else going on. She said each time she helped, she ended up gaining five pounds from eating cookie dough, chocolate chips, and frosting. Still, it sounded like fun to be around sweets all day. They were preparing a big three-layer red velvet cake. It looked like a wedding cake, really pretty with white and red icing. Eva had an artistic side she hadn't let truly shine yet. Her frosting roses looked real, not to mention yummy. For a moment it seemed like she was enjoying herself and not worrying about how much frosting she ate or when Caleb would text her.

Meanwhile, Phoenix had no idea, but I planned to spend the night with him later. It was hard to stay mad at him for sitting with Jackson, Sonia, and Gwen. It hadn't changed my strong desire for him, but I was still pissed he signed that card to Heidi. Tonight I planned to encourage him to sit with us at lunch next week, and maybe work up the courage to be closer to him and make a deeper connection to him.

Zara was on her way to the Youth Technology Conference to network with other bloggers and learn more about video producing and editing. I was proud of her for working up the nerve to get in her car and drive herself there.

I sat in the passenger seat with her tote bag, excited to test out my new purpose.

Zara looked tense gripping the steering wheel. Her eyes were wide with fear, as if it was her first time driving, and I had never seen her forehead create wrinkles like that. The radio played so low it could hardly be heard. When we got on the highway her phone buzzed, and she glanced toward her tote bag. It was probably Brett, and I could sense she wanted to answer it as she reached for her tote bag, but all she did was place it closer to her. As the phone was buzzing inside her bag, I wanted to say to her, *That's right; don't pull a Heidi.*

As she sped down the highway, I remained still and focused on syncing up with the energy coming from her. When I stopped being just a witness observing the actions of those around me and focused on the energies they gave off from inside, it was like meeting them again for the first time.

Her energy swayed rapidly, like happy lengthy squiggles. There was an aura of the sincerity and loyalty inside of her that I always knew was there. Her inner energy was inspiring to be near.

Within these hopeful vibrations, though, was a sagging pressure, a darkness shadowing over her belief in herself. It constricted the fluid movements of her high spirits and pushed her positivity off course. Like a runner who stumbled or twisted an ankle, her faith would try to steady itself on course again each time, to ease the conflicted uncertainty that tripped her.

Halfway through the day, when she walked out of a video production conference panel, waiting for her was a voicemail from her father, suggesting she come home early from the conference to study for the SAT. She rolled her eyes. It was only 1 p.m. She looked stressed at the thought of missing the rest of the technology conference and the dread of the drive home. She knew that before he left her alone to study for the math section of the SAT, her father would grill her about what she was going to do with the rest of her life.

I was so glad I didn't have to take the SAT anymore.

I swooped next to the sagging pressure building inside of her. She may have been worried about taking the SAT because she didn't do so well with her classroom tests. She felt hurried to think fast because the other students seemed to finish before her. I wanted to remind her that just because someone handed in their test before she did, it didn't mean they had all the answers right. There was nothing wrong with taking your time.

I was also trying to remind her that math wasn't everything, but she had to at least try. She would probably do better than she expected, and once she finished the test she could get right back to focusing on the things she wanted to. She was a self-starter and a great communicator, with a fantastic eye for detail. She was so courageous when she wanted to be.

She had a lot of skills, and I didn't want her to forget them.

Had she appeared on that fashion news segment after I died, she would have been great. I could picture her being a fashion journalist one day, or fashion expert on a network television show, or a host interviewing designers on her own television show one day. I wondered if she had these aspirations for herself and what the future would hold for each of us.

After I connected with her, amazingly, her walk seemed a bit less sluggish, like she had heard me and was agreeing that we all have to do things we don't want to, but we have to do them anyway.

Zara headed toward the parking with sort of a hippity-hop in her stride while texting Brett. I wanted to believe it had been me who made her feel better, even though it might have been his reply that sent a zing through her body. She could at least escape the torture of math and these thoughts of her future by six p.m., when he'd rescue her and take her out wherever she wanted to go.

I was happy she had him as an escape from the pressure, but I hoped she'd keep in mind my encouragement too.

With my new sense of being and connecting, I wanted to run to Phoenix and be with his soul. Intertwining with his soul would perhaps allow us to be closer than I had been with anyone. I didn't want to wait until tonight to see him. I was about to sprint to him, but something pulled me home in almost a warning tone, which seemed weird and a little scary.

My parents and I hadn't spent any quality time together in a while, so maybe this pull to come home was a sign for me to not forget where I came from, because I still had parents who also needed me. My desire for Phoenix wasn't everything—but it sure felt like it was.

I headed toward home. The pull was really strong, and it was like I was tripping over myself just trying to keep up with it.

It was weird to be pulled back home so soon.

I had been there early that morning. Before I had met up with Zara I caught up with my father before he left, pulling at his shirt and saying, "Come on, Dad, it will clear your head, let's go run on the trails by Willow Lake." He had considered it for a split second but decided not to put on his running shoes and just went to the office, totally ignoring me. I didn't understand why he was so hard to talk with; his soul only let me in for a short time, even though he smiled at the thought of me before he slunk back to his gloom.

He was probably busying himself with a new client and preparing a marketing campaign all day long.

Instead of nagging at him I ran the three-mile loop on the trails by Willow Lake by myself and I let it go, but I didn't like how my father now had a secret stash of Marlboro cigarettes in the back of the downstairs coat closet. He had always been against ruining his lungs with smoking and had quit for me—but not anymore, I guessed, when he grabbed a pack before heading out earlier this morning.

So, I'd spend the rest of Saturday afternoon with my mother, just the two of us, and I headed upstairs—I figured we both needed it, some mother-daughter time. Even if she didn't want to do much, though, it was fine with me—it would be easier to connect with her if she wasn't running around anyway.

The afternoon sun hardly lit up the house. Usually we didn't need to turn on the lights until the sun went down completely, but it was dim inside, the sun didn't care to shine on our home anymore.

It was too quiet.

My mother was still sleeping, and I noticed the sleeping pills on her bedside table. With the curtains closed, the room was like a cave and the air was cold like a tomb. I missed the way she would spring out of bed on Saturday mornings and prepare a big breakfast or bake muffins so that I would wake up to the smell of bacon or blueberries.

She'd always go to the farmers' market and make a yummy cheese and veggie platter in the afternoon or before dinner. Always so detailed, she loved to create a pretty presentation and arrangement, always using a colorful serving bowl or tray.

I tucked myself under the warm comforter next to her, on my father's side. I curved into the imprint his body had made on the bed sheet.

I had a feeling my father might not be home for dinner.

He had texted my mother a few times while she was sleeping, and her phone was beeping, but she wasn't waking up for it.

*Remember your car needs an oil change.*

*Let's go see a movie tomorrow. Or go out to get some food, even if it's just the diner.*

*Call me when you get up.*

After another hour of just lying there, I wished I could fling open the drapes and say, "Come on, Sleeping Beauty," Or, "Get up sleepy-butt," like she always said to me when I didn't want to get up for school.

She didn't wake up until almost three p.m. She put on one of my father's huge, bulky winter sweaters and went to the kitchen, sending him a text message that answered all his questions.

*I'm not feeling good.*

Then she stared in a daze at the icicles that dipped down off the roof while she washed some tomatoes. The icicles were melting, but it was hard to say when spring would ever come to Central New York. Sometimes it would snow even in May, like it had last Mother's Day.

I felt happy when she set out a green pepper, a can of olives, an onion, and a box of rotini and cut up the tomatoes. Water was boiling on the stove in preparation for my favorite macaroni salad. I missed her cooking. I wanted to be her sous chef. I was happy to see her cooking; she was being her normal self again. This was the way it was supposed to be. I tried to attach myself to her soul. I wanted to ask her how she was feeling and tell her everything I was doing, and tell her not to lose her faith, and that she was a great cook, much better than my friends' mothers.

I clung onto her like I was my little-girl self again, giving her a big bear hug. She felt warm and fluid. When I reached for her soul it was like I was flying down a swirly waterslide at an amusement park, and we braided together. We were connected and close. I could sense her gentleness, patience, and empathy coming through her inner energy. She was trying; I knew she was trying to find meaning in her day. I wanted her to feel okay again, and I sent a soft chill to her shoulders to let her know I was there, like I was leaning my head against her, and that she could count on me to care. But I'd soon regret sending her that chill carrying my care.

When it traveled down her spine she got goose bumps. My affection shivered through her whole body, but instead of comforting her it made her feel how cruel and harsh reality could be, and she became numb again. The purpose of things seemed fuzzy to her, like she couldn't count on the days or weeks, or time, or the thought of me to make her feel better again. The future was purely unpredictable, and she didn't want to give today a chance. Her soul told me that waking up and trying had been a mistake as she abruptly turned off the stove in a matter-of-fact way.

Then she put the can of olives and box of rotini in the cupboard and put the tomato slices she had cut in a plastic container; she collected the green pepper and onion and threw them back in the veggie drawer in the fridge. Cooking time was over.

I separated from her soul the moment the stove turned off, but it felt more like I was ripped away. I didn't want to be tugged off and it hurt, like I was a clinging Band-Aid being yanked off a wound when I wasn't done trying to heal it.

Her eyes looked down and her breath got heavier as she started to cry and wrote on a notepad her feelings to my father. At first I thought her note was going to be sentimental, but it wasn't.

*James, I'm so sorry. I don't think I'll ever get out of this. I don't know how to live with my pain. I'm hurting so much, I just can't live like this. Please forgive me. I love you, Gracie.*

Bewildered, I followed her as she grabbed her keys and purse, threw her coat and winter boots on, and hurried toward her car.

I threw myself in the passenger seat, muddling over why she wasn't allowing me to connect with her, and felt the intensity of the engine as the car blazed toward Route 370.

At first I thought maybe she just wanted to go for a drive. Maybe she just needed to clear her mind or get out of the house for a little while. If only that was true.

It was unusual for her to drive so fast when there was so much slush in the road, and she had a focus in her eye while peeling down the road that made me more nervous than the speed of the car.

She zoomed past the village of Willow Ridge, past the wooden cross and red ribbon she had stuck at the side of the road for me on Vine Street—not even looking in its direction to see that the rain had pushed it flat to the ground—then we surged onto Route 370.

I guessed we were going all the way around Willow Lake.

The sun was going down, and the cool air was making the slush turn to ice. I wanted her to turn around.

She was scaring me.

It was like she was looking further away than where the road went, into a place that was beyond her. But I knew that place well: It was the place I now lived; it was the place between regret and pain and purpose, that distant place within the air and clouds. And she was looking for a way in.

As she pushed on the accelerator, I thought of the note she'd left for my father on the kitchen counter and wondered if this escape was what she meant when she asked for his forgiveness.

The car started to fishtail as she drove dangerously close to the car next to us, oblivious to the howling horns of other cars. I was getting very nervous and whined, "Mom, slow down! Watch out!" But she didn't hear me. It was like she wanted to be that close to a crash.

Like she didn't care if she got in one.

Hurt someone. Or herself.

I couldn't believe this. I didn't expect that when I connected with my mother's soul I would be trying to convince it that life with warm flesh and a heart beating was better than being dead in a car crash. But here I was as we flew around Route 370. My mother had tears running down her face now, hardly able to see the cars around her. Not caring, not looking. We were sliding around, out of control, and she could easily ram into another car or fly through the railing of this bridge and into the road below. I hoped she wouldn't. I hoped to God she would get out of her trance.

The cars around us were honking and giving us nasty looks as we wildly passed them all. They thought she was a maniac. I thought she was being one too.

As each exit passed, she pushed on the accelerator harder, and I tried to push my need for her against her anguished soul. I wanted her to think of my father and Evan and go home, back to the kitchen to cook macaroni salad. I pushed harder and touched her apprehension for a moment, but quickly I got swatted away. She may have felt a twitch of my voice within her consciousness crying for her, screaming at her, "Mom, what are you doing? Where are you taking us? Slow down! Be careful! Please, Mom!"

But her pain was settled in deep.

I had to do more than cry.

The wind was picking up, and I had a feeling it was going to make this ride even crazier. I wanted her to worry about her life and the lives that she could collide with when we skidded across the lanes like her car was a carnival ride.

As she almost collided with another car, I wanted to grab the wheel and say, "What about me? I need a safe place full of warmth and love when I visit home. Why are you doing this to me?"

I felt forced to stay with her in this moment and hated her for taking me on this ride. It wasn't fair she wanted to give up so soon, and right when I had found my new purpose.

I was so angry and disappointed—I could have just zoomed out through the roof or the windows. But I was scared to leave her, because I didn't want to wonder what would happen if I did. If something bad happened, I felt like it would end up being my fault because I didn't stay.

We had almost rounded the lake; I just had to get her closer to Exit 36, our exit home, and everything would be okay.

As we drove across another long highway bridge, she kept calling my name and saying how sorry she was as she swerved back and forth between lanes, each time getting a little closer to the concrete railing. I imagined the car slamming into it at full speed, flipping over the railing and landing on the oncoming traffic below, and her being alone there with me.

After a few tries I could have given up. I didn't want to be there anyway. I tried to fight through the pressure of her pain and anger and agony.

I didn't want to have to help my own mother. This wasn't my job. I wanted to just go home and watch her stir the mayonnaise into the pasta salad.

But I had to save her. As much as I missed her and wanted to be close to her, I didn't want her doing anything crazy. I didn't want her here with me in this life after death. I wanted to keep visiting her at home and see her get better. And as selfish as it sounds, I didn't want her soul meeting up with me and telling me what to do or not do, where to go or not go. I wanted to visit her when I wanted, on my own terms.

We weren't going to go around the lake again. Not today.

It was like pushing a door open with a dead body lying in front of it. I didn't want to shove through, but I had to do something. Before she decided enough was enough and sent us flying only God knows where next, I needed to get ahold of the love that was buried in the pit of her in a sensitive but powerful way and make it spark.

She could hardly see through her tears, as the world around us whirled past the car. I tried to suction to her soul again as it started to rain. She hated driving in the rain, and I clasped against her and told her how it had only been a couple weeks; she needed to give herself more time. It was going to hurt; it was going to hurt perhaps a lot more. I was still coming to grips with all these changes too, and I needed her to have faith for both of us.

I could sense a warmth coming in the distance, something that held love.

Something that had to do with us.

I told her that at the end of this bridge we would almost be home. There was something at the end of this bridge that would make us feel close, I could feel it coming, and it would help her calm down.

When she turned on the windshield wipers I knew we'd see it.

A beautiful woman flaunting a diamond ring and a gorgeous diamond necklace.

It was the billboard for the jewelry store where she bought me the silver "e" charm necklace after I received a medal at the regional middle school track and field championships in seventh grade. It was the first real piece of jewelry I had owned. I had worn it every single day since. She had wanted the necklace with her after I died. It was still in her purse, and after seeing the billboard she seemed to catch her breath a little, in the remembrance of better times and maybe believing that we both would always have those memories. She started to focus on the road. I wanted to say, "See, see? I'm never too far," when she reached toward the passenger seat and from her purse pulled out my "e" charm necklace, bringing the charm to her lips like it was a rosary. Among her deep breaths I knew we were on our way home.

I felt strangely proud of her as we drove back through the village of Willow Ridge. When we got to Vine Street, even though it was raining, she pulled over by the side of the road to fix my cross so it stood up straight again. She dutifully tied the ribbon pretty again, as if her sole mission while driving around the lake was to come back and fix that cross.

Beyond the loss of me and all that wasn't fair, beyond this pain she was feeling, she had a purpose still. There was something to live for still. I knew if she found her inner strength and courage, there would be something in her life to remind her of it.

When she got home she immediately scribbled over the note she had written to my father, ripped the note off the notepad, then took it to the paper shredder in my father's office and shredded it to pieces.

For now the day she almost gave up would be our secret. After taking a sleeping pill she'd be out cold well past the evening. I kissed her cheek and said through our warm connection, *Mom, please don't ever do this to me again.*

Now that my mother was safe at home, I wanted to see Phoenix. I really needed to relax in his arms. Before going over to his house, I prepared myself for spending the night with him. To calm my nerves, I envisioned what would happen. First I would brush against his hand and tussle against his messed-up hair, then share with him the things I had been doing and how hard it was for me sometimes. I would press myself as close as I could to his heart. We would both feel a deep connection. I would have one of the best nights of my life.

Well, that was my plan until my fantasies were cut short. I suddenly felt an unusual impulse to visit Evan. I should see him. That asshole. He had no idea how much his mother was hurting. And shame on him for living it up at college while she was driving around like a wild woman on the highway. He'd left me, his little sister, to pick up all the pieces and hold the family together, when I myself was dealing with so many things.

# Careful

## DON'T JUDGE WHAT YOU DON'T KNOW

Evan lived with some of his buddies off campus in a house they rented together. The house had a basic couch, a huge plasma television, dartboard, and Ping-Pong table but none of it amused me. The smell of Thai food was in the air, and when I passed the kitchen a cute guy wearing workout shorts was chomping down on Pad Thai. Another guy chugging iced tea out of the jug caught my attention. I headed up the stairs toward the bedrooms.

I peeked into all four bedrooms. Down the hall from Evan's room was Gregory's. I had seen Gregory before. He was one of the buddies Evan met up with and ditched us for this past Christmas Day. Gregory was writing on a notecard and seemed really busy with it.

Evan's room was so much more neat and organized than when he had lived at home. It smelled better too.

He was on his computer, working on some engineering project even though it was a Saturday night.

I wanted to tell him all about my insane drive with our mother today. Eagerly I went toward him, hoping to give him a sense of worry and surround him with my message that he should call Mom and check up on her.

When I aligned with him it was like giving someone a high five, even though we hadn't done that since we were kids. His soul seemed to recognize me, although I didn't recognize his.

I wasn't connecting with the baseball-player-turned-pothead brother I thought he was; he was someone else. I could see him more truthfully than I ever had. In this room his energy was a lot more upbeat and present than I had known him to be. I could tell he was comfortable here. His true self.

He was totally different.

Had I known this side of him, I would have had the brother I wanted.

When I saw a newspaper clipping of my obituary on the tack board, I felt like I had missed out on having a friendship with him.

Maybe I should have asked him if I could visit him here and spend time with him, more often than just his infrequent visits home. He could have shown me what college life was all about. I was enjoying getting to know the vibe of my new fun-loving brother, but was distracted when an envelope whished under his door.

Evan smiled, like this type of thing happened to him often.

When he reached on his dresser for the pocketknife to rip open the envelope, I saw the black knight chess pieces that were missing from the set in his bedroom at home.

That's where they were. He had them all along.

It made me smile to know he had brought the memory of us playing chess to college.

I looked over his shoulder as he read the note card. It had an illustration of a lion and mouse on the front, and the sender wrote in pretty handwriting.

*Thanks for the chat last night, baby. You really mean a lot to me. I'm glad I have you in my life, and sometimes I feel like all I have is you. I love you. You are my courage every day.*

*Xo Gregory*

It was sweet but...weird.

Evan read the note a few times and his energy was gracious, as if he was happy Gregory was in his life too. I slouched with confusion in his desk chair as Evan put the card next to the black knight chess pieces on his dresser and left the room.

Then I heard the door of Gregory's room open and close.

I wasn't sure, but maybe the distance that had formed between us in the years before I died was actually because of the truth he was hiding from all of us?

Suddenly, I thought of Christmas again. I felt bad about my stupid comment that he would probably think the sweater I had picked for his Christmas gift was gay—I now felt I shouldn't have said that. I wondered how it had made Evan feel.

# Careful

## THINK BEFORE YOU SPEAK

When I left Evan's place, it was that perfect time of day when the air changed and the soft light after dusk became a deep blue before night started. The rain had softened but the air still felt damp. I loved how the moon was shining on Willow Lake, and it made me feel calm—finally. I was less than a mile away from Phoenix. It had been the longest day ever. I was so close but still so far from him, feeling a little like a dog being pulled around on a chain.

I didn't normally take the time to notice Gwen's housing development when I passed by it on the way to Phoenix's place, but this time the air was hissing at me and dragging me inside—wanting me to see something—even though I didn't want to go there.

Even though it was freezing and the wind was picking up, Gwen was standing with her parents in front of their house like she couldn't even feel the cold. There was her sister Olivia, standing outside too. They were all crossing their arms. Gwen looked dolled up and about to go out. But she wouldn't be using her car.

All four tires of her car were slashed, and there was an enormous long gash that ran around the whole car, probably from a key or blade. The headlights and taillights were all bashed in.

I watched from the tree in Gwen's yard, resting and watching her go around her car, pointing out each severed tire and the intense damage. Gwen wasn't used to being assaulted like this; she was getting more and more angry.

I couldn't believe it. Seeing Gwen and Olivia's faces in complete shock looking at Gwen's car was a great surprise, but what surprised me more was the familiar essence in the air.

Jett's impulsive energy lingered in the air around the car, and at first I was delighted that she caused this wreckage. I knew Jett had the potential to vent her anger, but I didn't think she'd really do it.

The tree in Gwen's yard was swaying aggressively back and forth. While I slid down the trunk a new rush of excitement quickened my pace. The wind was really picking up now, and I planned to ride it all the way to Phoenix's house.

Just as I started ascending into the night sky, I noticed something at the end of Gwen's iced driveway. A chain of dark gold was glaring at me. It looked like it could be Jett's bracelet. Curiously I descended back down toward it and its familiar glint of gold. Just as I did, a long tree branch swung and broke off, landing in Gwen's yard, right in my path. It spooked me, a reminder that catastrophe came without warning.

When I reached the exit of Gwen's housing development my night plans to see Phoenix took a different turn.

I wondered if Zara and Eva knew what Jett had done. Or, maybe they had been a part of it. I actually wouldn't have been surprised. I went to find them.

Parked in the dark alleyway behind the Walmart, Zara and Brett were in the backseat. She sat on top of Brett, wearing a sweater that was covering only part of her butt and her hot pink thong with her jeans flopped next to them. She was French kissing him and moving her hips slightly back and forth, the front of her riding up against him. Her hands were unbuttoning his jeans, then pushing them down to his ankles. She held him ready while he fumbled to unwrap a condom.

Half naked, Zara looked too busy to have been plotting to slash Gwen's tires, but I stayed anyway. I had never seen how Zara acted around Brett in this way, and I was curious if she was as lively and sensual as Jett was with Kyle.

It was dark and hard to see, but from the movements I could make out, their lovemaking wasn't a combined effort while their bodies came together. A few times Brett's body thrust upwards, but Zara was giving more.

Although they were as close as they could be physically, it was obvious to me they weren't totally in sync. In a place within her, deeper than he could go, she was disconnected from all feeling. It was like a barrier inside separated her from the path to her pleasure. Her mind wasn't really into it, wasn't surrendering to the feeling.

As he breathed heavily, encouraging her and kissing her, she focused on her hip movements. There was an aerobic style in the way she performed her up and down sequence, changing her pace from spurts of charged momentum to gentler stimulation from circling her hips around slower. The tighter he held her, the closer she felt to accomplishing what he wanted her to give him.

Unfortunately, the hurry of it all didn't work for her. Her body took longer to warm up than his did, and her mind had just begun to relax only moments before he warned her that he was going to finish.

It pleased her that she had pleased him. His eyes were full of admiration as he zipped up his jeans, fished for his keys, and started the car, but as she put her jeans back on there was quietness about her, an unfulfilled craving that still wanted to be reached and released. It seemed like part of their routine; her feeling of enjoyment always took second place.

She really desired Brett, but he was self-indulgent, and it was all about his enjoyment. Or maybe he just didn't know how to please her, or maybe they both didn't know. Still, a part of me felt like Zara had been ripped off, and it made sense why. Brett's father was a shady used car salesman who ripped off even his family members. Maybe Brett had inherited his father's selfish way of screwing people out of getting their fair share.

I wondered if Zara was happy with her relationship with Brett and if he'd eventually take care of her needs.

∽

Naively, until I had seen Zara and Brett going at it, I had assumed that when you gave yourself to a guy it would be transforming. The feel of him would seep through your whole body and mind, loosening up what you kept inside so you could give him the fullness of yourself, and you would naturally feel enraptured by the experience. But no matter how deep his body went physically or how strong his feelings were, the emotions felt inside the body weren't always reciprocal. It seemed like you could give a guy all you had and then be left wondering what you received.

I wondered what Phoenix would be like if I wasn't dead—if he'd be the generous type, a giver, careful. If he'd caress my skin…

Zooming past the traffic, I took a shortcut to Eva's by bolting through the ghetto part of Willow Ridge. I normally would have hesitated to take this shady route, but sometimes it was exciting to be in places I wouldn't normally be, especially when no one knew you were there.

I floated up to Eva's bedroom. After a day of baking, she had a little frosting on her sweater. She was spending her Saturday night on her bed, writing another poem in her journal and eyeing her phone constantly. I settled by her closet door, near a handbag hanging on the doorknob. It was the handbag she had bought at a second-hand store recently.

She didn't look like she had been out with Jett, slashing tires.

Her face was pale, and she was breaking out with acne.

Sitting uneaten on her dresser was a plate of yellow rice and beans and chunks of chicken that were now cold. That was strange too. She usually at least ate the chicken. She checked her cell phone again. Caleb hadn't texted her back yet, and it was getting late. She looked a little crushed. It went to show that just because Eva had given him her affection, it didn't mean he would call her his official girlfriend. I doubted he ever would. I didn't understand how Eva could put up with him treating her as an easy come, easy go.

She kept checking for the light on the phone's screen that meant she had a text message or the humming vibration of someone calling her.

She sat there waiting for her phone to make a sound. I was sure the moment she forgot about him and got busy doing something for herself, the phone would probably ring, but also I knew it was easier said than done. Infatuation was an unbridled and complex compulsion that could smother the brain.

I concentrated on linking up with Eva's energy. It was quivering and whirling around within her, like a flimsy spiral staircase that went round and round forever, causing knots in her stomach and self-doubt in her mind. Inside it was a maze that reminded me of a chicken running around with its head cut off. There was a lot of love inside, an unestablished inner love that wanted to present itself, and this self-honor beamed through her veins, but it stayed wanting, unchanneled, unacknowledged.

When I reached this discouragement embedded in her, I tried to untie the distressing knots in her stomach by sending her some of my own inner confidence, hoping my faith would speak to her heart and remind her that she deserved better and was wasting too much time on Caleb. I wanted to believe that she would gain an amount of love equal to what she was willing to give, but I worried that her willingness to give it all away to Caleb would leave her heart wounded and waiting.

At least she could busy herself with something that brought out her creativity—like I had seen when she was putting pretty frosting roses on the cake.

The sound of Eva throwing the pen and journal to the floor with a big whoop unlinked us. Then she threw herself back against her pillows, and I pulled back near her closet door again.

For a moment I thought she could see me hovering there, because she was peering curiously at her closet door, like she was staring at me.

Really she was looking at the handbag hanging on the doorknob.

The handbag was somehow speaking to her. She scooted off the bed with a peculiar eagerness in her eye. Then she was reaching for the handbag, and studied it carefully.

She put the strap of the handbag over her shoulder and examined the strap and how it attached to the body of the bag. Her fingers went over the leather trim of the handbag, and she took notice of its seams, shape, and structure.

While she studied the bag, I could feel someone creeping up against Eva's bedroom door. It was Marcella, Eva's younger sister, and her friend Gemma. They had a habit of spying on Eva.

Perhaps Eva could also feel that someone was lurking outside her door, because just after I felt someone there, she whipped open her bedroom door and yelled, "Back off!" then slammed the door in their little faces.

I felt bad for Marcella. I knew what it was like to have an older sibling yell at me and slam the door in my face; I still remembered those times Evan had done that to me before he went to college. I started pacing around Eva's room, thinking about how my parents didn't know that Evan was gay and how Zara and Eva didn't know what Jett had done to Gwen's car.

I could feel Eva's energy become antsy, like mine. She pulled from her dresser drawer a pair of ratty jeans that had frayed along the bottoms. She picked at the hole in the knee, actually trying to rip the material and make the hole larger. Then she hurried to her desk, where her fingers began hitting her laptop keys and punching into the Google search bar: handbag pattern.

We scanned through the search results and found a pattern for a small tote bag. Soon her printer was spitting out so many diagrams and templates she could hardly sit still to look them over.

Being resourceful, Eva went to her jewelry box; a thick silver chain necklace she never wore would make for perfect straps for her tote bag.

Then she thumped down the stairs and past her mother, who was sitting in her comfort zone on the couch, watching TV. She went to her mother's sewing basket and was pleased to find dark blue thread, the needle case, and the scissors.

She brought the materials back up to her bedroom and became absorbed in her creativity. It was an Eva I hadn't seen before.

I settled next to her as she started cutting the tote bag pattern and set the pattern on one of the pant legs of her jeans. There was a determination on her face I hadn't seen before as she hunched over the jeans and drew the outline of the pattern on the denim with a black Sharpie pen.

I was looking forward to what she'd create when Caleb texted her.

Go figure. Of course, she had waited all day for him to text her, and the moment she got busy with something for herself, he finally did and asked her to meet up with him at the pool hall.

I pulled back and settled near her closet again.

I understood her eagerness to see him, but it was also annoying to watch her text him back immediately that she'd meet him there. She sprang off the floor, already deciding her handbag project could wait.

I could feel a vulnerable nervousness form around her as she leaped toward her closet, and me. The adoration she felt for him fizzed around her. As she started stripping off her clothing, I went to the other side of the room, to give her some space.

I wondered if she was wrong to be at his constant beck and call, or if she was finally getting what she had been waiting for in the first place.

While she was standing in her bra and underwear in front of her closet, flipping through clothing selections, there was her prom dress, still in its protective plastic. She stopped suddenly and looked back over her shoulder and around her room carefully, as if she had heard something. The heat was on, the room was warm, but she wrapped her arms around herself and rubbed up and down her upper arms. Her eyes panned the room again. She felt a chill from the pulse of my movements, and maybe she sensed that someone was there…watching her?

She became quiet, and her expression grew curious, as if she knew I was there. When she realized she was standing there half naked, and that maybe I could see her, she grabbed her cream sweater dress and quickly threw it over her head.

I had seen her wear the cute cream sweater dress before, but now it looked slightly loose on her and didn't cling as tightly around her hips. I figured that the sweater dress had stretched out, although she did look slightly thinner around her thighs.

She chose to wear the tall black boots and some sexy black fishnet tights, which made the casual cream sweater dress more provocative. In front of the mirror she seemed pleased with her backside but not with the pouch that formed on her stomach.

I thought she looked pretty regardless, and if I was alive I would have bounced my hip against hers and told her so.

Her movement slowed down, the room got quiet, and from the bottom dresser drawer Eva dug under some shirts, where she pulled out a bottle of hidden pills.

She tilted the bottle carefully so it only made a soft rattling sound, and a little round pink pill landed in the palm of her hand. She slipped it into her mouth quickly, holding it there while she went to the small bathroom across the hallway. Putting her mouth under the faucet, she swallowed a huge gulp of water and down the pill went.

I hoped it was just a vitamin, but I wasn't that stupid.

In the car, a Spanish song pleaded softly, and all I could make out was "*bésame*" in the background. Snow flurries hit the windshield. I tried to channel Eva's inner energy as she looked out the window into the night sky, humming to the song, not saying a word to her mother. She just wanted to get there and get out of this car. She felt trapped as the ever-constant passenger, always waiting for a ride or begging for one because she was too scared to schedule another driver's test, too afraid that she might fail it again—and too nervous to try, because I had died in a car crash.

As her mother drove, Eva's heart raced faster and faster, but the increase in her heart rate wasn't only from her anticipation of getting closer and closer to the pool hall. The pink pill was dissolving in her stomach, and there was a burning forming in the center of her chest. There was cramping and congestion in her stomach, but Eva seemed to push aside the agitation of these internal side effects. I felt uneasy about it, though.

Eva got a few stares from dingy-looking guys as we entered. Caleb was leaning over the pool table and aiming his stick at the cue ball when we arrived. He was playing with some other guys I didn't recognize, and they all reeked of cigarettes. Caleb's pool stick aimed, and then the cue ball blasted across the table. Her heart was throbbing the way it always did before she saw him. We were almost at Caleb's pool table when Eva sort of tripped over the gooey soda-stained carpet. With her arms out to catch her balance, it looked like she was reaching for Caleb with panic in her eyes as her arms came forward.

I wanted to tell her that no one saw it happen, but we both knew everyone there had. However, she was comforted when Caleb gave her a hug and asked if she was okay; his hands squeezed her waist in a flirty, intimate way. As she took off her coat, I watched him and his hands carefully. He was a lot more caring for her at the pool hall than he had been at school among our friends. I had never seen him smile at her in that warm way, but I wasn't ready to call him a good guy.

Eva spent the next thirty minutes sitting on a stool while Caleb played another round of pool; she was transfixed by his every move, her eyes following him around the pool table.

I couldn't look at Caleb without thinking how I wished he would tweeze his eyebrows. They were almost connected. I didn't know which was worse, his hairy eyebrows or his thick sideburns. He scratched at them a few times before aiming his pool stick.

He'd been so annoying to sit behind in biology class. I had often told him to stop rustling his bag of chips, or purposely cracking his knuckles during note taking. There was a water dispenser in class, and Caleb enjoyed chewing on his plastic cup all through class, cutting the rim with his teeth and ripping thin plastic strips that sprouted like branches of a tree, which he'd flick his pen against while the teacher was talking. I thought he lacked common courtesy. Not everyone wants to be distracted by you decapitating your plastic cup.

I was getting bored, more like furious, watching him now. He wasn't even that good at pool, and a couple of times the cue ball went flying off the table. I considered leaving, but the energy around me felt like an itch I couldn't scratch. Something was coming. So, I waited for what came next and focused on the vibrations in the atmosphere.

They looked like a real couple on a date when Caleb and Eva walked hand in hand over to the café counter. I followed them as the unsettling feeling became eerie and more evident.

At the counter, Caleb scarfed down the fries drizzled in ketchup, and Eva bit the tiniest morsel off the edge of the fry that he held in front of her mouth.

While he slurped his soda I stayed by Eva, hanging in the air that outlined her body, and focused on sending a current of my energy to hers, like a nudge to her side telling her it was time to go.

My current of energy appeared as a strong chill, a long, cold tingling on her upper arms and shoulders, like a draft in the air. I knew she felt it when she rubbed her arms up and down quickly to warm herself and then leaned against Caleb, causing him to put his arm around her. Only my intention wasn't to get Caleb to put his arm around Eva.

Caleb seemed surprised Eva was cold and said, "Really? I thought they gave you hot flashes."

I regretted making her feel cold.

"Yeah, I guess I get both," Eva said while rubbing her arms again and looked down to her stomach and her hips. I wished she had worn something warmer; her cream sweater dress wasn't that thick.

"How many are you taking a day?" Caleb's tone was more controlling than concerned.

"Just two." Eva's eyes were searching his for approval.

Before he could answer she asked him with hope in her voice, "Do you think they're working?"

Caleb eyed Eva up and down, and his furrowed brows arched. He scratched at his sideburns.

"Yeah, you definitely lost some," he said, impressed. "Let me know when you run out. I'll get you another bottle."

I hated that he seemed proud to be her supplier.

Yeah, they definitely were not vitamins.

I wanted to hook up with Eva's inner voice again, to send her another warning sensation telling her not to let Caleb control her, but before I had a chance to connect I pulled away when Caleb asked her, "So, are you girls still going to prom?"

"Yeah, I think so." Eva sounded only slightly unsure.

Eva was about to get what she had been waiting months to hear.

I wanted to be happy for her, but I just couldn't be when Caleb finally put it out there by saying, "We should go together."

She cleared her throat, then again, this time harder and louder, as if clearing away her insecurities. She was floating, with the biggest smile on her face when she told him, "Yeah, we should."

I circled around Eva, and when I interlocked with her energy I could sense the fluttering in her stomach and her arms tingling. It was similar to what I had felt after Phoenix texted me and asked me to prom, while in the dressing room at the dress boutique—it seemed like yesterday.

Her longing for Caleb to truly affirm they were doing more than just having fun with each other had sat at the bottom of her throat during the past year. Now "going together to prom" meant being seen together in front of the whole junior class, walking hand in hand, smiling together in photos that they'd look back on years from now as keepsakes, and in years to come the songs they danced to would always bring back the memories of prom night.

Or at least that's how it would be for her.

Despite my hard feelings toward Caleb, I knew that if I were alive Eva would have texted me later about it. I would have written back "OMG" with twenty exclamation points and a few smiley faces, and I would have squeezed her hand and squealed with her for her happiness when I saw her on Monday.

When my energy met hers, a warm spark seared through me as her self-esteem grew. I sprung to the ceiling of the pool hall; I was enjoying the sensations and felt a little spoiled to be able to plunge into Eva's moment.

While skipping around the walls, I spread out an impulse of warm-heartedness among everyone there and thought of Phoenix.

Reliving the memory of when we all went to Harbor Fest last October I felt lucky again. We were playing carnival games. Phoenix had won a prize from the balloon and dart game, and he offered me the choice of the prize. I picked out the rearview mirror silver ladybug car charm and considered it good luck. While my car was in motion it always spun round and round, until the day I died, of course. Who knows where it is now? It probably got taken with the wreckage of my car or was flung to oblivion.

I started to shrivel up thinking about that, and I deflated to the floor just as Caleb said to Eva, "You might have to get a new dress; the one you bought will be too big for you by then."

*A new dress?*

I dwindled in the air by Eva's feet, jerked by his words.

She first smiled at him, like it was a compliment that the diet pills would make her skinny and in need of a new prom dress.

"Well, you can shop for a new dress with me then." I stepped back a little, away from her, when she said that to him.

She already had a dress; she didn't need a new one. A thick foam of resentment formed around me, foggy and heavy, while I imagined her shopping for a new prom dress with Caleb. I didn't understand how she could even think to erase that memory of us together at the boutique and just get a new dress, like it was whatever.

It was time for me to go, I headed for the door.

I could almost hear myself cracking a pool stick in half, and I wanted to throw all of the cue balls against the walls of the pool hall and bust up the place. I wanted to give her the evil eye, push her against the counter, and tell her how much this hurt.

She had to know. I couldn't let her get away with this.

I was skittish, on pins and needles, and I sent my frustration to her as a clammy trembling in her stomach. Then I did it again, and this time a little tension hit her shoulders and trailed down her backbone.

She felt that one, and I knew it when her face made a slightly thoughtful expression as if she was debating something. She then shifted her weight from one leg to another and rubbed her shoulders again like they were tense and sore, while saying to Caleb, "Or, I could always have my dress altered. I don't think it's returnable."

That sounded better, but still I blazed out of the pool hall, unsure if there was a line between keeping the memories with a lost friend alive and making new ones with the love you've been waiting for.

I'd wait until Eva got home. I'd get her to throw out the pills, somehow convince her that she didn't need them, that she didn't need to lose anything to gain love. I'd let her know that she was stunning in her original prom dress and wouldn't need to go shopping with Caleb for a new one.

The night air got colder and colder, and I swayed back and forth, feeling strangely betrayed on the way to her house.

I waited near a cluster of landscaping rocks that sat under a fresh layer of snow, near the steps of Eva's townhouse.

I pressed against the rocks and snow, trying to shove the anger I felt outward into something stable and firm. I kicked it like a soccer ball a few times, but of course it didn't move. Soon I just slouched on the biggest rock letting the snow fall all over me.

It was past midnight when the lights of Caleb's car appeared and then faded into the darkness. I straightened up as Eva pranced up the driveway. Her body looked loose and perky, and there was a lively, whimsical bounce in her stride. Her face was rosy and her hair was tangled in a mess, as if Caleb's hands had been frisking through it during the past hour.

As she got farther up the driveway and closer to me, I started to simmer down; it calmed me that she looked so blissful. Maybe I was wrong to judge Caleb. I knew it was he who had made her feel so lighthearted.

Her boots made a trail of prints on the fresh snow as she darted up the short path to the steps in front of her townhouse.

For a moment I tried to imagine them dancing together at prom in a tight embrace.

But my thoughts of them together split with Eva's body coming close me. She came clobbering down with her arms flailing, legs slipping and stumbling, and I dodged out of the way to avoid the slam and crack of Eva's right knee pounding against the rock I had been sitting on.

A high-pitched wail vibrated through the neighborhood. Eva was howling, and I wondered if maybe my energy near that rock inspired her fall. She lay there in the cold snow, curled up and reaching for her knee, unable to get up, screeching for help. The lights inside her house turned on.

I knelt down near her knee; her muscles were already going into spasms and swelling up.

Trying to send a calming sensation directly to the muscle tissue around her knee didn't work. So I took a different approach, adapting with her mental tolerance for the throbbing pain. I wrapped my arms around her and sent a gentle pulsation of waves, like a soothing hush, to her soul. My message found the path from her nerve endings to her thoughts and inspired her patience for the sharp stinging ache she felt around her knee. Soon she took a deep breath as her mind tried to focus on something else, anything else, like the cold snow.

I wrapped myself around her as the night wind hissed and whisked over her face, until her mother and sleepy-eyed Marcella found her lying on the ground. Her knee was much worse than it looked; it was fractured. I stayed with her until they all peeled down the driveway and went to the nearest emergency room. I was still a little upset at her, but she'd be okay. I had been freezing for hours and felt like an ice cube. It was my turn; I wanted to feel some warmth tonight and knew just where to go.

# *Careful*

## NOTICE THAT THINGS HAPPEN FOR A REASON

I gravitated to Phoenix. I wanted to see him when he was awake. Unlike other times, tonight he was snoring loudly in a deep sleep; as I got closer to his bed, he let out another snort, puff, and blow.

He was lying on his back, with the covers barely over him. I tried to keep my eyes above his waist, but it was hard since, as usual, he wasn't wearing anything.

I hovered over his body to be closer, wishing I could lie on top of him for a moment and hear his heart beating, feel his breath on my skin, and rub against him. Even with his mouth open, taking air in and pushing it out with a wuffle, he was cute. While I shadowed over him, he changed his position, grumbling a little, then grabbing his pillow tighter until he was lying on his side with his back facing me. His snores became soft murmurs, like a purr.

There was a soft glow coming from the streetlight that hit the curve from his neck to the end of his shoulder. It was perfect. Besides his brown eyes and the scar by his eyebrow, I had always thought his shoulders were the sexiest part of him.

I descended closer to his body, and then as if I were a pair of hands I massaged down his neck to his shoulder. His lips twitched as if he felt something, but I couldn't be sure he did.

At his shoulder I latched on, molding myself against his back. I stayed there for a while collecting his warmth, wishing I was alive.

There were so many things I wanted to share with him, and it seemed like the moment things were so close, they had been torn away. I could sense that he felt the same way—or maybe it was just my own hoping.

I pictured him sitting among Jackson, Sonia, and Gwen in the cafeteria, signing the card for Heidi. I saw the way he had become distant with my friends. I didn't want him to forget or to cut out my friends just because I wasn't there, and I wondered why he was holding back from talking to Zara, Eva, and Jett. While hugging him, I told him to stop by our lunch table on Monday.

While joined with him like that, I condensed my whole self to a smaller form and focused on his lips. I wanted to give him something. I wanted to be close. If I were alive, I would have waited for him to make the first move, but there was no point in that now, so I went for it. My whole self pursed together and gently pressed against his lips, staying there for a moment and then pulling away slowly.

I wanted to tell him how soft his lips were.

Some goose-bumps appeared on his arms, and he reached for his bed sheet and pulled it up to his neck. He might not have noticed my presence or my touch, but my devotion for him trickled through him.

About an hour later I noticed the time: 2:12 a.m. It was strange because the numbers were the date that I died, February 12th. Maybe it was a sign.

I stayed next to him, snug against his back, and waited for dawn, thinking that if it wasn't for Zara and Brett's relationship, I might not have even talked to Phoenix and surely wouldn't be in his bed now.

A text message Brett sent to Zara a year ago turned out to be very important to all of us.

Basically, for the sake of friendship and doing what one of your best friends begs you to do, we all submitted to her desire to see Brett that night.

A pile of Brett's friends, including Caleb and Phoenix—guys we recognized from our classes or in the hallways, but who hadn't said much to us at school—were playing a beer game.

Zara, Eva, and I had settled on the couch. We took the red plastic cups that Brett was distributing. Jett had gone out to Brett's porch. She had skipped the red cup altogether and didn't stay long at the party.

But I had started to feel less like we were pressured to be there and more thankful towards Zara, once I was sitting near Phoenix.

He sat there so carefree and comfortable in a leather reclining chair. I remember he nodded hello and a rush of exhilaration ran through my body. My stomach flipped with a nervous anxiousness, like it did before a track meet.

Just like now with him in his bed, back then I had an immediate interest to know more about him and be near him. It felt beyond my control, like something else was coordinating our lives and bringing us together.

My underwear that night wasn't exactly sexy or cute, but Caleb had given Eva and me huge white T-shirts when a group of us went in the hot tub.

Caleb and Eva had been eying each other and were already holding hands under the water.

I wouldn't hold Phoenix's hand that night, but our toes would touch in the water.

His foot had brushed across mine when he jumped into the hot tub and sat across from me. Then his foot lightly touched my toes again while everyone was laughing or blabbing about something that didn't matter to me in comparison to the fact that Phoenix's body—even if it was just his toe—had touched mine. His foot found mine again through the commotion of sixteen legs spread out in the hot tub, softy grazing over it, back and forth a couple of times. A fizzle of excitement ran up my leg and sent a chill down my arms, even though my skin was boiling in the water.

Our eyes glanced at each other, and I gave him a little smile to let him know I knew he did it on purpose, but then I looked away. It was too good to be true.

I was fizzling.

I could have easily run home in minutes, but I wanted Phoenix to know exactly where I lived, so I asked him to walk me home.

He slipped on his jeans quickly, and I cannot be positive he even had on underwear because he had thrown his drenched boxer briefs in the dryer before we left.

I still remember the feeling of walking next to him in the dark, glancing at his face as we talked a little while heading toward my housing development. In just a few more minutes I would be home, out of his presence, alone in my bed and thinking of everything he had just said, imaging him walking alone under the streetlamps with his hands in his hoodie pocket, and thinking about his feet touching mine in the hot tub—I wanted it to last.

Even now, those feelings are so vivid, like emotional time travel. People say memories are what matter, and they are. My memories were not locked in my body or left inside the creases of my brain under the ground in my casket; they were unconditional, and I carried them along with me in this new state of being wherever I went.

That party at Brett's house was almost a year ago. Zara hooked up with Brett that night and became exclusive afterward, Eva kissed

Caleb and was still to this day trying to be exclusive with him, and I had met and lost the one I wanted. A lot had happened to all of us in a short time, and I understood now, more than ever, how being in the right place at the right time could work for you or against you.

It was peaceful there, in Phoenix's bedroom against his back. Nothing else mattered, not even Heidi coming to town could irritate me tonight. I streamed over his toes, which to him would only feel like a dust particle or the smallest creep of a bug bed passing by, but it was me—waiting for dawn, thankful to be with him.

## DON'T LOSE VALUABLES

The snow had picked up over Saturday night. Another blizzard was in the works, and I didn't want to move from the warmth of Phoenix's bed. Being with him all night and this morning, watching him take a shower, had softened my mood.

On my way to see Jett at her photo shoot, I soared high above the houses and streets of Willow Ridge, feeling lucky I had stayed around and not gone to heaven—I had still gotten my chance to be close to Phoenix, and I wanted more time with him.

When I arrived at the photo shoot I didn't rush to connect with Jett like I had originally planned. I had wanted to put pressure on her conscience, telling her it was stupid to mess up Gwen's and Sonia's cars, but it seemed she already knew what I would have told her.

Sitting in the hair chair while a hairstylist attached extensions to her head, Jett rubbed her hand against her bare left wrist.

Imagining if it was possible to get caught for the property damage, she seemed fidgety and skittish. Whenever the hairstylist pulled a little too hard as she put in the hair extensions, Jett's face would scrunch. Her scalp grew sore for the look of longer, thicker hair, but she didn't complain—I understood how sometimes it took pain to get the job done, like how running always involved pain from pushing myself to go faster while I crossed the finish line of a race or battled a competitor to win it.

The photographer, salon manager, and crew might have thought Jett was poised and such a sweet model, but I knew differently, and I was nervous for her.

Last night payback was on her mind, for what Gwen and Sonia did to her car in the school's parking lot, and her heart was beating fast while she focused on her hate for Heidi.

She had been slick about her siege, tucking her black hair in her jacket and wearing a winter face mask to disguise herself. She had used her mother's Garasuki knife, which made stabbing into Gwen's tires quick and easy.

Jett went for the tires first. With each jab, she had thought of me. Then she scraped the knife's blade at an angle against the doors and went all the way around the car with it. Lastly she made one more round, this time with her mother's Genno hammer. She wacked the headlights and taillights, and then afraid someone might hear the smashing noises, she made a run for it to her car, parked a few blocks away.

A couple of miles away was Jett's next target—Sonia's car. There was only time to blast the side mirrors when the motion detector light came on. Scared of getting caught, she sped to Kyle's—not saying a word to him about what she had just done.

Quick and sneaky as she had tried to be, Jett hadn't hurried away from Gwen's car without a trace. While Jett had been in action, her gold bracelet had come unclasped and fallen on the iced driveway. It was that tarnished gold that had caught my eye.

The next morning, Gwen's father found the bracelet at the end of the driveway and asked Gwen if it was hers. It wasn't Gwen's, but she took one glance and knew whose it was.

The gold chain-link bracelet was tarnished. Jett's mother had worn it when she was our age, Jett had told us. Three small charms—Japanese symbols for strength, love, and faith—hung from it. It had been on Jett's left wrist ever since we entered high school, and I had never seen her without it.

Gwen, who knew Japanese, remembered seeing the strength, love, and faith charms on Jett's left wrist. The bracelet was Jett's signature piece of jewelry.

⌒

Today at the photo shoot Jett looked dove-like and harmless. The job was for a popular hair salon in the village of Willow Ridge that wanted to promote its hair extensions for prom with window displays and an ad in the newspaper; on the Internet there'd be a video demonstration of the before and after. Jett's already long hair was even longer and fuller with the extensions. Her hair epitomized the sleek look the salon knew so many girls in high school wished they had.

The photo studio was bustling. The photography assistants were adjusting the massive photographic lights for the perfect lighting, and other assistants were scurrying from place to place, helping with this or carrying that. It was all happening so fast.

Jett would get a variety of up-dos and styles done for each promotional shot. All eyes were on her, and she loved the attention, like always. She would be here all day because the makeup had to be changed and freshened for each new hairstyle.

While the makeup artist prepared her face, Jett was backtracking her steps from last night in her mind. She had realized only when Kyle asked her about it before they went to bed that her bracelet wasn't on her wrist. She wondered where she could have left it. She hadn't left it on Kyle's bathroom counter before her shower last night; it wasn't on the floor or under a pile of her clothes. It wasn't in her coat pockets, and she didn't need to check her purse for the fifteenth time. She tried to remember if she was wearing it during her attack of Gwen's and Sonia's cars. Who was she kidding? She always wore it. It was gone, and Gwen had it.

She looked angelic in front of the camera. It seemed like it took a lot of focus to stay so still as the photographer told her how to tilt her chin, where to look, and what type of expression to make. She had to "Stay just like that!" while doing her best not to mess up the perfect placement of the hair extensions and look comfortable while wearing a variety of different poufy prom dresses that were all a bit too small or too big.

Last week, I had wanted her to book this job, despite the fact that anything prom-related was a reminder of my death. Being seen in the salon's window display and in newspaper ads as the face of this salon was more proof Jett could make it in New York City as a model. Everyone would see it; it would bring just the confidence Jett needed.

Last week between my rounds with the girls, Mila, Jett's modeling agent, texted her to ask if she was available today, and Jett was submitted for the job. I had followed her modeling comp card, and it landed at the photographer's studio, where the salon manager and photographer were deciding on a model.

The manager of the hair salon and the photographer were also reviewing online beauty portfolios of local makeup artists when I arrived. They talked about how the look for the shoot should be fresh and clean, then gradually get more glamorous, letting the hair extensions and hairstyling be the main dramatic factor.

I sat with them and got excited when they landed on a certain makeup artist.

She didn't have as much experience as the other makeup artists being considered, but her work was impressive. What really caught my eye was the makeup she used.

When I saw in her bio that she was associated with a new makeup brand called Ella Estella, I fizzed like carbonated bubbles in soda. It was so cool—almost unbelievable—that a cosmetics brand had my name in it.

It was too perfect, too much of a coincidence to not have Jett see it. I knew when she saw it she'd feel hopeful. She'd feel a reminder of my belief in her aspirations. I wanted this makeup artist to be booked, and I wanted Jett to be the model for the job.

They weren't originally going to use an Asian. They had wanted a blond Caucasian model.

"What do you think of her?" the photographer had asked the salon manager, handing him Jett's comp card. They stared at the close-up beauty shot on her comp card, imagining if she was the right girl for the job.

As they were evaluating Jett's beauty, I focused on what features they were paying attention to, and then my hopeful energy streamed through their unconscious, nudging their decision in Jett's favor— they had no idea. Or that's how I think it happened.

For the next shots I watched Jett pose and smile at the camera. They told her how absolutely stunning she looked, and I felt proud that I was friends with a girl who might be a big model one day. She was gorgeous in the beautiful gown, which was a similar style to her own sultry sequined prom dress.

I wanted her to see my sign. She was so preoccupied with fear of getting caught for property damage or getting away with vandalizing Gwen and Sonia's cars that she hadn't taken her usual interest in what brands that makeup artist was using. I wondered if she'd notice my name on the label.

When the makeup artist took all the makeup off Jett's face to create a totally new look for the next shot, she reapplied a moisturizer and a primer to Jett's face; it wasn't the Ella Estella brand.

For a moment I worried my sign would be ruined.

The makeup artist was in a crappy mood and didn't seem to want to be there. It was disappointing to watch her puff on a cigarette in between curling Jett's lashes and lining her eyes with white eyeliner, until she began smearing light pink lip gloss on Jett's small lips. I got excited when I noticed it was with an Ella Estella product.

Thankfully, Jett struck up a conversation with her to make the experience of getting her makeup done less depressing. I shuffled around with anticipation when Jett finally asked, "Are there any new brands you can suggest I check out?"

"Hold still. Look down." It was like the makeup artist didn't hear her or want to hear her. She focused on Jett's upper eyelid, trying to get a perfect light pink line across it to play up the light pink color on her lips.

Finally Jett's face was done, and she looked at herself in the mirror.

"Oh—that's so pretty! I've never used a light colored eyeliner or lip gloss. What kind is it?"

Bingo!

"It's this new brand; it's hard to find in stores so I ordered it online." The makeup artist pulled the lip gloss back out of her kit. "It's called Ella Estella."

She handed it to Jett.

"Estella?" Jett asked her.

I wanted to say to her, "Yes, Jett, Estella! I'm here! I'm here, you crazy girl!"

The makeup artist spoke for me instead.

"Yeah, Ella Estella. I did the makeup at this charity runway show last weekend for a breast cancer foundation, and they were one of the sponsors. I used their makeup on all the models. It's really great stuff—a little pricey, but they've got really good lip glosses. I'm surprised you weren't there. You would have been great for the show."

The makeup artist handed the lip gloss to Jett, who studied my name as the makeup artist told her, "You can keep it. I have more."

"Thanks." Jett didn't mention me or my death to the makeup artist, but her face lit up a little as she held the lip gloss, like she knew something no one else did. I could sense she realized it wasn't just a coincidence.

After the shoot, in her car before she drove home, she pulled the Ella Estella lip gloss out of her purse and took a picture of it with her phone, being sure the words "Ella Estella" were clear to see, then texted Zara and Eva the picture with:

*OMG! Look what I got at the shoot today. Spooky. I think it's a sign.*

Before she got home she applied the lip gloss a few more times. I beamed the whole time while riding home with her.

That night she had a lot of homework to catch up on, but before she started it, she texted Zara and Eva again:

*Very important! Let's meet at Lilly's Café for breakfast before school.*

# *Careful*

## FOCUS ON THE REAL PURPOSE OF YOUR PURSUITS

Monday morning brought the first week of March, and Willow Ridge was covered in snow. On the way to Lilly's Café, I noticed all the flowers—especially Phoenix's long-stemmed, white roses—that had been laid out on the mound of dirt in front of my gravestone were now brown and mushed, flattened under the snow.

My ruby-red headstone was blanketed in snow so that I could hardly make out my name engraved on it. My grave was just another white, round, lonely hump in the cemetery. I hated how the rainstorms and blizzards in Central New York in the weeks after my death struck against my grave. I hoped it would be more beautiful to visit in the spring.

In Lilly's Café, Jett sat in a booth by the window, sipping her coffee slowly. She felt stupid sitting in the booth by herself, but I was there right next to her, waiting with her.

Jett kept rubbing her hand against her left wrist, where her gold bracelet had been. I noticed her earrings; they had Japanese charms that matched her bracelet. The symbols for strength, love, and faith dangling from her ears caught the morning light each time she moved.  With the hair extensions still in she looked glamorous simply wearing her tight jeans and an oversize gray sweater that was probably Kyle's. Her eyelids were extra dark and smoky today, and I admired the sexy swoosh of black eyeliner that came off the outer corner of her eyes.

On the table her laptop was open with her calculus e-book on the screen, and her spiral notebook lay open. She had a pencil in hand, ready to write, but she was finding it impossible to focus while debating if she was going to tell Zara and Eva what she did to Sonia and Gwen's cars. She swayed the Ella Estella lip gloss back and forth on the table. The sounds in the diner seemed to get louder with each second: the man turning his newspaper, the old ladies gossiping, the clanks of the plates hitting the tables, and the spoons hitting the sides of mugs as customers stirred their coffee.

I wondered, too, if she was going to tell Zara and Eva what she had done.

I could see Eva through the window. She was trying with difficulty to get out of her mother's car with her crutches. She yelled something at her mother, then slammed the car door and slowly lagged toward the café's entrance.

I had yelled at my mother like that before, and now wished I hadn't thrown a hissy fit when she'd forgotten to buy the cereal I wanted. I didn't get to have it on the morning of the day I died. It seemed stupid now to complain over something so trivial when there were always plenty of other things in our kitchen cabinets to eat. I hated myself for being so finicky, and I regretted being unappreciative for the things I had. I wondered if one day Eva would regret slamming her mother's car door.

"Eva, over here!" Jett shut her laptop and waved franticly before getting up to help Eva hobble in with her crutches and leg cast. Eva had texted the girls about her fractured kneecap and about Caleb sealing the deal to go to prom with her. She was worried now that she would still be in her cast during prom. It would be so embarrassing to hobble around with a cast and crutches in a beautiful prom dress while everyone was dancing, but at least she'd be in Caleb's arms.

With today's snow, Eva was wearing a puffy winter coat that made it hard to maneuver around. Her big school bag swung against the crutches each time she made a move. She was obviously frustrated. It was hard enough finding something to wear with a leg cast that extended up past her knee; jeans were impossible to put on. In the end, she'd gone with a maroon wool skirt because it was the easiest and warmest thing she owned, though it itched like crazy, and a fitted turtleneck that she tucked into the skirt. Both showed off her hourglass shape. On her hurt leg, over her bare toes she had a sock that stretched up her cast to her calf and then wore a thick knee-high sock and one tall high-heeled boot on her better leg. It looked a little weird, but I smiled at Eva's handmade denim tote bag on her arm. She had finished it, probably in between learning how to use her crutches last night, and it looked like something from a department store. There were also a couple Band-Aids on the tips of her fingers, from the sewing needle most likely.

With the cast on, it was a challenge to get her legs under the table as she sat down across from Jett.

When she finally settled in she looked totally worn out and defeated, perspiring with mortification. She feared that later she'd be run over by the other students at Willow Ridge High School—people like Heidi's boyfriend, Jackson, who had no patience for slowness and gimps.

Eva ordered her usual tea with lemon and, remembering Jett's text message, pointed to the lip gloss on the table and asked, "Is that it?"

She reached for the lip gloss and observed the light pink color.

"Yeah," Jett said with a smile. "It's just too much of a coincidence, isn't it?"

Eva stared at the words "Ella Estella."

Twisting the cap off the tube, she said, "That's just crazy." Then she applied a small amount of the pink gloss to her lips and rolled it back across the table to Jett.

When Jett said, "I think it means something," Eva looked at her curiously.

"Like she's trying to tell us something?" Eva wondered.

"Maybe…" Jett said, sure that there had to be a purpose behind seeing my name on the lip gloss label, a purpose beyond herself.

As the waitress came over with the hot tea with lemon, Jett's eyes panned over Eva's denim handbag. She silently admired it; she never would have assumed Eva had created it.

A few moments later the bells on the door to Lilly's Café chimed and in walked Zara, looking tired from studying for the SAT all Sunday.

She was flaunting a navy and cream look today, sort of sailorish, with her navy peacoat, cream sweater, navy skirt, cream-colored tights, and navy booties that gave her some extra inches. I liked the way she had wrapped that silk blue and white flowered scarf around her neck so neatly.

She rushed to our booth and held up one of Eva's crutches and belted out, "Holy shit, honey! You were serious? I would totally bust my ass using these things!"

Zara leaned into the booth and gave Eva a hug, still holding one of the crutches.

"Yeah, I know." Eva covered her eyes with her hands and said, "I can hardly walk. Everyone's going to be staring at me. How am I supposed get into my stupid dress let alone dance?"

She kept shaking her head in distress. "Why is it when something good finally happens for me, this had to happen? I don't know if I can even go to prom like this."

Zara wouldn't accept that. "Yes, you will. Screw it—let them stare. Even if we have to carry you in, we will!" Grabbing a red Sharpie out of her bag she asked energetically, "Can I sign your cast?" Zara always liked to be the first to leave her mark on things.

Eva slid out of the booth, and Zara bent down, practically showing her ass to the whole diner as she excitedly signed Eva's cast.

She wrote in her pretty cursive, "To the hottest legs in town. Get better soon, baby doll," then added a big heart and smiley face and signed her name. I remembered all their heartfelt words when they had signed my casket.

Scanning Eva's legs and body Zara asked her, "Are you on a diet, girl? Your legs look thinner."

"Nah, I've just been eating less," Eva said and stretched her lie more. "I'm so sick of how my mom gives us so much food. Seriously, I feel like a cow every night."

Zara smiled and looked her up and down again, then said, "Well, I wish my mom made me a big dinner each night. I want a real home-cooked meal one day."

She settled into the booth next to Eva. "Oh, I love this place!" Zara searched the menu as if she hadn't already seen it about a hundred times before. Like I assumed she would, she ordered the veggie omelet with a coffee.

Then Jett started to explain her urgent reason for getting together that morning. She didn't say a word about what she had done to Gwen's and Sonia's cars over the weekend, though.

"Okay, so at my photo shoot the makeup artist gave me this lip gloss…"

Zara immediately cut her off and looked at Eva. "Oh my God, I love your bag! Where'd you get it?"

"I made it," Eva said sheepishly and handed her denim bag to Zara, who flung it on her arm.

"Can you make me one?" Zara asked. She was very impressed.

"Jett, isn't this cute?" Zara imitated one of Jett's modeling poses.

"Yeah, it's cute…" Jett didn't care about the handbag.

"You guys, I gotta tell you something. Look!" Jett held out her hand. She held the lip gloss between two fingers and waved it like a wand in front of Eva and Zara to get their attention.

"The makeup artist at my photo shoot said she used Ella Estella makeup on the models at a charity fashion show, and she gave me this." Jett handed the lip gloss to Zara. Zara's eyes got wide. She dabbed a little on her lips after studying the packaging carefully.

"Wow. That is just too crazy." Zara continued looking at the brand name of the lip gloss and then rolled it back to Jett. Zara opened her compact mirror and, watching her lips, made kissing sounds. "I wonder if it's at Sally Beauty. This color looks good on me too, don'tcha think?"

"Yeah, it looks pretty on you. Do you want to go to Sally Beauty after school?" Eva asked her.

"Listen—I'm talking about Estella!" Jett lightly dropped her fist on the table.

Eva and Zara got quiet.

"I'm saying, stuff like this doesn't just happen." Eva and Zara nodded in agreement, and I wanted to say to them all, "You're right; it doesn't. I helped make sure you'd see it!"

I enjoyed them all talking about me, and even though I could feel their affection for me, it was quite a surprise when Jett said, "And…maybe we should do something for Estella. Something in her memory. I think this is a sign that we should do something that represents the friend she was to us."

Zara arched an eyebrow and smiled. Eva also looked intrigued and nodded her head. I was curious what Jett was going to say next, too.

"I mean, Estella was so caring and positive." It was like we were at my funeral again. Jett shook her head in a sorrowful way. "She always saw the good in people. She always was so nice to everyone."

It made me smile, but I wasn't always *that* good a person.

"And there's so much she will never get to do now. So much she wanted to do."

Talking about sentimental things actually made Jett feel uncomfortable, so she looked out the window and said quietly, "I still can't believe this happened."

"I know." Zara looked regretful and said, "I miss her voice and advice." She was thinking about the conversations we'd had recently about how her father didn't understand that she could spend hours on the computer blogging. "I should have let her talk more. I always talked over her, and she hardly ever got a word in."

Zara didn't need to feel guilty about that. I wanted to tell her it was okay. I didn't have as much to say as she usually did.

Eva put her hand to her mouth and looked like she was going to cry into her teacup. Zara reached for her hand, while Eva said, "It's just, that week she died…she wanted to order a big batch of oatmeal raisin cookies for the first day of outdoor track practice, and I forgot to tell my mom about it."

I wanted to tell Eva it didn't matter anymore; I'd never get to run this coming outdoor track season anyway.

They all sat there for a moment, staring at the empty seat next to Jett, where I used to sit. Their stares made me feel kind of awkward as I floated over my seat.

Then Jett broke the silence, getting back to why she wanted to have this breakfast. "We should do something for her. Something she would have liked."

To our astonishment Jett whipped out a notepad and said, "I have a list of nonprofit organizations that we could work with on the weekends, and upcoming events in the Syracuse area if we have time. I think it's something that would be good for us to do together."

I thought it was a fantastic idea, although Eva looked a bit unconvinced. Arching an eyebrow she asked Jett, "So you really think you'll be available on the weekends?"

"Besides that hair salon job, I haven't booked shit in weeks!" Jett had some bitterness in her voice, and I could sense she was serious about making time for others.

Zara, always down for social activities, blurted out, "I'm in! Sounds fun!"

While Zara was sifting through Jett's list of nonprofits in the area, her energy was flowing rapidly. I could tell she was pondering something daring, conceiving something great and complex, imagining if it were possible, before she said on a whim, "You know, we could create our own charity events. Maybe even start our own event planning company that works with nonprofits."

Jett and Eva were sort of in shock with the idea. So was I!

Donating time to a cause for a few hours was one thing, but starting a whole company sounded awfully tough — but also exciting at the same time.

Jett was intrigued too and asked, "So what do you mean? Do you mean we would have a real business?"

"Yes! Why not?" Zara said excitedly. "It could be in Estella's memory, and we could create our own charity events right in town to benefit good causes!"

Zara started to explain how easy it would be to get the word out. She was a marketing queen when it came to social media. She used the Internet and social networking every day; she was a wiz at building an online following. It would be a snap to link their event planning company's blog to Zara's blog; everyone would know about it quickly. It would be easy to promote their events since Zara was already so connected.

All this talk about a company created in my memory made me feel hyper. Jett was nodding her head in sync with Zara's every word, I was also agreeing, but Eva's face was stiff; she seemed iffy about the idea and was struggling to picture the reality of it. I could sense she wasn't sure she wanted to be a partner in a company that would be a constant reminder that one of her best friends had died. She was still really shaken up over my death, but even with her dismay, Eva asked Zara, "So what would we call it?"

Zara started rambling ideas with the enthusiasm of a cheerleader, "Estella's Bitches! Estella's Event Planning Hotties!" She started laughing; she was obviously kidding around, trying to make Eva laugh, but she kept going.

Eva and Jett rolled their eyes at the sarcasm in Zara's suggestions, and they all started searching their minds carefully for the perfect company name.

I could sense that Eva wanted to share something good; maybe she was visualizing how her idea would look on a business card. I waited with anticipation for her to speak, but Zara beat her to it with, "I got it! Why not just Estella Productions?"

"That's great! I love it. Simple, professional, to the point. Perfect!" Jett was sold, and she smacked her hand on the table hard as if there was no point in offering more suggestions.

We all looked at Eva, and Zara said, "What do you think?"

Eva hadn't had a chance to spit out whatever name she was crafting in her mind. We could all tell that it bothered her, but she agreed that Zara's suggestion was best, and that is how during breakfast at Lilly's Café that Monday Estella Productions was born.

It was thrilling for me to think that a company was going to be named after me.

Now that they had a name, Eva was immediately curious about what the company would stand for. "So what type of charity events would we create?"

"It would be for people our age, it would get them off their asses, and it would encourage them to be involved with something beyond themselves." Zara said in her matter-of-fact way.

"We could inspire teens through events we produce to help others and the environment. They would volunteer their time and contribute to the events we host. It would be philan-philan-thra—I can't say the word."

"Philanthropy." Eva could always be counted on with her expertise in pronouncing words we could hardly say.

"Yes, Phila-nthra—I still can't even say it." Zara was laughing, but we all got the point.

"So we'd be like an event planning production company, and we'd work with other nonprofits and host events for them?" Eva asked.

"Yes. We could work with them, or to get started we could just plan our own events and donate the proceeds to organizations we like. Organizations Estella would have liked." Zara already seemed sure it would be great.

Zara's grandmother had died of breast cancer, and she wanted to do something for a breast cancer nonprofit. I thought that would be perfect. It made me think of my own grandmother, who died when I was twelve, and how odd it was that I hadn't run into her soul at least once since I'd died. But I'd think about that later, because the girls were onto something really good, and I wanted to be a part of all the details.

Jett was concerned about recycling. She was shocked to find out that some of the makeup artists on her shoots didn't even recycle the plastic from the packaging that so many cosmetics brands came in, and just threw them in the trash. Jett thought it would be cool to do an event at the school that involved students bringing their cosmetics packaging in to be recycled. That seemed like a good one.

"We could hold our own fashion show!" Zara was all smiles thinking about that.

Then Eva chimed in, "Wasn't Estella going to work at the youth running club this summer?"

Zara remembered reading the name of the running club in my obituary and said, "That's right—McClure Bowerman Youth Track & Field Summer Club. She used to run for them."

I hated remembering that. It would have been fun to help teach kids the basics of sprinting and gaining endurance on the track.

When the girls agreed to donate proceeds of their first event to the club, they thought I would have been proud.

I was.

There was a seasonal membership fee to join the McClure Bowerman Youth Track & Field Summer Club. Kids from all over the Syracuse area ran, and a lot of parents couldn't also afford expensive new running shoes each season, so the club recently started a nonprofit called Speedy's. The donations helped pay for uniforms, running shoes, running apparel, food, and drinks, among other track meet necessities to support unprivileged kids who ran for the club. They needed as much help as they could get. I wanted the girls to know about Speedy's.

"If we're really going to start a company, we first need to make it official." Zara clicked the Google app on her phone and scrolled down the results, determined to find out how to start a small business.

I was also curious what "official" meant. Soon we all realized that starting a production company meant not just planning fun charity events and doing exciting, thoughtful things for the community; they would also have to take on the responsibilities that came with being professional for it to be successful.

From Zara's Googling she landed on the New York Department of State's Division of Corporations website.

"Look at this." Zara passed her phone around so we could all see the screen.

It seemed complicated. Words like "Types of Partnerships" and "Employer Identification Number," "Incorporating Your Business" and "Register a Doing Business As Name," jumped at them. It wasn't something they could do alone. Zara was reading off the details from her phone, and it clearly read in the "Forming a Business Corporation in New York" section that they had to be at least eighteen years old.

Eva had a nervous look on her face, and Jett said disappointedly, "Oh well."

Zara would turn seventeen in late March, and Eva and Jett had summer birthdays to wait for before turning seventeen; eighteen felt like a long way away. And that reminded me, I wouldn't be having my seventeenth birthday in April.

Maybe this was all over their heads and starting a company was out of their league, but Zara eased the wrinkles forming on their foreheads by saying, "Don't worry. My father can help us with this stuff." She was right. Even though her father didn't totally support her blogging, he was a business lawyer, and he would understand this legal language better than they could.

The girls hadn't totally decided what their first event would involve or where it would be, but I was impressed and excited that proceeds would be donated to the McClure Bowerman Youth Track & Field Summer Club. Within a matter of minutes I was seeing a totally new side of my friends too. For as long as we had known each other, we had never created anything together like this.

Looking at the time on her phone Zara said, "We gotta get going. Let's talk about this more at lunch, or you guys can come over after school."

Zara asked for the check. With Jett's coffee, Eva's tea, and Zara's omelet and coffee the bill wouldn't be much. Jett reached for the check. As she did, Zara noticed Jett's bare wrist.

"Where's your bracelet?"

Jett looked down at her wrist and Zara snatched the check from Jett's hand and started to pull out her wallet to cover the bill with her credit card.

Jett suddenly looked worried. "I think it fell off somewhere or something because I can't find it." Jett put on a sad face, knowing there was no doubt that it had come off during her secret tire-slashing escapades over the weekend.

I wished Jett had told them the truth.

As Zara looked at the total of their bill her eyebrows rose in a startled way. Then her face froze, as if she were seeing a ghost.

"Look!" she handed the receipt to Jett, who then passed it to Eva.

It was for $12.12.

I had died on the 12th.

I had nothing to do with that one, but it was pretty ironic anyway. It was cute how Zara kept a copy of the receipt and said she was going to tape it inside her sketchbook.

Zara held up her coffee cup, then Jett held up hers, and Eva held up her teacup, and they did a toast.

"To Estella!"

Their cups clanked two more times, once with Eva saying, "To the inspiration of our company."

And then again when Jett added, "To someone we will never ever forget."

I missed them so much.

If I had been alive I would have totally teared up, but instead a rush of gratitude swam through me, and I shimmied around each of their shoulders.

Really, the lip gloss was just something I had wanted Jett to see, in hopes that it would give her a sense of confidence for her own future, but instead it had made her think of my future, the things I wouldn't do. Thinking of what had happened to me made them consider the good they could still do for others. I realized how much could transpire just from seeing something like the lip gloss with my name on it, something that held hope and sparked the inspiration for so much more.

While they all left the café, Zara prancing, Jett strutting, and Eva staggering, I did a loop around the parking lot, feeling energetic and charmed. It comforted me to know that if they gave the company and themselves the chance, I would be there to see them rise to the top.

I would be right beside them as a guardian for their plans. Perhaps it was true, that time might be able to heal all of us and that friendships could live on. I had a feeling that by the end of the week the sun would warm up our town and all the snow on my grave would melt.

# *Careful*

## THE UNEXPECTED DOESN'T KNOCK FIRST, BUT IT CAN LEAVE A MARK

The energy around them was rippling with anticipation for what could transpire from Estella Productions. An unstoppable excitement ran through them, like they were carrying an exclusive prize in their pocket.

As Eva gimped down the hallway, Jett and Zara were her safety patrol, making sure there was a clear path so she wouldn't get bumped and shoved as the hallways became more crowded.

Jett tried to act normal while on the lookout for Gwen and Sonia. She kept her facial expression calm but not too calm and tried to be friendly but not too friendly, while waving quick hellos to a few familiar faces in the hallways. To me she seemed tense and had a nervous look in her eyes. I wanted to tell her to relax—although I was also on the lookout.

After dropping Eva off at her homeroom, Jett hardly said goodbye to the girls and went to her homeroom to finish her math homework—not because she cared about math but because she wanted to avoid the hallways and the chance of running into Gwen and Sonia.

I went with Zara to her locker. On the way we passed my locker and I cringed, thinking about the day Principal Falcon cleaned it out and found a stash of tampons and that extra pair of underwear I kept in the back just in case I miscounted the day and got my period unexpectedly.

Just before reaching Zara's locker, she and I noticed that there was something stuck in the slit where it opened. Intrigued, Zara opened a little envelope with a "Z" on it.

At first she thought it was a romantic gesture from Brett, and as she opened it she thought the butterfly design on the card was cute.

But she knew it wasn't from Brett or any friend when she read what was inside:

*You don't have a chance, bitch. She'll break your bones.*

Zara looked both ways down the hallway, but they were clearing out. She read the card again carefully. A sick feeling went from her stomach to her throat. She felt like someone other than me was watching her as she stuffed the card under some notebooks at the bottom of her locker and hurried to her homeroom.

Throughout her morning classes Zara tried to forget about the butterfly card while she focused on her idea for Estella Productions' first event. She wrote in her sketchbook:

*A Fashion Show*
*Featuring local boutiques*
*During the week or on a weekend?*
*Sponsors?*
*Publicity?*
*Gift bags?*

When the bell rang, Zara swerved into the claustrophobic foot traffic of the halls, the toes of sneakers nicking the heels in front of them, shoulders bumping into backs, elbows into ribs, and stomachs smashing against backpacks at a standstill. She only had one class to go before lunch and seeing the girls. While walking with her thoughts blossoming, she wasn't paying attention to how everyone she passed seemed to be eyeing her carefully, but I noticed.

The air had shifted from being light and smooth to now seeming dense and cloudy to me; it was difficult to travel through the whiff of smog.

Something scandalous was building in the air, making it feel thick, and I could sense a shadow creeping up on Zara as a large hand tapped her on the shoulder.

Zara looked extra small and timid next to Erica, a well-known volleyball player in our grade who got to the point quickly: "So, why are you talking about Heidi like that?"

Zara was stunned and sure Erica had heard the wrong thing. "What do you mean?" she asked.

As students rushed past them, someone banged into Zara's bag a little roughly.

Totally serious, Erica told Zara, "Everyone's saying that when Heidi comes back into town, you're going to confront her. Are you?"

The thought of confronting Heidi was so ridiculous to Zara that she softly laughed. It was almost hilarious—but it wasn't.

Erica didn't think it was funny at all; she wanted an answer.

Zara scrambled to get her words out while shakiness ran through her body. Her chest sank like she was losing air. Her whole body squirmed, like a fish swimming around a fishbowl with a crack in the glass, panicking for more time. I wanted to hold Zara's hand, wishing I could speak up for her, until finally she spoke. "I wouldn't do that. I don't even know where she'll be. And I'm not going to talk to her anyway. Who told you this?"

Erica wasn't buying it.

"Well, everyone's talking about it. I saw it this weekend on Heidi's fan page. The comments were written by Zara K. There aren't many girls around here named Zara, ya know?"

Of course Zara knew, but that didn't mean she wrote it.

"What did the comments say?" Zara asked. I could sense her heart beating faster.

"That you were going to do to Heidi what she did to Estella…"

Erica had her hands on her hips now; she was obviously not on Zara's side of this.

Zara tried to open The Annex site on her phone but it was being slow. Even if her phone was loading the site it wouldn't have mattered. Zara wasn't a fan of Heidi's page, she didn't have access to view the whole page and she couldn't comment on it, or remove anything, and she'd never have joined her fan page anyway.

Standing there in the now nearly empty halls, with Erica staring her down, Zara stared at her phone, totally dumbfounded, unsure of what to do, saying over and over to Erica, "I didn't write that…I didn't do it…I wouldn't write that…It wasn't me. I swear it wasn't me."

I started pacing around Zara. I would have loved to be alive, standing there to throw in, "Don't believe everything you read, Erica."

Maybe Erica could see the sincere worry in Zara's eyes or felt my words, because before she turned toward her next class she offered to Zara, "I'll try to tell people it wasn't you, but I don't know if they'll believe me."

Then Erica said, "It's all over Heidi's page, everyone has seen it."

*All over* and *Everyone* echoed in Zara's ear, as the Internet browser on her phone finally loaded and she tried to sign into her Annex account.

Nervousness was building with each second. Her password didn't work anymore.

She took a deep sigh, knowing someone had hacked into her account.

Worried what else was corrupted, she checked her fashion blog next and found over a hundred anonymous new comments on it, bashing her, calling her a stuck-up skinny bitch, saying the navy skirt she wore today made her look like a whore. One comment said that Zara had nothing to offer this world but her big titties.

She had to delete them but couldn't do it in class, and the bell was about to ring.

Even if she erased the comments, her name and reputation had been compromised, she knew she'd lost a huge chunk of her following. Her blog would receive the highest amount of hits it ever had, but it wasn't because she was respected. Everything she had worked for was being squashed with hate.

Her eyes looked off toward the doorway of her history class. Being seen was the last thing Zara wanted, so she put on the saddest most emotionally anguished face she could—it wasn't hard to fake—and went right to her teacher's desk. I would have done the same thing. She didn't even have her period or cramps, but she got out of her class and spent it in the nurse's office, lying on a cot with a heating pad on her pelvic area, safe and warm under a blanket. Using her phone she signed into her blog and started deleting the comments. For a moment she wished she were dead. When I thought of Phoenix and not going to prom, and everything else I'd miss or not be truly a part of, I knew it was better to be there on earth alive, even with the assholes, than dead.

Completely under the blanket, Zara curled up around her phone and texted Eva and Jett a longer message than usual:

*Someone hacked into my Annex profile. There's some shit on Heidi's page. I didn't write it. It's bullshit. Meet me by my locker before lunch. WTF?!!*

～

At Zara's locker they all studied the butterfly card and envelope. Zara appeared very paranoid, looking back and forth down the hallway and tapping her foot, while Eva inspected the handwriting and determined, "It's from someone who knows how to do calligraphy."

I noticed Eva had about fifteen new signatures on her cast and was holding a small bouquet of roses from Caleb. He had surprised us all. Eva's injury was working out for her after all, and she smelled the flowers, deeply inhaling their scent.

After Jett analyzed the butterfly card she declared, "That's harassment. Keep it."

Zara put the card in the back of her locker, and they headed toward the cafeteria. Jett anxiously bit her nails while Zara walked at an even slower pace than Eva, who was struggling to shuffle along in her crutches.

"Don't worry, no one's going to mess with you," said Jett, but her words didn't console Zara. I was also on the lookout for the unexpected.

Today was meatloaf day, and the cafeteria reeked. It wasn't long before I felt an icy gust in the air as Sonia and Gwen appeared and headed for the food line, with Jackson following closely behind.

Their heads bobbed and their hair swayed back and forth, while they laughed about something outrageous. It wasn't hard to miss their matching red stilettos, red nail polish, and bright red lipstick.

"Yuck," Jett said smelling the room. "It's probably the meatballs and burgers from last week all mashed together." She made a gagging sound. Eva was drained. Her underarms hurt from the crutches, and her whole body was aching. She threw her body in her chair, wishing it was her bed and that she could take a nap.

Eva had forgotten her lunch, but when Jett offered to get her something from the salad buffet, Eva said she didn't want anything.

She couldn't have cared less about lunch, probably because her diet pill was taking its place. As she yawned, I wanted to roll my eyes at her and tell her that maybe she was so tired because she wasn't getting any nutrients from all those diet pills.

Uneasiness was consuming Zara as she settled in her seat. Her eyes were alert as she panned the whole cafeteria, still thinking about the butterfly card and who might want to break her bones. I quietly sat on top of the table trying to feel out the differences in the air density, focusing on any little change in the landscape.

Phoenix would be here soon.

I was on the lookout for him. He was on his way; I could sense his calm, cool, collected walk and his charismatic energy coming close.

If I had skin it would have been all prickly while waiting for him, and my blood would have warmed.

Warmth wasn't all I could feel though.

When Jett came back from the food line with a fruit drink, she said to the girls, "Maybe we should wear matching shoes, nail polish, and lipstick tomorrow." She then rolled her eyes at the other side of the cafeteria, at Sonia and Gwen.

"Don't even bother noticing them," Eva said in a sleepy voice. She looked ready to rest her head right on the table.

To distract herself from wanting to look over at Sonia and Gwen and their matching shoes, Zara pulled out her sketchbook and said to Eva and Jett, "So, what do you think about a fashion show for our first event?"

She started sharing her fashion show ideas but Jett and Eva were only half-listening. Their eyes were on something else.

"I think Phoenix is coming over here," Jett whispered.

I straightened myself up.

It felt almost weird for Phoenix to be standing there now. Not knowing I was there, Phoenix seemed nervous talking to the girls.

He held his two slices of pepperoni pizza, waiting to be invited to sit down.

I tried to control myself from wanting to connect with Phoenix's energy again like I had on Saturday night. In my boldness of pressing against his lips and caressing his shoulders, I had become even more infatuated with his brown eyes, his every breath. I wanted to be close and hear him tell me again how he got that scar by his eyebrow when he was nine by hitting a rock while dirt biking and flipping over the handles at full speed—he could have been killed. The scar was so sexy. When he glanced over at my chair, waiting for the girls to tell him he could sit with them, I wanted to be able to smile at him again.

He was such a gentleman. Brett would have just loudly plucked a chair, and Caleb wouldn't have thought to have any manners at all while scraping the legs of his chair loudly against the floor.

Jett was eyeing him carefully and waiting for him to speak first.

The moment he asked how they were doing, Jett snapped at him sarcastically, "Look who decides to finally say hi."

Jett had a right to be mad, and I knew she was doing it for my sake, but I swooped next to her and nudged myself against her shoulder to say, "Come on, tell him he can sit down with us."

Phoenix ignored Jett's remark and asked Zara and Eva what they were up to, but they didn't make much eye contact with him and focused on all the signatures on Eva's cast.

Zara, though, moved her sketchbook and bag so Phoenix could sit next to her.

He sweetly told Eva he was sorry to hear about her fall. When he asked if he could write something on her cast, she of course welcomed the attention and hunted in her handmade tote bag for a marker.

I wanted badly to be Zara, sitting next to him.

He wrote: *We all fall sometimes, but what matters is getting back up! Feel better soon! Phoenix.*

It made Eva smile.

I remembered him sending me a similar text message after I told him about a disappointing track meet one weekend; it had made me feel better.

After he signed Eva's cast, Jett started hassling him. "So, what, have you had enough of the laughing over there?"

Phoenix started chomping into a slice of pizza. "They aren't that bad. They're just hyped up because Heidi's coming into town."

I hated that he acknowledged that Heidi was coming back.

From the start I had a bad vibe about Phoenix sitting with Sonia and Gwen, but at least he was sitting with the girls now.

I moved closer to him, making myself as thin as possible to fit between his chair and Zara's. While he ate his lunch, I almost forgot I was dead. I was so relaxed and comfortable with him taking space at our table again, the way he had done so often before I died, but Jett wasn't with me.

"They're always staring at us," Jett snuffed and rolled her eyes.

When Phoenix told her to ignore them, she wanted him to know how hard that was to do.

"Well, at least they can see their best friend again. At least their friend is still alive and breathing and not getting moldy under the ground." That one was harsh. I could feel Phoenix's energy wanting to break away from the table and leave, but he stayed glued to his chair, chewing his pizza slowly, listening to Jett say, "I thought you'd be there for us—for Estella."

The sound of my name startled Phoenix like a gunshot, and he started coughing, choking a little on his pizza.

Jett ranted at him more as he downed most of his soda and cleared his throat.

"You really don't even know the type of crap we've been dealing with. It's like you don't even care. Do you?"

185

She didn't wait for him to answer and threw at him another question. "Do you even miss her, or are you too busy at their table now to remember you were supposed to go to prom together?"

Jett had hit the bulls-eye hard.

I will admit, I was swimming in it when Phoenix said, "Yeah, I remember. It's not like I forgot."

I felt all tingly and toasty hearing that.

He seemed surprised that Jett would bring up prom. Maybe he hadn't assumed that I had told the girls about his text message asking me. Maybe he thought I never had the chance to tell them before the crash.

I wanted him to go on so I could hear him say he missed me. He collected his thoughts and finally said to the girls, "I'm sorry."

I suddenly felt like rubbing his back and comforting him. His head was down; his second pizza slice was getting cold.

But sorry wasn't enough for Jett, and she snapped at him, "Yeah, well, I bet you haven't even gone to her grave!"

A part of me wished he'd felt his life spin out of control and sunk into a deep depression from losing me.

Eva and Zara looked at him curiously. They were shocked at Jett's bluntness, but also impressed. I knew he hadn't gone to my grave.

"Not yet…I'm sorry…I will…I'm just trying to do the right thing." He said it quickly, like he wanted to avoid the thought of visiting my grave and was still figuring out what the right thing was.

"What, by ignoring everything and us?" Jett was really on a roll.

"I was friends with Jackson before all this." Phoenix knew the girls knew this. I could hear the frustration in his voice, like maybe he wanted to leave our table and regretted stopping by.

"Were you friends with *them* too? Why are they always looking over here?" Jett glanced toward Sonia and Gwen as if she didn't know why they were staring and that maybe it was because of her bracelet being found on Gwen's driveway.

"I don't know, but I wouldn't worry about it." Phoenix took a bite of his cold pizza. I wanted Jett to tone it down a little and let him just finish his lunch in peace.

"Did you know my car got trashed in the parking lot?" Jett brought her voice down and was now almost whispering. "And Zara got a strange letter in her locker and is getting harassed —"

"—It was just one stupid note," Zara insisted, while wishing she could have believed her own words.

Jett kept shaking her head, growing madder.

"And Eva can't even function in English class— "

Eva's eyes whipped in Phoenix's direction. "—I'm fine really, I'm fine."

Through her clenched teeth Jett said, "*They're* doing this," and quickly looked at Sonia and Gwen.

I could see concern in Phoenix's eyes. He told the girls that Sonia and Gwen just wanted attention and to ignore them. But ignoring them would now be impossible. If only he knew that Jett had already secretly done damage.

Wanting to end the conversation, end this lunch, end this day, and get home as soon as possible, Zara started scribbling in her sketchbook her favorite fashion silhouette that she always drew. But when Phoenix asked what she was working on, she said, "Nothing," and flung the sketchbook in her bag. Eva was tapping her better foot nervously.

Thankfully the tenseness in the air dispersed a little when Phoenix said, "The guys are going to the billiards on Saturday night if you girls want to stop by."

Jett let out a huge bored sigh. She couldn't care less since she hated billiards. Eva was quiet; of course she wanted to go, to spend more time with Caleb, but she was curious what Zara would say.

Zara wondered why Brett hadn't told her about going to the billiards on Saturday night.

"Yeah, Brett told me," Zara said confidently, though it was a lie. It was strange Brett hadn't told her about this.

For a moment, the shortness in Zara's voice made Phoenix feel like he'd said something he shouldn't have, but he didn't dwell.

I was sad when he started to collect his tray. He had to meet his counselor to talk about college applications.

He gave them his adorable little boy smile that I had always loved and said to us, "Alright girls, I'll see you tomorrow." His smile always made his cheeks and chin form a perfect heart shape.

Walking with him toward the cafeteria doors, I was longing to know him again, wishing Jett hadn't been so hard on him, but happy that she had gotten him to admit that he hadn't forgotten what could have been. I believed with my deepest conviction that he had stopped by our table because he felt I would have wanted him to.

After Phoenix left, the air in the cafeteria still felt warm, but gradually it got cool and morbid.

Jett went to throw out her fruit drink, and Zara tried to get the girls back on track with ideas for the first event for Estella Productions. They didn't seem to notice, but I did, how the room was unusually calm and hushed.

A dim overcast was moving across the room and was creeping toward our table, like when the sun is going down and darkness starts to eat up the light that shines across the floor.

Across the cafeteria, Sonia and Gwen collected their things and then began walking fast, swinging their arms, as they got closer and closer to our table. I went to meet them. Sonia's red hair was swaying back and forth with her hurried stride; she took a big swig of her soda with her eyes fixed on our table.

At the same time Gwen was focusing on the back of Jett's head, radiating a determined, unstoppable force. With each step toward our table, more and more rage poured off them.

I picked up my pace and hustled with them, trying to communicate with their intentions and pull the reins on the fury they held inside, but I failed to find out what they wanted to do in such a short time. Their hateful stares at Jett, Zara, and Eva penetrated our table and told me it wasn't good.

A trail of curious groupies, including Jackson, swarmed around Sonia and Gwen like a stadium of devoted supporters, just waiting for something to happen. I wanted to tell Jett, Zara, and Eva to leave the cafeteria, but there was no time to send them a message, to encourage them to leave. It was too late.

Jett turned her head quickly. Gwen tapped her on the shoulder, like a woodpecker, hard and intent, and said, "Did I tell you I like your earrings?"

It wasn't a compliment, though. Gwen looked down to Jett's bare wrist and back to her earrings.

Jett froze like a statue with her mouth shut tight, at first listening but not looking directly at Gwen. Eva's and Zara's hearts were beating fast; they were unsure what was happening and why Gwen and Sonia were at their table.

Jett's eyes followed Gwen's hand as it came closer to her face and reached for her earring. Almost delicately Gwen touched Jett's earring with her fingers, and the tarnished gold Japanese charms flickered from her ear. Almost like a rehearsed line in a play Gwen sneered, "I think I've seen a matching bracelet like that somewhere."

Gwen took a step back and ran her hands through her hair like she was irritated, then handed her schoolbag to Sonia. I wanted to throw up when Gwen dug into her pocket.

"This looks just like a perfect match, don't you think?"

She had in her hand Jett's mother's gold bracelet and held it up for everyone to see the similar glint of gold from the charms. Then she threw it hard at Jett's face, almost hitting her in the eye.

Surprisingly to Zara and Eva, Jett let the bracelet fall to the floor, like it didn't hurt her to do so.

Zara and Eva recognized the bracelet and looked even a little glad that it had been found. Zara bent to pick it up, but Jett grabbed her arm and looked at her as if to say, don't you dare.

Following Jett's lead, the girls collected their tote bags; they weren't interested in more harassment and thought it would be better to just walk away, but it wasn't.

Gwen pushed her hands against Jett's shoulder, holding her so she couldn't leave. She got close to Jett's face, whispering in her ear loud enough for everyone to hear, "You think you can mess with my car and get away with it?" She called Jett a crazy bitch and forced Jett's shoulders back into her chair, so that every time Jett tried to stand up she got thrown back down. After a few more shoves Jett's chair fell backward onto the floor with a high-pitched clatter and bang. It was terrible to see Jett on the floor and hear the shrills of laughter.

If I could have pushed Gwen through the cafeteria windows, I would have.

The sound of Jett and her chair hitting the floor echoed throughout the cafeteria, but amazingly the four teachers on cafeteria duty, deep in conversation about their 401(k)s, didn't even glance our way.

Zara helped Jett up, who was obviously in some pain and shock.

Eva stood up with her crutches, wanting to help even though she couldn't walk without a struggle.

For a moment I thought, that's it. That's all Gwen wanted to do, just embarrass Jett some more, but I was wrong.

Gwen stomped on the bracelet with all her weight and crunched it into little pieces.

"How do you like this?"

With her red high heel, Gwen kicked all the little pieces at Jett, Eva, and Zara, while everyone watching laughed, including Jackson.

"I don't care. That's not mine," Jett said, acting careless, and kicked aside the pieces near her. But I could tell she wanted to cry.

Zara and Eva were dumfounded. We all knew it was Jett's bracelet, and they were holding the little tarnished gold pieces in their hands, unsure whether to save them or flick them aside like Jett had done. They still didn't know that Jett had actually caused this encounter; they thought Gwen was just acting crazy and that Jett didn't dare act like she cared about some tarnished gold bracelet that was her mother's.

"If it's not yours, then whose is it?" Gwen's choppy bangs accentuated her eyes, which were piercing into Jett's. With each word, she pushed Jett harder and harder and soon she was pressed against a wall.

Each slam of her shoulder blades hitting the wall reminded me of the car crash and my chest concaving, my broken shoulder and arm, my shattered collarbone, and the moment I realized I was dead.

"Leave her alone. She didn't do anything," Zara said, defending Jett and trying to pull Gwen away from her, but it only sounded like a little girl's whine.

Gwen was busy smacking Jett's head and reaching for her earrings, while Jett was covering her face with her hands and using her elbows to block the hits.

"Oh look who's talking, Little Miss Talking Shit Priss." Sonia thought Zara was such a wimp and figured she would be very easy to knock down, so I spread myself over Zara's shoulders, wishing she would notice she could scoot over Jett's fallen chair and make a run for it.

"You think YOU can talk shit and get away with it?" Sonia's face was getting closer and closer to Zara's, and Zara was pulling her face farther and farther away until it was like her neck was going to snap back. Zara kept telling Sonia to stop it because she didn't write anything about Heidi, but it didn't matter.

Sonia wouldn't believe it. "Oh, yeah, then tell me who else in this FUCKING town is Zara K.? Who else would write something like that about Heidi?"

The soda can in Sonia's hand was whipping all around as she stabbed the air with her other hand, pointing her red fingernail at Zara's face, raging on and on.

Just as the bell rang, Sonia slammed the soda can against the cafeteria floor, blasting soda all over Zara's cream sweater. The swarm of students around them didn't care about the bell; their next class could wait, they weren't leaving. Instead, they were texting their friends that a fight was going on and to come check it out.

Seriously, this wasn't something for anyone's entertainment, and I was down at their feet practically begging them to defend Zara or go get a teacher.

Sonia's face was getting redder and redder as she reached for Zara's throat, digging her nails into Zara's silk blue and white flowered scarf and her neck. She simultaneously took her other hand and pushed Zara's shoulder back, jolting Zara and her tote bag to the floor. Her sketchbook with her notes for Estella Productions and makeup bag and schoolwork were scattered on the floor beneath her. Everyone was waiting for Zara to thrash back, but she didn't.

Fright and disbelief spread across Zara's face. The squeeze around her neck hurt, and she wasn't used to being pushed around. I stayed close by, like her bodyguard, ready for whatever might come next.

Sonia's finger resembled a hawk pecking at its prey against Zara's arm while she said, "She—" peck, peck, "thinks—" peck, peck, "she can—" peck, peck, "talk shit—" peck, peck, "and get away with it."

A terrible cunning laugh came out of Sonia with each stab of her finger, and her energy was hissing, ready to strike harder. Zara pushed her hand away each time, which only made Sonia more intense. She shoved Zara again, this time into the table behind her.

It was embarrassing. I hated seeing Zara trapped like that, especially when she tried to get up each time but was pushed back against the table.

She was practically lying with her back on the table. At one point, her skirt flew up all the way; I didn't want the crowd of onlookers to see.

"Get the FUCK off me!" Zara screamed. She was a good screamer. She used her knees to kick Sonia's stomach, but it only made Sonia smack Zara's face harder.

There were two fights to watch now. Gwen and Jett were reaching for hair and breathing heavily. Both of their arms were flailing around in a crazy way, slapping at each other as they uncontrollably stumbled between the cafeteria tables. The students watching were starting to get rowdy and loud, egging them on, all eyes going back and forth between the two sets of action.

So much was happening at once I didn't know how to help.

Eva just stood there frightened, too scared to jump in to help Jett and Zara. And it wasn't like she could do much, hardly able to walk.

Sonia had a nice grip on the pretty silk blue and white flowered scarf around Zara's neck, and I could see in Zara's eyes her fear of being choked while lying there helplessly.

I pulled at Sonia's arms with all my might. She was pressing down on Zara's throat with one hand and using her other arm like a strap across Zara's torso to restrain her from going anywhere. She leaned over Zara, yelling that she was a dumb, dirty little slut who had no respect and deserved to die like her friend.

That really pissed me off.

Zara couldn't sit up enough to get off the table, harnessed down like that, so I pushed myself against Sonia's back, but of course she didn't budge. I had never physically hurt anyone in my life, but as Sonia was mauling her fist towards Zara's face, I wanted to reach deep into Sonia's chest and squeeze her heart until it bled. I wanted to show her what death really was about and drag her body down into the dark hole where my body now lay.

Eva and I weren't sure who needed more help, Zara or Jett. I wished Eva would use her crutches to bust their heads.

Gwen had a strong grip on Jett's long black hair extensions and yanked a huge chunk out of her head. There was an obvious patch missing from her head, and her scalp was starting to bleed where the long hair had once been. Students were kicking around the strands of hair on the cafeteria floor. Jett also got hit in the nose, which was bleeding now, and Gwen wasn't done with her.

While being choked by Sonia, Zara's face was getting really pink and she had tears in her eyes.

Seeing blood on Jett's face and hearing Zara's desperate gasps, Eva screamed at the top of her lungs, "Stop it!" She swung her crutches like a baseball bat, sending a huge whack against Sonia's legs that made Sonia loosen her grip on Zara's neck and go for Eva. Sonia pushing Eva to the ground, grabbing a chair to hit her with it—that's when the four teachers on cafeteria duty finally turned to see what was happening.

The teachers—two male and two female, who I recognized but didn't have any classes with—started to come over as Sonia beat the chair against Eva's legs.

One male teacher looked pretty strong and tried to separate Gwen and Jett, while the other took the chair away from Sonia and held her back from kicking at Eva. The female teachers told the students watching to go to their next class, but of course they weren't listening.

Jett caught her breath for a moment after being separated from Gwen. Released from Sonia's choke hold, Zara coughed while inhaling air. They looked a mess, but there was no time to clean their faces.

Being bridled up only made Sonia and Gwen angrier. Even in the teachers' grip they were like slippery eels and tugged themselves free, and it all began again.

But much worse.

When Sonia and Gwen kicked at the teachers and freed themselves, they bulleted right for Jett and Zara again.

Hand in hand Zara and Jett plowed out of the cafeteria together. Their tote bags, the notes for Estella Productions, and Jett's mother's bracelet didn't matter. Zara's soda-stained sweater and Jett's missing hair were the last things to worry about now. Zara's neck had Sonia's grip marks on it, and Jett's nose and scalp were bloody, but we'd think about that later. Right now we needed to get away from those crazy bitches.

Sonia flew down the hall after us, her red hair bolting in every direction; she was fast in her red heels. Gwen sprinted right behind her, her hair whipping back and forth like a witch's.

Students were trampling each other to get out the cafeteria and follow us. The teachers were trying to flee from the cafeteria too.

Jett was yanking on Zara's arm, pulling her to keep up. I hoped we could outrun everyone. For a minute or two we just stormed ahead like we were winning the 400-meter dash down the hallway. I could hear Eva yelling in the distance, "Zara! Jett!" But we didn't stop.

We all knew Zara was a professional at walking in the highest of heels, but running down the slippery hallways in her booties was not easy for her. Jett was faster than Zara but not by much. Neither of them were meant for the track team.

I wanted to grab their hands and pull them along to the science wing, where there was an exit out toward the soccer field and the old busted tennis courts. They didn't have their coats on, but it would be a perfect escape.

Viciousness was clamoring near; it suffocated the air around us. I could only watch as Zara gasped for air while slipping. Jett was panicking, not knowing where to run next. I wished they had more endurance. They just weren't fast enough to escape what was coming behind them.

While running after us, Sonia and Gwen were both pulling off their red stilettos. Sonia was gaining on Zara, clawing at Zara's back with the heels of both shoes.

Hugging Zara's back, I hoped to block the stabs of the heels of Sonia's shoes, but it didn't matter. It was just too easy, and soon enough the heels of Sonia's shoes were scraping down Zara's back, right through me, puncturing her cream sweater and the skin beneath it.

From the impact of the stabs Zara tripped, twisting her ankle. Her scream echoed through the halls as Sonia pounced on her back, scrambled to hold her down, and sent deep whacks into her back, holding the heel of the shoes like a weapon, like they were knives.

Gwen collided into Jett, smacking her in the head with her shoes and then pushed her against the lockers.

I wanted to smash Gwen's face against the lockers, and would have at least tried if I was alive.

Zara was trapped against the weight of Sonia on top of her. I wanted to jut in and grab the shoes out of Sonia's hands, but now that I had the confidence, I couldn't do anything.

All the love I held inside felt useless with so much horror surrounding me and pounding on my friends.

To worry me more, an audience of students had caught up to us now and was surrounding us, cheering on the fight, wanting more; Jackson was watching too, behind a few rowdy sophomore boys.

I flared up, almost hitting the ceiling, wanting to warn Jackson to just wait until Phoenix found out. If Phoenix had been there he would have stepped in and helped Zara and Jett. He wouldn't have let them go through this.

After hitting Jett a few more times with her shoes, Gwen threw her shoes to the floor and starting reaching for Jett's earrings ferociously, trying to rip them through her earlobes. I wanted to yell, "You've done enough. Leave her alone!" But I couldn't vocalize it, and my message was only like a faint whisper of persuasion, seeping over the ignorant hearts around us. I looked around for someone to cut in and stop the fight; I could feel the debate going on within the minds of the onlookers. All of me concentrated on someone stepping up to help. I could sense a few people wanted to — but no one did.

I was twisting myself into a knot, rustling around, not wanting to look at my friends going through so much torture.

Sonia smashed the side of Zara's face against the cold floor, then dug her nails into the back of Zara's neck, goring her, before using the point of the heel to stab her shoulders and spine, over and over. Lying there, Zara was looking like roadkill already. I shriveled up, scared that her bones were breaking from the stabs. I didn't want to look, but it was hard not to watch, like I was seeing a house burning down with people stuck inside.

Gwen had gotten ahold of Jett's left earring and, repeatedly calling her a stupid bitch, yanked the earring out of her earlobe, creating a slit that quickly started gushing blood. Gwen dropped the earring on the floor, and soon it drowned in a puddle of Jett's blood. With her bloody nose, bleeding scalp, and now her ear, a trail was starting to run down Jett's neck from her left earlobe. She hardly had the strength to stand, but she went for Gwen with any energy she had left and spit in her face.

That wasn't good. I really wished she hadn't done that; I couldn't take it anymore, when Gwen took out another clump of Jett's hair and then punched her in the jaw. Jett's whole mouth was full of blood.

A roar went through the halls. The surging energy of the watchers only made Gwen more forceful. Feeding off the intensity, she grabbed her shoes off the ground and slashed the heel of her stilettos across Jett's face quickly and aggressively, just like Jett had sliced her car tires. She went ballistic, clobbering Jett's face back and forth.

I wanted to hide inside a locker and pretend I couldn't hear their cries and feel the horrendous pain of Zara's and Jett's souls, and my soul too. I wasn't a great friend; I couldn't be counted on to be the type of friend they needed right now.

It wasn't easy for Eva to rush down the hall clumsily on her crutches. She was waving one of her crutches in the air, pushing through the mob to get to Zara and Jett, yelling, "Get out of my way!" As if her yelling would make a difference or be heard over the cheers from the other students—the malicious spectators, just watching as my friends were getting their asses beat. I wished I could have taken the place of Jett's cheek and chin, and taken those deep hacks to her face. I would have taken them all. I curved myself around Jett's face like two soft hands cradling the wounds that I knew would not heal easily.

That was it. Jett fell to the floor, and I couldn't save her—I couldn't even help her.

I knelt down near her head, cupping myself around her left earlobe, praying medical help would be here soon but knowing it might not be.

I knew Jett wouldn't be modeling for some time after this. I wasn't sure how bad it was, but her whole face was red, puffy, and bleeding. She was panting and crying, struggling to open her eyes, like she might die right there in the hallway.

Gwen had been brutal about it. I really believe she wanted to do more than hurt Jett for what she did to her car. She wanted Jett to feel as ugly as she did sometimes, permanently scar Jett's beautiful face, and ruin her pride.

I weaved through what was left of Jett's hair, trickled down her face, and kissed her cheek. I wanted to clean up all the blood that covered her face, which would never look the same again.

And I thought of my face, totally unrecognizable, under the ground.

I wasn't sure Zara would ever be the same again either. She looked like a lamb before the slaughter. As Sonia put her red shoes back on, I noticed blood had seeped through Zara's cream sweater, which looked like it had red polka dots all over it.

The outrageous vengefulness coming off of Sonia was deeper than her loyalty for Heidi. I could sense a beastly jealousy coming loose. It gave Sonia fulfillment to see Zara's face pink with tears in her eyes, mascara smudging down her cheeks, and her lip gloss smeared on the floor. Each stab to her sweater had torn Zara's stylish image, and it thrilled Sonia to see all of her being made ugly. Envy was deep inside of Sonia. To her Zara was a perfectly proportioned, spoiled show-off, rich bitch, and egotistical know-it-all, and this perspective only presented more reason for Sonia to smash her resentment into Zara's back. Sonia knew Zara was capable of success in ways that she would never be, and was determined to make sure that could never happen. It was impossible for me to break through to Sonia's resistant soul, to remind her that there would be severe consequences waiting for her one day, but I tried.

During each wham of Sonia's shoe kicking and bashing against Zara's skull, I wished I could have been the fluid around her brain and act as a cushion, hoping there wouldn't be a change in the way her brain functioned. Then again, maybe her brain wouldn't matter, because Sonia was planning to kill her, if she hadn't already.

Jett was just lying there, out cold. Gwen also put back on her high heels, knowing Jett wasn't able to fight back. Then Gwen stood next to Sonia, telling her to do it.

When Sonia kicked at the side of Zara's stomach and ribs, each kick went right into the pit of me, crushing my faith, showing me that reality was brutal and unsympathetic to our innocence.

Zara looked lifeless, her eyes closed, knocked unconscious. It was unbearable. Sonia gave Zara one more kick at the side of her head, right near her temple. She was ruthless and merciless, and everyone made a terrible "ouch" sound.

I sent my strength and patience to Zara's soul, as Sonia finished her.

I felt pathetic sending her my hope. I prayed that each kick, punch, and hit wouldn't hurt as much as it looked like it had. I sent my warmth to the areas on Zara's body that had been beaten on.

I shook myself with outrage. How could no one feel ashamed?

Rushing toward them now, finally, the four teachers on cafeteria duty showed up, along with a few other teachers who heard the noise of a beatdown in the hallway.

Jackson started to peel out with the other cowardly students, as if he hadn't been an eyewitness at all. I rolled myself up; it was a test to my patience not to be distressed over the gruesome details he'd report to Heidi. If I had been alive, and if I had been the type of person who didn't hold back from saying the things she wanted to say, I might have grabbed his sleeve and told him he was the most disgusting person I had ever seen, a true scumbag, a coward and a loser, for not doing anything when it was obvious that my friends were hurting way beyond getting a little roughed up. He was an asshole, and I clung to the soles of his feet as he headed down the hall, sending my anger up his calves and to his heart.

Strands of Jett's natural beautiful long hair and the hair extensions splayed across the floor. Zara's silk blue and white flowered scarf lay in the distance; it had fallen off as she ran down the hall. A path of blood streamed between my friends.

I was so worried for Jett and Zara I didn't even get excited when Sonia and Gwen were dragged to Principal Falcon's office.

The other students were dispersing now for their next class. They had seen the highlight of the day. I wanted to tell them all to go to hell. I hated them all for just watching and now joking about how Gwen had ripped Jett's earring out of her ear and sliced her face like a maniac. They made hand motions like they were holding swords and slicing the air, and others were reenacting how Sonia had kicked Zara's head like a soccer ball. It was a disgrace. All they had to do was step in or get a teacher, but they didn't. Their eyes saw the brutality, and all they gave was ignorance. I was sure I couldn't ever forgive their weak souls.

I had loved going to Willow Ridge High School. I once had pride for our student body while singing the school song, but I didn't anymore.

The school nurse was on her way. It was ridiculous how slow care came. Eva let her crutches fall to the floor and was lying on the ground with Zara and Jett. I was glad Eva had collected Zara's silk scarf and Jett's earring off the floor.

As ambulance sirens moaned in front of Willow Ridge High School and Jett and Zara were each placed on stretchers, it reminded me of the moment I was forever changed and how hard it was to accept that things would never be the same again.

## NOTICE YOUR INNER BEAUTY

After the fight the wind felt different on my way to the hospital. It was moving very fluidly, creating cursive letters that seemed to spell my name within its sway. Immediately memories of my grandmother came to me, but I couldn't feel her energy near.

Maybe I was so busy connecting with the souls of the living that I hadn't allowed myself to notice the souls of the dead, right there around me trying to communicate. But I knew we'd get to say hello at some point.

Right now all that mattered was getting to Zara and Jett.

Zooming past the village of Willow Ridge toward downtown Syracuse, I was consumed with images of the deep gashes on Jett's face and Zara losing her breath before being stabbed repeatedly by Sonia's high heel, and a despair surrounded me with every stride.

Strangely I felt closer than ever to my friends.

On my way to the hospital I could feel words from Eva coming at me. Even from a distance I could hear what she was thinking. In her mind she was telling me to make sure Zara and Jett would be okay, asking me to be by their side. It was a little awkward when she asked me to make sure Sonia and Gwen would see the wrong they had done; she even asked me to hurt them somehow.

I would have loved to smack some sense into Sonia and Gwen or choke hold them, at least for a few seconds. Actually I wanted to do more than stab them or make a lasting impression across their faces, like they had done to my friends.

My effect had to be greater than that, more significant than physical pain or a cut to the skin that might heal with time. I wanted to access a life lesson that would forever change Sonia and Gwen in an emotionally draining way; they would feel sorry to know what it was like to truly feel pain. I just needed to figure out how this lesson would show up in their lives.

The highways were like one long track to me, so I stretched as far as I could and bolted, arriving at the hospital just as Jett and Zara were being injected with IVs.

The next days were a rush to and from my friends' hospital rooms. I was by their sides every day, but when Jett said my name out loud she was spending her last night in the hospital.

She had been there for five days and was touching the bandages across her face in disbelief. Bandages were on her head too, over her scalp where her long dark shiny hair and the hair extensions had been. She could hardly move her swollen face and sometimes was still spitting out blood.

Terror was in her eyes, like she had already seen what it looked like under the bandages.

Her voice came to me like a soft whimper. She was really pouring on the hope when she said, "Estella…please, help me…please, I need you."

My heart fell and I rested near her hand as she told me how much she missed me; she said she was glad I wasn't there to see what a terrible person she had been.

Only I knew about everything that had happened, and of course I forgave her when she said, "I'm so sorry, Estella. Please forgive me?"

She told me how much she hated herself. Crying wildly and loudly, knowing the life she wanted was over, her dreams to model in New York and move there with Kyle were crushed—no models have scars this frightening, she thought. She didn't want Kyle to visit her in the hospital, or even tell him what happened. Having him see her battered face and the deep slashes all over it—she would never. To see the shock in his eyes would kill her; she already wanted to kill herself.

She lay there in her hospital bed feeling safe, though, protected from the outside world—it was more comforting to be there than at home.

In the hours after the fight a hot zap, that was electrocuting and loud, entered Jett's hospital room. Her mother's energy was violent and wanted to beat and punish her for being dragged out of a big real estate closing meeting and hurrying to downtown Syracuse during rush hour. When Jett's mother whipped open the door, she didn't run to Jett's hospital bed and bundle her close to her chest and tell her it would be okay; she didn't cherish her in any way. Jett got a big bitching, about how incredibly stupid she was and how awful she looked and how Jett had done this to herself. I gripped the side of Jett's bed and wished her mother would just leave. If there weren't so many doctors and nurses around I swear her mother would have yelled even louder. I felt so bad for Jett and cuddled next to her after her mother told her that their lives were both ruined now.

I wanted to take her someplace safe, where she wouldn't feel so horrible. There had to be a way to escape the pain, and Jett was searching for it when she imagined the life ahead of her and the embarrassment of living with her mistake every day. Never looking in the mirror, avoiding sunlight, ducking and dodging people, and the effort of making sure no one ever saw her face again.

She was thinking about death, questioning whether living with a face so ugly was worth it. I could relate—sort of.

Say I did survive the crash, I wouldn't have wanted to walk around with my face looking how it did; it had looked so distorted with my features all smushed in and lopsided. If I hadn't died, I was sure I would have wanted to live in isolation looking like that. But maybe I'd find meaning in my life again...somehow. I desperately wanted Jett to hang on to the hope that she could still have a life that was worth living, no matter how ugly she felt right now.

An advantage of being shapeless was that I could easily slip under Jett's bandages and kiss her wounds. From both sides, her whole face was carved up. From her upper cheeks, over her nose, and down to her chin, it looked like a tilted tic-tac-toe board had been ripped across her red, puffy face with long thick chops and slashes. The nurse tried to comfort her with the option of having plastic surgery, but Jett knew her mother could never afford it—and her mother hated her.

She thought of me and put her hand to her face, imagining how my face might have looked inside my closed casket.

Suddenly Jett and I had a lot more in common. Our faces had both been permanently changed. Only she had the choice to live with it or not.

The nurses said that Jett would have to wear the bandages every day for another month to let her face heal, but the scars would be impossible to disguise or cover up completely—even with makeup she wouldn't look the same.

Facing the end of how things used to be was my daily struggle. I missed having a body and a face, my green eyes, I missed my red hair that was always frizzy, and I even missed my small breasts. But Jett still had her eyes, her nose, and lips even though the skin around them was thrashed. She still had her breasts, her legs and arms, all her fingers and toes, functioning organs and a brain—things I'd never have again. I'd give anything to smile again and laugh with the girls and I wished my lips could have really kissed Phoenix; I'd do nothing but homework for twenty years just to breathe again for a day. I wanted to hold Jett's hands and tell her how lucky she was still—although right now I knew she wouldn't believe me.

She had booked that dental office commercial and had been excited about it but obviously wouldn't be doing it now, and she let out another hard cry when the reality hit her again.

Having to tell everyone at Mila's Model Management about the fight would be too humiliating. Mila would tell Jett she had wasted her whole career on some stupid revenge plot, and it would only make her feel worse, more stupid and sorry for herself. Instead Jett sent an e-mail saying how much she loved working with the agency, but she didn't want to pursue modeling anymore, she couldn't accept any more modeling jobs for personal reasons, and that's it—modeling was over.

On top of these emotions was the fact that she had lied to Eva and Zara. They would never believe she had mutilated Gwen's and Sonia's cars; that wasn't something their friend would seriously do. I think she was deciding what do to about everything, because when the nurse came around Jett asked for a piece of paper and a pen. I went to check on Zara.

Every day I knelt down by Zara's hospital bed and brushed against her hand. She had more than 200 stitches on her back and shoulder blades and down her spine from the high heel stabs. I had lost count.

She looked like she was in a coma while lying there sleeping.

The kicks had cracked both her rib cages, and with the trauma to her spine and shoulder injuries it would be best if she didn't walk for a while. The doctor told us that using a wheelchair would help quicken her recovery, but someone else would have to push her around since Zara wouldn't have the strength in her shoulders to do it herself all the time.

Most of the time her mother was sitting in the chair next to me and holding Zara's hand; her eyes were red and she was praying, her lips trembling while asking God to cut her life short if it meant that Zara would be okay.

Watching her was almost as painful as watching my own mother cry for me to come back to life. I could feel Zara's mother's guilt, her wrongness swinging like a pendulum in the air, for how she had and hadn't been there for Zara; deep regret was all over her skin.

I, too, felt desperate for her to be okay; I searched my heart for a song that would let Zara know how thankful I was that she was my friend—maybe it would help somehow.

I started softly singing "Power of Two" by the Indigo Girls. Although I wasn't a great singer, suddenly the song had more meaning to me, hoping somehow the sacred lyrics would seep into her heart and around the bruises on her skull and frail body.

On that Saturday morning when she woke she was lightheaded, and the room seemed fuzzy but she had healed some more and her face looked rosy and pretty. She squinted from the lights in the room, but her eyes had a sparkle in them. I felt hopeful for her recovery when her eyes gazed around and found the familiar face of her mother. She had gained enough strength to sit up and in almost a whisper she said, "I saw Estella…We were sitting on top of a mountain, having a picnic. She was singing to me."

Her mother may have thought Zara was just confused, kissing her forehead and saying, "It's okay, honey," but I knew that Zara and I had connected on a deeper level.

When the nurse brought Zara's breakfast before she checked out of the hospital, a note from Jett was on the tray. Zara didn't recognize Jett's handwriting at first and was worried it was another threatening note, but it read:

*Dear Zara,*

*I hope you are okay. I miss you. Just a warning, you probably will scream when you see me because I look really ugly. My life is over.*

*Love,*

*Jett*

They would be on their way home, back out into the uncertainty of this world, but I wanted to tell Jett that as long as she was breathing, her life wasn't over—there was a lot more life for her to live.

## STAY IN TOUCH WITH THOSE YOU LOVE

Through text messages the girls planned to meet at Zara's Sunday evening. Jett might have the courage to show them what it looked like under her bandages.

When Jett and Zara left the hospital Saturday morning it was about thirty degrees out, warm actually for Central New York, and the wind had weakened. The change in the air made me feel light-footed. I was planning to do the three-mile loop on the trails by Willow Lake, but on the way there I was pulled toward the zip of my father's thermal running jacket, and I rushed to my house.

The ground crunched as my father started to run down the driveway; finally my nagging and gnawing at his heart had worked.

My adrenaline was already racing; I swooped beside him and easily got into our warm-up pace, like old times on Saturday mornings. Even if it wasn't on the trails by Willow Lake, we were still here running in our neighborhood, which was fine with me.

We used to have plenty of long runs through the neighborhood together; he always said the distance would help me with my speed.

He chose to go the hill route, which was my favorite. We had named the hill Ol' Blister because I had gotten one the first time I ran up it.

Whenever we went on runs together, I always guided us this way, over to the intense incline of the road, sometimes just to tease him that I'd beat him to the top of Ol' Bister, and then to the woods behind our housing development, because although I was a sprinter I had a lot of endurance from running this hill. Running this hill had made my calf muscles and arms strong from pumping them hard on the way up, and also made my stomach tight and gave my butt a shape I was proud of. I wished air could fill my lungs and I could feel the burn again.

On our way, I wanted to bump my father's elbow, give him a laugh, and say, "Your shoe's untied again, Dad." A few seconds later, he did stop to fix it.

The long incline of the road felt like a never-ending uphill, but afterward I loved flying down the smooth decline and the feeling of freedom and power as I let my body go as fast as it could.

I looked forward to reliving that feeling today, or imaging I was.

Running Ol' Blister took a lot of work and focus—it could be excruciating.

My father's eyes were concentrated at the top of the hill. I always hated looking up and knowing how much more was left. I just liked to focus on the final result of the rush from flying down it.

Usually on the way up, he had always told me to keep my chest and head up to save energy and to watch my posture while I attacked the hill, but I hated doing that.

This time, though, I listened and I kept myself upright, loose, and springy.

Side by side at a steady pace we made our way up, and I focused on my father's heartbeat and breathing. I could tell what point of the hill we were on just by his breathing. It started to get heavier as we ascended the hill.

Blood was flowing through his muscles, and his arms were pumping up and down swiftly as a few cars went by us.

I moved exactly the same way he did, or that's the way it felt, pounding my feet left, right, left, right, and swinging my arms back and forth, pushing off the ground on my toes, hands relaxed with my index fingers ever so slightly touching the thumbs, and there we were—together again in the momentum of his stride.

He started sweating. He was really feeling the burn now in his legs as we hit the toughest part of Ol' Blister. His arms were driving hard to lift up his legs, and his calves were feeling heavy; his throat was a little dry from his quick inhales and exhales, and he coughed a few times but kept right on.

I was so happy to be with him.

His muscles were working so hard; he was leaning his torso forward, his tendons were being strained, he was charging higher and higher up—he was really working it. All that mattered was getting to the top, and I kept telling him, "We're almost there, we're almost there, Dad!"

He looked like he was about to cry, and I wasn't sure if it was because he missed me or because he was tired.

Memories kept whizzing by us with each step, like the time we got lost on the way to a track meet when I was running for the McClure Bowerman Youth Summer Track & Field Club. We were on our way to Ithaca, and we were so late that I ran directly from the car to the starting line on the track. Literally the gun went off seconds later.

And there was the time when my shoe came off during a race at Manley Field House last year while running the 400, but I kept right on ripping up the track without my shoe and still got a red ribbon — and it was a close call. We both agreed if I had my other shoe on I would have won it.

I remembered a Chiefs baseball game on my 12th birthday. He had set it up so that during the seventh inning I'd see my name across the scoreboard. It was an amazing feeling when I saw it read:

*Happy Birthday Estella!*
*The Running Rebel!*

There were a lot of memories that we held on to, a lot of fun times that couldn't be erased. We were almost at the top of Ol' Blister, and once we hit the top I knew some of my father's sorrow would be at the bottom of our hill. He'd feel a bit of relief from knowing he could still make it to the top, despite now being a grief-stricken man who had lost his daughter.

We plowed right through the crest of the hill and kept going, gliding downhill together. There was nothing but an easy ride down.

As the road leveled, we whipped through the children's playground and right through an open field of slush and slop, and then we were on the trails in the woods behind our housing development.

It was a piece of heaven to be there again.

The woods in front of us used to be a lot bigger, but half of the trees had been cut down to make our development, and although the houses were pretty and new, I hated that the planted trees on our yards still looked like a cluster of sticks.

The ground was soggy from the melting snow, and my father clopped and thudded through the woods on the trails. Down some of the trails there was only running room for one, but it was easy for me to run beside him and dodge the branches of the trees we passed.

He was breathing heavy and pushed himself to finish the trail like he was pushing himself to carry on with life. The cool air filling his lungs was a reminder that he was alive.

The woodsy air full of pine attached to his jacket, but I couldn't smell it. I would have chosen to die a more painful death if it meant I could smell the soothing woodsy air.

When we came out of the trails, I wanted to run through them again, but my father headed back home. It was about to rain. But the wind was at our backs and it whistled at us; it knew my father and I would run again another time.

On the way home a rainbow that arched over our neighborhood was right in front of us. It was the strangest rainbow ever, dark on one end and bright on the other. Looking at the red, orange, yellow, green, and blue, we both felt a sense of peace to be with the beauty of our surroundings.

Inside, it was like the whole house had warmed up a little. I could feel the warmth within the house's energy coming off the walls; it was definitely warmer than it had been right after I died, or maybe the heater was turned up higher than usual.

Upstairs in my bedroom, my mother was wrapped in a blanket. She was cold, but there had been a lot of love in this house, and in time it would warm her again.

I plopped down next to her on my bed and started telling her about the run, but she continued to stare out the window, focusing on nothingness. She didn't care to look at the rainbow when my father yelled up to her that if she came outside she'd see it from our driveway.

In her hand was my "e" charm necklace.

Clutching it, she was in deep thought, somewhere between praying and contemplating. My bedroom had become her holy place. Sitting with her I rested my head on her shoulder and hugged her arm like I had when I was a kid and wanted her attention. I focused on the furthest memory I could recall that we had together: I was three or four, wearing a yellow summer dress she had made for me, and we were collecting small stones at Willow Lake.

Goose-bumps appeared on her arms like she remembered too.

She rubbed my "e" charm against her fingers. I felt like it was the perfect way to connect. I compacted myself and swirled around her fingers and looped my love through the curves of the charm. Amazingly, for a moment, she looked at the charm curiously, as if she had felt my warmth coming off of it, and she broke the silence in the room with the whisper of my name.

"Estella…" She took a deep sigh and spoke to me like I was there beside her listening, and of course I was.

"I miss you. I'm sorry if you've had to see me like this. This isn't easy. I don't know what to do…I don't think I'll ever get over this."

It was like each word floated in the air like dandelion wishes around me, and I wanted to make one of hers come true. Tears were forming in her eyes. She put her hand to her lips and after a moment wondered, "Why do the hours go by so slow but the days go so fast?"

I had no idea but also felt the same way.

"I just wish you were here. How do I say goodbye?" she asked, and I wanted to tell her that she didn't have to say goodbye—I would always be with her. She never had to say goodbye or let me go, and I hoped she wouldn't.

A large tear rolled down her cheek all the way to her jaw, and she let it slowly fall onto her shirt. I wished I could have caught it in my hands.

She put my "e" charm up to her lips and kissed it softly, like it was the last step to saying her prayer, after telling me that she loved me and hoped that I was at peace. I wanted to assure her that I was at peace, even though I wasn't sure if I really was.

She moved to the edge of my bed still holding my "e" charm necklace, and I moved to my vanity table chair. Her hands pushed her body up off the bed gradually like she suddenly had arthritis and each movement was slow and took so much energy, and just as she stood up she went to my vanity table chair too, practically sitting on me. It was funny.

We both looked at her reflection in the mirror; she wiped her tears away with her hands and brushed her curly hair with my brush.

The things I had last touched were now her treasures.

I missed how her fingers brushing through my hair when I was a kid made everything seem okay.

Holding my "e" charm necklace, she also picked up my perfume bottle. She squirted some on her wrists and when she smelled them, her nostrils filled with the scent of me.

Holding the bottle in her hand, she started listing off the errands she'd been running that had involved me, and I listened carefully.

"Well, I had to cancel that order for your running watch."

I didn't know she was getting me a running watch. It might have been something she had purchased for my birthday, since she always shopped early for things.

"I canceled your eye appointment too."

I didn't mind about that one, since I'd always hated the eye doctor and the machine that blew air into your eyeball, but that running watch sounded cool.

"I guess I should start creating some bags for donation. You had so many dresses you never wore. That one from your seventh grade dance is still hanging up in the back of your closet. Remember when you went through that baggy jeans phase?"

She laughed sort of, thinking about that. I remembered. Anytime Zara whipped out a photo of me from middle school wearing baggy jeans, I would snatch it out of her hand and want to rip it to shreds.

It surprised me how much I cared, but I did. It bothered me that my mother had thought of making donation bags of my clothing for the Rescue Mission. It felt too soon to start giving away my life.

"It feels different now, like it's all gone. It's not fair, it's just not fair."

I didn't think it was fair either, how you could be here one second with the future to look forward too and gone the next wondering if the time you had on earth was well spent.

"I've canceled your e-mail account, Evan's going to look after your Annex account, everything's done, and nothing's left. Monday I was going to turn off your phone but...I'll turn it off later."

She took a great sigh, placed the perfume bottle back on my vanity table and put my "e" charm necklace back in her pocket, preparing to leave. Before she reached my bedroom door she turned back and looked toward the window, as if she thought that's where I was, and said one more thing to me. "I wish you were here. It's not the same without you—it's just not."

I liked it when she said that; I circled my room slowly as she turned off the light and shut the door quietly.

The remnants of my life were being canceled or were in the works to be donated to the Rescue Mission, and I wondered when my phone would be turned off. What was next to go? Maybe creating donation bags and shutting off my email account were symbols that she was coming to grips with my passing? But just because she threw out elements of my memory didn't mean her pain or the truth of it would be gone. She didn't need to get rid of stuff yet. I wanted her to just leave everything the way it was.

That night I felt like going to the track at Willow Ridge High School. I didn't mind that the track was wet and cold; I whipped around it a few times feeling like my fast self again, remembering how great it felt to be dedicated to something and the rewards that came when you gave it your all. And if you worked hard you might leave a long lasting legacy. It made me think of my friends and all we had been through recently.

I wanted to reach in their hearts and remind them that they had bright futures ahead.

There was a time when things were simpler—when we didn't have to deal with responsibility, when we didn't go behind each other's backs and inflict revenge against others, when we thought twice, when we didn't keep secrets from each other, and there was less to worry about.

I remember when the future didn't matter as much. We could almost picture it, but it was still far away and blurry, waiting for us—but it could wait because we were going to enjoy what was happening now, and nothing was more important than the now.

Nothing could hurt us, let us down, ruin our plans, or break our hearts, because bad things happened to other people, it seemed. But we all knew differently now.

I wanted the girls to feel positive despite their injuries and all the changes going on around us. I felt they could start anew through Estella Productions. Togetherness would heal and inspire them. I wanted them to carry through with their plans and wondered if they actually would.

I wanted to get through to them.

While going around the track once more, I remembered that time I was driving to school and the car in front of me had a license plate that read EMRUNNER. I found that so cool and ironic because it was my initials with the word runner.

Suddenly I felt compelled to find the car with that license plate; I had plenty of time tonight.

Knowing the girls were going to get together tomorrow evening, I would try to see if it was possible to coordinate it, inspire the right movement of energies, so that the driver of EMRUNNER would just so happen to be driving in front of Eva's mother car. I wanted Eva to see it on her way over to Zara's.

## VALUE EACH DAY

While Zara and Jett were in the hospital, there had been some changes on our Willow Ridge High School terrain. Jackson changed his lunch to a different time period, to avoid us probably.

Phoenix was feeling disgusted with him after finding out he had watched the whole fight and done nothing. He sat with a new crowd at lunch, guys from his architecture design class. It brought out a whole new side of him to talk about something other than lacrosse, and I imagined him one day as a successful, world-renowned architect.

Between my visits with Jett and Zara in the hospital, I'd try to slip away and spend time with him, but I only managed a couple of visits. After school I rode with him to pick up his little brother, Paxton, who Phoenix always called Pax; he went to the school for deaf children about thirty minutes away. On the way Phoenix and I shared some alone time.

In the car I told him how Zara and Jett were doing in the hospital, but mostly we would sing together and jam out to the rock music he liked. I wished he could have felt my happiness as he tapped his hand against the steering wheel, but maybe he could a little. He smiled when the song "Wonderful Tonight" by Eric Clapton came on, and he kept it on—maybe because he knew I liked that song.

He looked so cute when he was driving. With my happiness of having him near me, I felt even more close to him when his phone buzzed and he decided not to text back one of his architecture buddies while he was driving. Then at a red light when he scrolled down his recent text messages, I was able to see that my name and the last text messages we sent each other were there still.

I had known that he knew sign language, but seeing him do it was impressive. Even as he drove, he had full conversations naturally with Pax. It took a lot of patience just to share a simple thing like "How was school today?"

I remember he had told me once that his whole family knew sign language because they never wanted his little brother to feel left out.

I loved that I had chosen to adore a guy who came from a devoted family. I understood where Phoenix got the root of his goodness. I wanted his family to know me, and I wanted to know them. They made an effort for togetherness—a rare thing in the world I had once known.

For only part of the night I stayed with him because I didn't want to leave Jett and Zara too long, but while pressed against Phoenix's arm I felt that something was on his mind. It had to do with his future and the direction it was going, and it was complicated. A battle was going on inside his mind, one that made his face tighten and creases appear on the sides of his eyes. He felt miserable about the things people expected of him, the things he had worked so hard to do, things he used to want. He wondered why he didn't want them anymore.

I understood him and wished we could have talked about it, so I sent him a message that just because he's good at something, it doesn't mean it's the path his heart must take.

To be honest I was kind of happy that he was debating what's next, because before we all knew it, the future was going to be here. I was also wondering where time would take us. I didn't want time to take him away from me.

I wanted him in a separate world of our own, and wondered what his dreams were because I could sense they were about to change. He knew what I knew, that tomorrow was not promised. It was best to focus on what really meant the most and what really lifted the happiness we had inside—that would be time well spent.

While Zara and Jett were in the hospital, Eva had gained popularity; she liked all the attention she was getting. Caleb loved to remind her that by prom she'd probably lose ten pounds. With Zara and Jett absent she didn't need to be as careful when she snuck a diet pill before or after lunch. She didn't feel so idiotic using her crutches anymore. They made her body work hard just to walk, which meant constant calories being lost, which I'm sure she liked.

Without Zara and Jett to eat lunch with, Eva spent her lunch hour in her art class even though Sonia and Gwen weren't around to bother her. She had plenty of seat offers from other girls, but she was wary of Gwen's older sister approaching her. Olivia was proud of Gwen for marking up Jett's face, but lucky for Eva their paths never crossed.

One of her best friends was dead and two others were in the hospital. You couldn't help but feel bad for her and want to help her out. She kept everyone in the loop about Zara and Jett's recovery, and people who had never talked to her were now curious about her life and our lives. I thought the questioning was mostly superficial, but Eva was submerged in answering their questions.

Principal Falcon visited both Zara and Jett in the hospital. They told him what they could remember about the fight, but they were both on medication and kind of out of it; they didn't want to remember the bloody, painful details and also had a hard time recalling what happened vividly.

It never crossed Zara's mind that Jett had actually messed with Gwen's and Sonia's cars to prompt the fight—to her, Sonia and Gwen had purposefully approached them because they were crazy bitches who started rumors and fights.

Cameras in the hallways clearly showed Sonia and Gwen ferociously pounding on Zara's and Jett's bodies and faces, with the type of force that could do even worse. The video had been reviewed by district officials, so it was just a matter of time before Sonia's and Gwen's lives would start to unravel. All the good opportunities that waited in their future would slip away, just like that.

Sonia and Gwen had been arrested after the fight. They'd been suspended from school while Zara and Jett were in the hospital, and there was an expulsion hearing coming up. I didn't need to attend it; I already knew the decision from the district superintendent. Sonia and Gwen would be expelled for the rest of school year.

Only to Principal Falcon did Jett admit that she had damaged Gwen's and Sonia's cars, but slashing tires was different than getting your face slashed. She told Principal Falcon she had made an incredibly immature mistake, and that she'd take responsibility for the cost of the damage. She never assumed Gwen should be the one forking out money for her hospital bill, but Zara's father was after a lawsuit.

Jett's mother didn't have the time, money, or care to invest in Jett's rights, but Zara's father was sure the punishment Sonia and Gwen would get from the district superintendent wasn't enough. Zara's father was creating a case on their physical abuse and was going to push for Sonia's and Gwen's parents to pay for their medical bills. He thought at the least Sonia should pay for Zara's and be sent to a youth detention center, because he knew she was capable of being even more dangerous.

Principal Falcon understood when Jett said she didn't wanted to finish the school year at Willow Ridge High School, but told her to think about her future.

Jett had a long deep debate with herself about her life so far and asked me in her quietness, "What should I do, Estella?"

I couldn't plan her life and I didn't know what was next for her but it couldn't be worse. I knew her reflection was all she could see right now, but my response to her soul was for her to listen to her heart; I hoped she would.

## NOT EVERYTHING LASTS FOREVER

I was excited to see the girls all together again at Zara's house Sunday evening. The sun going down was my cue, and I starting out with a lot of speed, going faster and faster down each street, becoming one with the wind, taking a short cut through the fences and pushing off a few roofs to get there faster.

It was a smooth ride through the neighborhoods until a cold gust of wind collided with the batch I was riding on and spun me around like a merry-go-round; a queasy feeling came over me, and I felt heavy like I was carrying weights. My movements became wobbly and unbalanced. I even forgot which way I was going.

Everything was spinning and coming at me. The headlights of cars were glaring right at me. For a moment I wasn't sure I'd make it to Zara's. It was that bad, and it was the same weakening feeling I had that day Zara found out Heidi was coming to town, only a bit more intense this time.

Maybe I was just tired and nauseated from running around—I hadn't really had many moments to relax lately, or maybe it was something else, like an allergic reaction to something in the air. Maybe it was what I feared; maybe Heidi's excitement about her visit to Willow Ridge was trailing in the air and creating a sickening pulse that pounded down on what was left of me.

During the next days I'd continue to feel off-balanced sometimes, like Heidi's energy was near, cutting me off and making me feel like I was walking toward a dead end. The sound of metal crushing was all around and it wouldn't leave me alone.

Tonight I wanted to leave all my negative feelings outside and not bring them into Zara's house. But I still relished the thought of Sonia and Gwen failing their classes while being expelled for the rest of the year; their plans for a bright future would evaporate, and they would be left standing in a blackout of obscurity and lost opportunity. But that still wouldn't be true justice because they could have killed my friends.

When I entered Zara's bedroom I knew Phoenix had stopped by with Brett because his easy-going ambience still lingered in the air. Their *Get Well Soon* cards were on her nightstand, one from Brett and one from Phoenix. I pressed myself all over the one from Phoenix, just wanting to be near anything he might have touched.

There were also flowers on the nightstand from Brett and a few bottles of painkillers, plus other additions, like the wheelchair near Zara's closet.

Zara was lying in bed but sitting upright with pillows all around her. Her chest hurt when she breathed, and she now got very painful migraines. Sitting by her, I carefully checked on her bruises. They still were very sore, especially her shoulder blades. She had been very lucky—if Sonia had pierced her spine just a bit more deeply, she could have suffered a major spinal cord injury or maybe even been paralyzed.

Eva arrived with a box of chocolate chip cookies from her mother's bakery and placed them on Zara's nightstand. She was wearing her cream sweater dress again; it looked even baggier on her. I knew that Zara noticed Eva's dress looked baggier, but she didn't ask or comment about it.

After setting her crutches against the wall and giving Zara a hug hello, Eva asked about the flowers on the nightstand gushing, "Aw! Are those from Brett?"

Zara spoke slower than usual, as if her thoughts didn't come as quickly now, and said the flowers were from Brett. He wanted to know if we all wanted to do a limo for prom together—he could get them a great deal through his father's sleazy connections—but she sounded perplexed about the whole thing. I could sense that Eva was nervous that Zara wasn't sure about prom anymore.

With sympathy in her eyes Zara said, "Phoenix looked so uncomfortable when Brett mentioned prom."

Eva made a sorrowful face thinking of me. She remembered seeing the license plate of the car that was driving in front of her mother's car on the way over here. It was the EMRUNNER license plate I had made sure she'd see. Eva had said to her mother, "Look, that's so weird. Estella's initials are E M, and she was a runner." I was glad Eva was thinking about my passion for running, because I wanted the girls to talk about Estella Productions. I wanted their first event to involve running. I wanted Eva to speak up tonight and remind the girls of their plans. I wanted Jett to be reminded that she could find meaning in her future perhaps through their plans.

"Here." Eva handed Zara her school bag with her makeup and schoolwork inside, and her sketchbook that had fallen out in the cafeteria when Sonia had pushed her. Zara didn't care to open her sketchbook, but it rested next to her.

I could feel Jett's energy nearby, and a few moments later there was a soft knock on Zara's door.

"Are you guys ready?" It was Jett's voice. She was about to reveal her face, covered in bandages, to us.

They couldn't tell her what they really thought. I mean, friends don't do that, but Zara and Eva's "Oh my God, honey!" exclamation said it all.

A gray scarf was around her head, meant to cover the patches of missing hair. She stood there, like a mummy, with just the tip of her nose, mouth, and eyes uncovered, completely obscuring her beauty. She was holding back her tears as we all stared at her.

Wanting to cry, Jett glanced toward Zara's desk at the "Best Friends" frame and photo of us at the boutique trying on our prom dresses that memorable day that ended in my tragic death. We looked so pretty that day—our smiles were so big, our faces so full of life.

She also noticed the wheelchair by Zara's closet.

Eva hopped toward Jett, and Zara started to scoot to the edge of the bed, wanting to hug her.

Zara reached her arms out at Jett and smiled in a warm way, hiding her astonishment to see her friend look this terrible, and said, "Come here, honey."

It was sort of a wakeup call for Eva when she saw Jett. Having some stomach chub come over her jeans wasn't such a big deal anymore.

Jett sat on Zara's bed, right next to me, and peeled up the bandages a little bit so the girls could see what was underneath. Zara and Eva thought it was gross, but they made "aw" sounds with concern and their faces crunched up like they had a sour taste in their mouth.

Eva hugged Jett while trying to avoid her face.

"It's going to heal." Zara wanted to say something to assure Jett it would be okay and it wasn't as bad as it looked, although it was.

She asked Jett, "Did they give you any ointment? My aunt had back surgery and you can hardly see the scar now because she used creams on it."

Jett nodded and became really quiet.

Zara felt stupid. It was one thing to have a scar on your back, but another to have so many scars all over your face.

We all felt awkward talking more, because the truth was too bad to bear.

For once Eva felt like the prettiest one in the room. This new feeling inspired a change in her attitude—for this evening anyway— one that involved something she hadn't been good at: being positive.

Eva would have to use her skill for putting words together and creating beautiful poems and quotes to now encourage her friends to have faith. I let Eva's inner energy know that it was her time to rise up, be a leader, and think beyond outer beauty and diet pills. She had to remind Zara and Jett that their embarrassment over getting their butt kicked and their dramatic injuries wouldn't hold them down forever.

"Guess what?" Eva asked them like she had a surprise and reached inside her handmade denim tote bag.

"What? You know a face surgeon?" I wanted to roll my eyes when Jett asked that.

Zara did what I would have done, tapping Jett's arm and telling her again, "They're going to heal." Like me, Zara really wanted to believe Jett's face would look better one day.

"Hold your hand out." Eva said with a smile, and Jett did unenthusiastically.

After the fight was over and the ambulance drove away, Eva had managed to retrieve most of the pieces of Jett's mother's smashed gold charm bracelet from the cafeteria floor, but there was no way it could be put back to together again. Now the pieces were in a small cloth pouch Eva had made.

Opening the pouch and staring at the pieces of tarnished gold, Jett softly said, "Thanks," thinking about how her actions had ruined so many things. She started to sniffle and her tears streamed down the bandages. We all could feel her pain when she cried, "I'm so sorry."

She had immense guilt inside, for messing with Gwen and Sonia's cars, and for not being able to help Zara—she blamed herself for the fight.

"I don't know what to do." Jett let her body fall to the carpet still holding the pouch and closed her hand into a fist.

Eva let her leg in the cast sweep in front of her, and she went down to the carpet too. Zara, unable to move fast because of her back pain, was slowly making it off the bed to the carpet, and they hugged Jett together. I slithered off the bed and rested beside Jett's arm.

"It's all my fault—If it wasn't for me none of this would have happened." Jett looked so broken. And hearing Eva and Zara say it wasn't her fault only made Jett feel more like it was.

"It is my fault." Jett didn't want to admit that she snuck around and ignited the fight, but I could see in her eyes that she was about to share something important.

"You don't understand." Jett said. On the floor we sat listening to Jett tell us how she had lost her mother's gold bracelet on Gwen's driveway, and what she did to Gwen's and Sonia's cars. She asked us to promise not to tell anyone ever about it.

We all promised not to talk about it. Zara and Eva looked shocked and partially fascinated that Jett had the guts to do such vandalizing.

Zara felt it wasn't Jett's fault that Sonia had accused her of talking shit about Heidi and attacked her.

Jett was bawling so hard while telling us how ugly she was now, how she couldn't go back to school looking like this, and how her modeling dreams were over. It was tough to hear when she said that her life was over and how alone she felt, while her tears seeped into her bandages.

"You're not ugly." Zara dabbed Jett's eyes with a tissue and reached for Jett's hand.

"Seriously, would you want to be seen like this?" Jett let go of Zara's hand and suddenly didn't feel as close to us anymore as she started to get frantic thinking about how embarrassing she was now.

"You don't even have to hang out with me anymore." Jett started to get up off the carpet.

"Stop it." Zara grabbed Jett's shirt; she was acting ridiculous. "Stay here, you're not going anywhere." Jett slumped to the carpet again and covered her face with her hands.

Deep down Eva was glad she didn't look like Jett, but she knew what it was like to feel ugly. She rubbed Jett's back to calm her down and said sternly but sweetly, "We're here for you, you're not alone, we'll always be your friend, and it has nothing to do with your face. You're going to be okay. We love you."

Jett got quiet, perhaps wondering if it was true, that she should feel lucky to have such loving friends who would stand by her no matter what.

What the girls didn't know was that Jett also feared losing Kyle. In a text message she had told him that she was sick with strep throat. He had sent flowers to her house, and each day texted asking how she was feeling; he didn't care if she was sick, he wanted to see her. But Jett kept giving more excuses, like her period was coming and she had bad cramps, her grandma was sick in the nursing home and it might be Jett's last time to visit her, or she had a modeling job in Rochester and would be back too late to stay the night.

In the silence between Jett and us, Eva's phone buzzed loudly. For the first time she didn't text Caleb back right away but let him wait.

"Estella would still be there for you too." Eva said. "What you looked like had nothing to do with the fun we had singing karaoke, and your face had nothing to do with roller skating at Dance N Skate."

"Or riding the trolley," Zara suggested, and a giggle came out of her like a foreign sound we hadn't heard in a long time. In the summers at Willow Lake we always rode the trolley and jumped off it before it stopped. We thought we were so bad-ass.

"And it didn't matter what you looked like when we went sledding in middle school and I stuffed snow down your coat, or when we wrote that poem for Estella for her funeral or went shopping for prom dresses together." Eva smiled with the thought of prom and the poem they wrote.

Jett's mouth curved very slightly and the tiniest smile appeared. "I know, it's just…"

When Jett looked at Zara, her chin started trembling a little, like she was about to tell us something she knew we wouldn't like to hear.

"It's just…I don't think I can go to prom like this." Jett was ashamed she didn't have the love for herself anymore or the courage to show everyone what she looked like now.

I slowly moved away from Jett's arm and sunk low to the floor. I wanted to hide under Zara's bed and pretend Jett hadn't said that. Eva became fidgety playing with her earrings and chewing at her fingernails. She had bitten off the entire whiteness of her pretty crescent-shaped nails.

Strangely Zara, the one who was usually most excited about glamorous memorable occasions, didn't seem shocked. Looking at Jett and her mummified face, I couldn't be upset—more like I shouldn't have been upset, because I was actually very disturbed.

"It's okay, don't worry. I don't really care about prom." Zara laughed like it really wasn't a big deal at all. "I can't dance or even bend my body with my back like this. And I'll be using that for a while." She pointed to her wheelchair and hugged Jett again.

Like Eva, I felt unable to move suddenly.

"I just don't want you to be mad at me," Jett said to us all, but she could tell Eva was bothered. I couldn't believe this. It was like the walls around us were caving in.

"I'm not...It's okay; it's not the end of the world," Eva said without any concern in her voice, even though she was pissed.

Soon after the shocking news Jett went to the bathroom to fix her tear-soaked bandages, and Eva whispered to Zara, "You really don't want to go to prom?"

"Shh, I don't know." Zara went back in bed and pulled the covers up to her chin, like she was sleepy and in a lot of pain and didn't want to talk about it.

"Isn't Brett going to be mad?" Eva couldn't believe Zara really didn't really care.

But Zara said she didn't care and that Brett was pissing her off. He hadn't visited her in the hospital. Showing up a week late with flowers still counted for something, but she was angry he hadn't come to sit with her while she was struggling to breathe.

Eva stayed quiet with her dreary thoughts.

After seeing Jett and Zara in the hospital, it had crossed my mind that prom wouldn't happen, but hearing them say they didn't want to go to prom still really stung. My wish had wilted like a flower that someone forgot to water, and the day would never come. I couldn't count on anything.

Prom had been a beacon of hope for me; I hoped it would be memorable for us all. It wasn't easy for Eva to accept that prom wasn't going to happen either. Of course, I couldn't wear my dress or be there with Phoenix hand in hand, but I still wanted to see it happen for my friends. Who knows, maybe I would have been able to sway with the music beside Phoenix and we would have been able to dance together—sort of.

Not wanting to look at Zara or Jett, I dangled off the edge of Zara's bed comforter feeling droopy, like a huge wad of snot.

Eva looked really unhappy; her leg was healing and the doctor said she would be off her crutches by prom, but she felt it would be selfish to mention that now.

I tried to convince myself that skipping out on prom was the best thing to do, but I couldn't. I had a feeling they would all be full of regret. Zara would always wonder how pretty and romantic it could have been. Eva would be mad at herself for letting her friends decide things for her. Jett would wish she could have looked beyond her appearance and just lived in the moment with her friends. They would all regret forgetting about me and what I wanted.

I crouched down under Zara's nightstand and wondered if my own gown, which had been buried with my body, would stay white, or if over time it would turn to yellow or disintegrate completely. And if the words my friends and family had written on my casket would also fade.

It startled me when Zara's bedroom door opened and shut. Jett's energy appeared ready to broadcast something else.

Jett announced that she wasn't going back to Willow Ridge High School and would get her GED instead. It would be too humiliating for her to be seen right now by anyone other than us. She was looking at Eva and Zara for their approval, but at the same time I could tell she was going to do what she wanted whether or not they understood why. She didn't need to explain herself, we all saw the certainty in her eyes that she wasn't going to go back to Willow Ridge, and she asked Eva to help her collect the things from her locker.

A general equivalency degree, or what we liked to call a "good enough diploma," was equal to graduating high school, but it didn't involve the memories that high school was supposed to contain, like prom, like lunch with the girls, like being together every day.

Eva and Zara didn't argue with Jett about it. She wouldn't have to deal with everyone at Willow Ridge, their eyeballs, and their whispers—it might be best for her. Still, I didn't like the idea of my friends separating and our routine disappearing.

Jett seemed to relax after she told us what she was going to do. She didn't give us a full smile, but she looked more at ease while sitting on the carpet with us. Like we had been with Eva in the past about her appearance in dressing rooms at the mall, our sensitivity immediately turned towards Jett's obvious insecurities, and we were careful not to be offensive.

"Okay," Zara said. "It will really suck, but if it's what you want, it's okay."

It was like everything was falling apart. Eva thought of our lost prom and how I was buried in my prom dress. She thought about what I'd say, what I'd do, and how she hadn't been initially totally excited over the idea of starting a company with the girls, but now it seemed like the only thing that would keep us all together. Eva looked at Zara and then Jett. "Okay, so we won't see you in school, but are we still going to do Estella Productions?"

I crawled out from underneath Zara's nightstand.

This was just the conversation I wanted the girls to have.

Jett didn't look too interested but said quietly, "Yeah, I guess."

Zara sighed like she was debating everything. "My dad read some of the comments that were written about me on my blog and on my Annex profile. If he catches me using them again he's going to take away my computer. And I don't think right now is a good time to ask him about starting a company."

It was like each stiletto stab to her back had also jabbed at her confidence, and it was gone. Her go-getter attitude was too, like it was all a big waste of time to grow her fashion blog and be known as a fashion expert, or eventually become a successful stylist or have a goal at all. Now it seemed like a pipe dream that she could never live up to. She thought creating a company that hosted charitable events would be another thing to be put down for, have rumors spread about, or even get in a fight over.

"But your dad didn't say Jett and I couldn't blog, right?" Eva asked. She had on a sneaky smile and proposed, "Jett and I could write the blog if you just show us how to create one."

Zara didn't look enthused at the idea of starting another blog.

She started opening the box of chocolate chip cookies that Eva had earlier placed on her nightstand and handed the box to Jett, who took a cookie and said hopelessly, "To hell with being skinny and modeling."

Jett chewed the cookie slowly because her jaw still hurt. She didn't pass the box to Eva. Although Eva liked to give us treats from her mother's bakery, she always said, "No, I'm fat enough," to sweets. But this time to be more united she said, "I'll have one."

With the cookie in her mouth, Eva nudged Zara's sketchbook toward her and said, "Come on, let's work on our first event."

Zara flipped open her sketchpad at first reluctantly, and after glancing at her notes about a fashion show she closed it abruptly and said, "I don't know if a fashion show would be the best thing to do right now. Can we do something else?"

"Okay?" Eva was puzzled, since Zara was the fashion expert, after all.

"I mean, no offense but..." Zara was trying to find the right words to say it nicely, but they looked quite opposite of a group of trendsetters.

"It's not even us, it's just that I want to take a break from fashion meaning everything, and Estella wasn't even into fashion."

I wanted to say to Zara, "Hey, I had some cute outfits!" But she was right—fashion wasn't my forte. My white prom dress was the most stylish thing I had ever owned.

Jett had considered Zara's fashion show idea back at Lilly's Café but now said, "Yeah, there's no way I am going to be in a fashion show or a part of one."

And that was that.

234

So, again they thought of the perfect event to define their company and my memory. I thought the fashion show was something they could still pursue, maybe sometime later. For now all they had to do was think about what I loved to do most. They were already planning to give the proceeds to the McClure Bowerman Youth Track & Field Summer Club, and since running with my father it now seemed so obvious to me what they should do for an event.

I spread my idea over them; there was no other idea that would be better.

After they blurted out a bunch of mediocre ideas, finally, it clicked with Eva. She remembered the EMRUNNER license plate and how ironic that was and said, "What about an event related to running, like a Sprint-A-Thon?"

That was what I wanted to hear!

Eva thought for a moment and then said energetically, "Estella ran the 400 dash, so the race could be the 400 dash, one lap around the track. Anyone could run it, and we'd get the students to collect donations for their race."

All Zara could think about was running down the hall while Sonia had chased her, and she said, "I'm not sure I'm going to want to run a race."

"Yeah, we all know what happens when we try to run." Jett said, remembering how she had dragged Zara down the hallway but they weren't fast enough to outrun Sonia and Gwen.

It was just one lap around the track, but I understood their hesitation and lack of interest in running. Even for the sake of me.

"You don't have to run it," Eva assured them. It was about getting the other students at Willow Ridge to be a part of the Sprint-A-Thon and raise funds for the McClure Bowerman Youth Track & Field Summer Club.

"We'd call it The Run with Your Heart for Estella Sprint-A-Thon."

It sounded kind of long and a little corny, but it was thoughtful of Eva, and I loved it. "You don't think students would run a lap for Estella? It's not that much running," Eva said, eager to get Zara and Jett on board.

"I don't know, run for fun?" Zara asked, unconvinced the Sprint-A-Thon was a good idea.

"Estella did every day. She loved running, it was fun to her, and she will never run again." I liked how Eva whiplashed their emotions and struck their hearts, just like that.

Reminding Zara and Jett that I would never do what I loved ever again made the air around them change, and it made Zara think.

After some visions of me running and remembering the conversations we used to have about my running lifestyle, Zara could see why the Sprint-A-Thon was the perfect event, and she agreed with Eva.

Zara and Eva looked at Jett, trying to see her expression through her bandages.

"I really don't want to be around people for a while, but I could help out with the other stuff," Jett offered.

"Yeah, that's okay, we can do a lot right in this room. We're going to create posters and a blog, round up volunteers, create a pledge form—there's a lot to do." Eva was starting to sound like the old Zara, the way Zara had always triggered our energy and gotten us pepped up.

"So, do you want to create a blog?" It was cute how Eva looked at Zara with a hopeful little smirk.

"Go to my blog. In the upper right corner it says, 'Create a New Blog,'" Zara said, as if it was the simplest thing in the world to do.

Zara directed Eva and Jett on the basics of blogging, and soon they had set up an Estella Productions blog account. It was cool to see my name as part of a blog.

Considering my speed, the girls chatted about how the focus of the Sprint-A-Thon races would be endurance. They imagined students running a lap, 400 meters in my memory, and asking to get sponsors for their lap, with pledges starting at five dollars.

They could group the runners by each runner's personal prediction of their race time, by how many seconds they thought they could run the 400 dash in. The Sprint-A-Thon would start with the qualifiers, where every runner would run. Then there would be semifinals for the top twenty runners, and finals for the top ten based on their running times.

"We could design T-shirts and even give out trophies to the top ten sprinters," Eva proposed, and we all thought it was a good idea.

The girls looked at the calendar, and easily enough they picked my birthday, April 26th, a Saturday, as a potential day to hold the Sprint-A-Thon.

Because of the fight, Zara and Jett both had easy access to talk with Principal Falcon. They'd ask him about using the school's track.

The schedule for home outdoor track meets hadn't come out yet. If there wasn't a home track meet or another sport scheduled on the field that Saturday morning, it would be really amazing to hold the Sprint-A-Thon on my birthday. In fact it was all I wanted for my birthday.

Their planning reminded me a little of my parents planning my funeral, all the many little details to consider.

Jett wasn't going to be at school anymore, which made me unhappy, but they would all meet up again tomorrow and every day this week to talk about the Sprint-A-Thon and Estella Productions.

On the way to Zara's earlier that evening Jett took the back roads, but now since it was dark out she wouldn't have to worry as much about anyone seeing the bandages on her face. She was in less of hurry to get home to her disappointed mother, so she offered to give Eva a ride.

When they got to Eva's place, it was genuine how Eva grabbed Jett's hand before she got out of the car and assured her, "You're going to be okay, girl."

I knew Eva had always thought Jett was pretty and skinny, but now Eva was noticing that friendship meant more than how she had previously compared herself to her friends. Her comforting words stayed with Jett all through her ride home. Sometimes the care from others can help you find your own faith in yourself. The sun would shine again, for all of them, and I'd be there this week when Zara and Eva had their meeting with Principal Falcon about holding the Sprint-A-Thon at the school track. The girls figured if they got the track date they wanted, it would be a sign that it was all meant to be. Lucky for us, I would be trying to make it happen from behind the scenes, or doing the best I could.

# Careful

## KEEP SAFE WHAT'S SENTIMENTAL

Jett hid the pieces of the gold bracelet in the back of her underwear drawer. Seeing Jett's push-up bras bursting from the drawer made me think of that padded strapless bra with the tags still on it in my own underwear drawer, that stupid padded strapless bra that stole precious minutes of my life while I purchased it. It was the one thing I wished my mother had thrown out. I felt like it was bad luck to keep it around.

Jett was hoping her mother would never ask about the bracelet — maybe her mother would never talk to her again. Deep down Jett knew she'd be mad at herself for the rest of her life for letting Gwen smash it into a million pieces; it was her favorite bracelet, and it couldn't be replaced.

Because Jett didn't want to face the students at Willow Ridge High School, Principal Falcon had arranged for her to finish the year at the Alternative High School, located in a separate building near the village of Willow Ridge, where she'd start this week. She could always come back to Willow Ridge High School for her senior year if she wanted to, and she would be able to attend graduation next year with Eva and Zara, he said.

Perhaps after the summer, after the scars had healed a little, she'd return. At least that option was always there.

After avoiding him for so long, she had to face Kyle. Well, not exactly—she wouldn't dare let him see her face. She wasn't ready to see his eyes become worried for her and their future. She wanted him to remember her as beautiful, not as the ugly person she felt she was.

It wasn't right, and she hated breaking up with him over a text message, but that's what she did.

He kept asking to see her, to talk about it, but she told him, "We are at different points in our lives." He knew she wasn't telling him the truth and accused her of cheating on him, even though she wasn't. She told him it was over. It was easier for her to handle his anger than the truth that she didn't think he'd love her with all those scars.

Without Jett as a ride, Eva asked Caleb if he could pick her up for school Monday, which he did, but he didn't hide his disturbance at driving through her ghetto neighborhood, which made Eva feel bad. He always made her feel so sorry.

With her crutches, Eva couldn't exactly push Zara's wheelchair, so after Zara's father dropped her off at school, Brett met Zara at the entrance and wheeled her to her locker. I could tell he was embarrassed pushing Zara in a wheelchair—he hated doing it, and Zara also looked uncomfortable being pushed around like she was helpless.

Brett wouldn't be able to wheel her to all her classes, so a student from each class was assigned to help her get around.

Phoenix sweetly offered to push Zara's wheelchair to and from lunch, with Eva hobbling beside them on her crutches.

At first Zara still made the effort to look stylish while sitting in her wheelchair but soon she gave up trying so hard because she was often too tired to care about looking the part of a fashion expert. She had started wearing the type of typical T-shirts and casual sweaters I had worn to be more comfy during her recovery.

After lunch Phoenix dropped Zara off at her locker. Brett and Caleb would be there like usual and they'd all chat, mostly about what they were going to do over prom weekend since they wouldn't be attending prom together anymore. I didn't like listening to them make other plans.

Brett's parents had a cottage on the Finger Lakes. Everyone could come up, and of course Phoenix was also invited. I hoped he wouldn't go. There was a beautiful lake right here in Willow Ridge. They didn't need to go trekking up to the Finger Lakes just to do the same thing they could do here, but whatever.

Surprisingly at lunch that Monday I noticed that Eva ate. Not a full meal but a small fruit parfait and a few bites of salad with cucumbers and tomatoes. I was proud of her for not taking her diet pill for a couple days. During lunch Zara was sketching something in her sketchbook; it caught my eye because it looked like a track shoe with wings. She had drawn many variations, some simple and some more detailed. It was clever.

I was happy when Phoenix stopped by their table again. Zara showed him her drawings, and he showed her some of his architecture sketches; he was working on a design for a house in the shape of an oval, with a spiral staircase made of glass and floor-to-ceiling windows. I could picture it and thought he was so inventive. I wished he was showing the sketches to me, and I wondered why Zara was drawing the track shoe with wings.

Earlier that morning there wasn't time for Jett to stop at the cemetery, but I could tell she wanted to visit my grave and talk to me. On the way to the Alternative High School, she stopped at the side of the road where I died in the village of Willow Ridge; she walked over to the cross my mother had put in the ground. The artificial flowers looked wilted and tattered from the wind. It made me smile when Jett pulled a big, fat green elastic ponytail holder out of her pocket and looped it on the top of the cross; she remembered I had always tied my thick curly hair in big, fat elastic bands to keep it out of my face while I ran.

Under her coat she wore a turtleneck sweater, with the neck of the sweater pulled up past her chin purposely, like she wanted to hide at least the bandages on the lower part of her face. While looking down at the cross and touching her bandages she said, "Well, Estella, wish me luck. I'm going to need it today."

Monday evening the Estella Productions blog had a green background; Zara thought it would be nice because of the color of my eyes. From the folder of photos on Zara's computer they added some of my favorite photos of all of us together.

At the top of the blog they added the mission of their company.

*Estella Productions is an event planning and production company that was created in memory of Estella Marie Montclair. We host fundraising events and awareness campaigns that inspire teens to volunteer their time for charitable organizations that affect the well-being of people, animals, and the earth. We aim to be an example of compassion as a common sense.*

It made me feel all fuzzy and warm.

The entrepreneur mind-set in Zara was being awakened again, and she suggested that they get business cards. They easily could be ordered online and arrive at Zara's by tomorrow evening.

On Tuesday it was depressing for me, but the girls decided to sell their prom dresses on eBay. They were going to use some of the money to prepare for the Sprint-A-Thon. I could tell Eva was not fully happy with the idea of selling their dresses. Prom was truly gone, our moment to wear them again was gone, and I secretly hoped no one would bid on the dresses because I wanted them to be preserved in my friends' closets as a memento of our friendship.

While working on my biography for the blog, Eva seemed distracted as she typed *Estella Marie Montclair was born in Syracuse, NY...*

She was having a hard time focusing on my life description when she really wanted to see Caleb. I wanted to tell her that this was more important.

She checked her phone and started texting him that she couldn't meet up, even though she wished she could. He was offering to pick her up at Zara's.

"What are you telling him?" Zara was curious, but she also wanted Eva to focus.

Eva lied to her.

"Nothing," Eva said while eyeing the medication bottles on Zara's nightstand, "just that you're doing better and that we're working on the blog."

In that moment I wanted to be Eva. She had a zing running through her skin while reading Caleb's text. But I didn't want to be his decoy, like she was. She was considering sharing with Caleb the medications Zara was taking, since he had asked. He probably wanted her to snag a couple for him to sell.

It bothered me how Caleb put Eva up to this scheme of stealing medicine Zara needed.

After texting Caleb back that she would try to get him a couple of painkillers, Eva started Googling my name.

I had Googled myself before plenty of times, and at first it was exciting to see my name being typed into the browser, but it was disturbing when the first thing that came up was my obituary.

There were pages and pages of horrendous photos of the crash, my car, and Heidi's car. In one photo, probably snapped from someone's phone that pulled over to see the wreckage, you could almost recognize the curl of my hair in the driver's seat. He probably sold the image to the newspaper, and the thought of that made me mad. Seeing it reminded the girls that Heidi was coming into town this weekend, but no one brought it up.

There were video clips online from the news segments about the crash, and each headline involved the words "death," "killed," or "died." I was angry that those words were now coupled with my name.

A silence fell over them all when Eva said, "Maybe we can use her obituary?"

It was like my stomach dropped, and I floated down to the floor and under Zara's nightstand.

"Yeah. I guess." Jett scanned down my obituary.

Eva was adding words to my obituary like "exceptional" and "bolting speed" to make my biography sound even livelier.

I thought they were doing a good job with it, but Eva seemed concerned and asked, "Maybe we should call Estella's mom?"

I peered out from under the nightstand.

Eva wondered if maybe they should have asked my parents about doing Estella Productions in the first place, and if it was okay with them.

I already knew my mother wouldn't mind; it seemed like just the thing to lift her up and make her feel that some good could come from my death.

Eva held her cell phone in her hand and wondered if it was too late to call, looking a little nervous about being the one to do it.

"It's only 9:05," Jett said.

"You want to call?" Eva asked her.

Jett shook her head not wanting to be the one, so Zara said, "I'll call."

It wasn't too late, and I zapped to my house.

My parents were in the living room watching a movie. My father was taking another sip of his Peroni beer—he had already finished four and looked sleepy. My mother was resting her head on his shoulder, wearing her big tortoiseshell glasses, which were a sign she didn't care how she looked, when the phone rang.

My mother got up slowly and finally answered it.

The sound of my friends all speaking into the phone as Zara held it, saying, "Hi Mrs. Montclair, how are you?" poured right into my mother's heart. She hollered to my father from the kitchen counter, "James, pause it. It's Zara and the girls."

She started to get a little choked up telling them she was doing okay; how it wasn't easy and it wasn't the same anymore. She told them how much I had loved being their friend and what good friends they had all been to me. They all started getting emotional at the thought of me.

After a deep sigh my mother changed her voice to sound less sad and asked Zara, "So, what are you girls up to tonight?"

After pausing the movie my father waited curiously, while my mother listened to Zara explain their plans for starting Estella Productions. "We want to do something for Estella. We've been thinking of holding a memorial Sprint-A-Thon at Willow Ridge High School in her memory and donating the proceeds to the McClure Bowerman Youth Track & Field Summer Club. We are having a meeting with Principal Falcon about it tomorrow, but we wanted to make sure it was okay with you and Mr. Montclair."

I sat on top of the counter as my mother wrote down "Estella Productions" on a notepad and then the words "memorial Sprint-A-Thon" and "in memory of Estella" and "proceeds for McClure Bowerman track club."

She wrote my birthday, April 26th, on the notepad and stared at it, hurting to know it was coming up, and circled it a few times.

Looking up toward the ceiling—maybe at God—she was listening carefully and nodding her head, taking in everything Zara told her. She was pleased with their thoughtfulness and told them how much I would love this.

I shimmied around the kitchen. It was amazing how I could frolic from one moment to the next and be there when the pieces of things came together.

"You know," my mother said, "the director at the McClure Bowerman Youth Track & Field Summer Club launched a nonprofit last year called Speedy's, which would be a good place to send the proceeds."

I was so happy my mother told the girls about Speedy's.

She shared with the girls the director's name, Scott Arthur, and went to get his contact info. I was skipping around behind her like I was a kid again as she hurried back to the living room and flung open the lower drawer of the armoire that held important papers.

I was so happy my mother was offering to call Scott and give him the heads-up.

When Zara asked my mother about getting local sponsors for the Sprint-A-Thon, Accelerations, the running store where my father and I bought my running shoes came to mind, and my mother said, "Let me get back to you, I think we know of a place."

My mother's sunken heart was being lifted a little thinking about Estella Productions, and I hugged her while she told my friends, "I'm so glad you girls called. Let me know if you need anything."

After the call, my mother went back to the couch and held my father's hand, telling him about Estella Productions and the Sprint-A-Thon. A smile appeared on my father's face when she mentioned approaching the manager at Accelerations and asking him about getting involved. My father was almost crying thinking about that, and I was sure he'd stop over there over the weekend; he knew I wanted him too.

"See, Mom, good things can come," I wanted to tell her, and I flopped across her chest, squeezing her tight, sending her my message and love.

Fleeting back to Zara's, jumping on the first windy gust of air I could grab a hold of, I couldn't wait for our plans to come to life. I was having a hard time sitting still on Zara's carpet.

Zara was still holding her cell phone, scrolling down her text messages, and texting Brett again. "Helloooo, where are you?"

Her face looked concerned although she tried to hide her worry, but I also wondered why he hadn't texted her back.

Eva was talking about a shoe drive and thought of asking students to donate a pair of running shoes before the Sprint-A-Thon for Speedy's, so that even if they didn't want to get pledges for their race they could perhaps still contribute.

Zara gave her phone a rest and put it on the nightstand. If Brett texted, we'd hear her phone vibrate and we'd all know. She was really tired and didn't have much strength left to think tonight. But after talking to my mother, Zara wanted Eva to create the content for our first blog post about Estella Productions. They'd include a link to their prom dresses on eBay within the post, and also put it on my Annex memorial page.

They titled the post, "*Introducing Estella Productions, in memory of Estella Montclair.*"

I was all jumpy waiting for them to finish the post.

A mix of pressure and anticipation ran through me.

*Hi Everyone,*

*As you might have heard at school or in the news, our best friend Estella passed away recently from a terrible car collision on the day we shopped for our prom dresses.*

*With great sadness and grief we have decided not to attend prom. Instead we are selling our prom dresses and putting the money toward a production company we are launching in memory of Estella, called Estella Productions. You can find more about the events coming up for Estella Productions on this blog soon. Please check out the links below to the stunning gowns we are selling. Stay tuned for more details on our first event in memory of Estella. Students from Willow Ridge High School and anywhere can bid. The bidding is open and starts now.*

*Love,*

*Zara, Eva, and Jett*

I hoped that my memory could successfully be the pillar to keep their business plans strong.

Zara linked the post to her blog. Her hope was that her readers would see the post, bid on the dresses, and start to get curious about Estella Productions despite the rude comments that were posted recently about her. She also hoped that her father would forget to check her online status every day. He had agreed to help the girls set up their small company officially, which was nice, but he still didn't want Zara to be using social websites. She was supposed to be disconnected from the Internet world, which to her was like being disconnected from the whole world.

I felt strangely disconnected as well, unable to sign on to my account while people used the Internet to feel connected to me and my memory; I was surprised people still put thoughtful comments on my profile page on The Annex even though I'd never be able to write a thank-you in return.

It was different for me now—I didn't have the ability to respond in ways I once could, but at least I was getting a thrill out of the ways I could connect.

Sneaky me, I was there in Principal Falcon's office on Wednesday with Zara and Eva and their business cards. Before the meeting I had arranged that on his way to the school that morning Principal Falcon would see a girl with curly red hair running on the side of the road. He would do a double take, but it wasn't me; she was at least five years older than me and ran for exercise, not competitively. Seeing her reminded Principal Falcon of my passion for running, and the track records I had set for the school.

Coach Berlet joined them in their meeting, and he was almost tearing up when Zara and Eva said they wanted to do a Sprint-A-Thon in my memory and donate the proceeds to Speedy's. I think he even felt guilty he didn't think of it first. He suggested that the girls on the track team would probably volunteer their time for it, to help set up and check in the sprinters, time runners, and promote it. Coach Berlet seemed happy with himself for his suggestion, but also he seemed guilty for something that I couldn't place. There was a lot on his mind having to do with my absence, and I wondered what it was.

Zara and Eva set their goal to raise $2,012 dollars in pledges and donations, in memory of the month and day I had died. That was sweet, but this was their first event, so who knew how many people would want to run a lap for me and how much they'd raise for it.

Originally a big track invitational was planned for that weekend, but Coach Berlet would work it out to hold the invitational another weekend. So April 26th it was! My birthday gift came early this year.

I was excited and couldn't wait until race day, although the apologetic energy around Coach Berlet worried me.

On Wednesday evening, Eva started writing the first draft of their post announcing the Sprint-A-Thon. Zara sent an e-mail to Scott Arthur, the director at Speedy's, and heard back right away. Scott was honored to have Speedy's involved; he had been at my funeral and was happy that there was going to be a running-related event planned in my memory. And although I looked away, there had been a few bids on their prom dresses.

Jett wasn't at Zara's that night. She was happy to hear about us nailing my birthday for our first event, but she had gotten clip-on hair extensions and wanted to spend the night figuring them out. When Jett had the extensions clipped in, she'd feel a little bit normal again, but was having a frustrating time getting them to fully cover the bare areas on her head. Her scalp was sore. It hurt each time she clipped the extensions to the strands of hair that were left on her head. She got frustrated during the process because she wanted to make sure they were securely attached and wouldn't fall out when she moved her head around; she needed to practice making them look perfect, because it would take a long time for her real hair to grow back.

The week was flying by, and I was proud of my friends, but it was a little draining for me as they prepared a fundraiser that involved another race I wouldn't be running. It was all constant reminders that my days as a track runner were over, and it was excruciating. I wanted to be happy; I really wanted to ignore my feeling of lonesomeness.

The feeling of emptiness was always there, even though I wanted this event to happen. I had gotten what I wanted and didn't want to carry around my anger about dying.

I was being celebrated, I was being cared for, and I knew it was selfish of me, but I wished someone had been there, behind the scenes of my life doing what they could to make sure things turned out right for me and my life.

## MAKE THE MEMORY MEANINGFUL

On Thursday Eva had rewritten the post about eighty times until they were all happy with it, titling the post: *"Run with Your Heart for Estella at the Sprint-A-Thon!"*

When Eva pressed Post, we all felt antsy knowing the word was out. I felt all this pressure, actually, being the motive for the Sprint-A-Thon.

Next they put the Estella Productions blog link on each of their Annex profile pages. Now we just had to wait for interest to build for the Sprint-A-Thon and market the heck out of it.

While waiting for the first clicks and comments, Zara pulled her sketchbook out of her schoolbag and said to us, "I want you to see something I drew."

All week Zara had perfected her running shoe and angel wing sketches, and she was feeling more and more confident about presenting it to us.

"I drew this for us, in memory of Estella." Eva and Jett immediately smiled while looking at the illustration. It wasn't just a simple side view of a running shoe and angel wing—it was elaborate. The wing had many feathers, and the first and largest feather soared off the back of the shoe to create a long curve. Along the curve were the words "In memory of" with my initials E.M.M., and below that feather were many other feathers. They were all so detailed and almost looked soft to touch. Around the shoe and angel wing was a pretty lace design.

They said how pretty it was and how cool it looked.

Eva wanted to use it as a logo for posters, T-shirts, and marketing material for the Sprint-A-Thon.

After they got excited about that, Zara surprised us all and said, "I think it would be really cool as a tattoo."

A permanent, lifelong impression on their skin was a serious thing, daring and exciting at the same time.

They all wanted it, and weren't going to tell their parents, because what if one said no? The tattoo would be pointless if they all couldn't get it. They decided to get it on their lower back this Sunday. Zara figured the pain of it wouldn't be anything compared to how she had felt after the fight. There was a tattoo artist Jett had worked with who also did airbrush tattoos and body art for photographers. Jett swore the tattoo artist was exceptionally talented and safe; he would hook them up if girls promised not to tell anyone where they got the tattoos since they were under eighteen.

I never expected my friends to inject ink into their skin for me, but I was also jealous that I wouldn't be getting one with them this Sunday.

⌇

Awareness for the Sprint-A-Thon was already moving at a good pace, and I blushed and breezed down the hallways while hearing students say that they hated to run but would do it for me. Zara and Eva had handed out almost all of their business cards, and many students were impressed that they were starting their own company for me.

It had been a very tiring week for Zara in her wheelchair—she could hardly lift her laptop, her body was like a fragile old lady's—and maybe it was because of all their hustling and promotion efforts but Eva was now slower than usual on her crutches. It bothered me when a bunch of girls gossiped about how pale she looked.

At least it was Friday.

Jett had survived the first week of the Alternative High School. Without modeling and without Kyle, she started to think about what else she could do with her life and what other skills she had. She doubted that anyone would hire her looking like she did. I told her soul that when she was comfortable with herself again, she would build new goals and dreams, and other people would see the potential in her as well.

Tonight the girls were enjoying their Friday night movie ritual. Jett kept touching her luscious clip-on hair extensions, which made her hair so shiny and full again and she seemed less depressed, at least for the moment.

We were all cozy on Zara's couch. They each had a bowl of popcorn, and I wanted to taste the butter and salt. I wanted to tell Eva, "If you're not going to eat that, I will!"

She looked really uncomfortable; she kept moving around and adjusting her position. You could hear her stomach grumbling over the movie, and her dizziness made her want to vomit, although she hadn't eaten much today.

I had a feeling she was having another diet pill meltdown when she jumped up on one leg and hopped as fast as she could to the bathroom without her crutches. We wondered what was wrong.

She was in the bathroom for a very long time, and some awful sounds came out of it. We could hear her gagging and crying. The girls found her clutching the toilet seat and panting with dry heaves.

She looked extremely gaunt, and her forehead felt hot. Immediately Zara wanted to call 911 and get her father, but Eva said she just needed to lie down.

On the couch, surrounded by Zara's and Jett's closeness and care, Eva admitted something I never thought she'd say to the girls.

I held Eva's hand and kept telling her to tell them. She took her time to finally spit it out because she was so exhausted from gagging. "I've...been...taking...diet pills every day...even before Estella died."

Her eyes looked hollow and blank, and her mouth was really dry. Finally Zara and Jett could see how unhealthy she looked and how blind they had been not to question her about her weight loss sooner. Zara, still sore from her injuries, hurried to get some water and juice, yelling for Jett to stay with Eva. They told Eva to drink up and placed an ice pack on her head to relieve her fever.

Eva moaned, grabbed at her stomach, and told them how horrible she felt about herself, that she wanted to be skinny like them and had been hoping to be skinny for prom, and that Caleb had been giving her the pills.

"Where's your phone?" Zara demanded. Without waiting for Eva to tell her, she dove into Eva's purse, snatched it, and started dialing Caleb.

Aching and still dizzy, Eva had a hard time getting up off the couch. She yelled at Zara to give her the phone, frantically screaming, "Stop it, Zara! Don't call him!"

I rubbed against Eva's forehead and told her to calm down. Zara was ripping Caleb apart, telling Eva that he could have killed her, then bashing Caleb, he was a horrible person and that Eva was worth more than his scum ass. It was the best!

It was too bad for Eva. Zara didn't care that she was furious at her; Zara told Caleb that if he gave Eva another bottle of pills she would raise hell, and she hoped he'd go there. Zara was quite serious when she said Eva better stay away from him.

I wasn't sure what the door to hell looked like, or if it even existed. But I was glad after the crash, when I came back down from whirling around between life and death, that my world was still filled with the good people I had known. The typical asshole or bitch here and there made me feel thankful, because not everyone would end up in such a familiar place.

# Careful

## WHAT YOU WANT COULD BE RIGHT IN FRONT OF YOU

Preparing myself for the worst, Saturday afternoon I seeped through the thin layer of snow and went under the ground to check on my face and body. It had only been a month, but I looked dreadful, a lot worse than the day I died.

Although my face was smashed from the crash I could still make out where my eyes, nose, and mouth had originally been. I looked so disgusting—my pale skin was turning greenish, and in some areas it was purple and black. Sections of my curly auburn hair had fallen out already. I knew in time all of my skin and even the shape of my body would disintegrate—I feared to know what was going on under my dress.

Before long there would be nothing but my white prom dress, the satin blanket, and my skeleton stuck under the earth.

I shriveled up imagining it. Down here it was dark, an endless sorrowful dungeon. I didn't want to stay long, and felt relieved when a gust of warmth came down from above.

Above me someone was approaching my grave, and I zoomed up to see who it was.

There was Phoenix. I froze.
He was standing beside the mound in front of my grave.
I became nervous like a little girl.
It was exactly one month after I had died.
It was different when I visited him in his bedroom, because he might not have always known I was there, but I knew he was here, he was visiting me.

He stood there looking down at my grave. The snow had melted a little this past week, and my name could be made out clearly on it. He held a bouquet of yellow daffodils in his hand, the brightest yellow flowers I had ever seen. I fluttered around each petal, while he bent down to place the bouquet—my bouquet—near my grave. When he did I felt reborn.

The sun peeked out from the clouds, and sunlight was glowing on us both. It was serene, and he said softly, "I…just wanted to say hi."

He looked awkward standing there talking to me but added, "I'm sorry it wasn't sooner."

I wanted to jump in his arms so I swirled around him.

He quietly looked down at the earth in front of my grave—the mound of dirt had finally flattened out more. Maybe he was thinking about how my body lay below it. I could feel his thoughts of me; I could feel him remembering my curly auburn-colored hair when he whispered with his gentle heart, "I wish I could see you again."

It was the best thing anyone ever told me in my life.

I wished he could.

Actually, never mind. I was glad he couldn't see my distorted face rotting away below us, each day a little more.

I reached for his hand even though I knew it wouldn't work.

I wanted him to stay with me here all day, especially when he put his hand in his coat pocket and pulled out my silver ladybug charm that had hung from my car's rear-view mirror. He had won it for me at the Harbor Fest last October. It had been missing since the crash, and I couldn't believe it was in his hand.

On the way to the cemetery he must have pulled over to see the cross my mother had placed near the site of the crash and found the ladybug charm at the side of the road, peering out from under the melting snow.

He was now giving it to me.

At the ground near my gravestone, he pushed away some melting snow and stuck the chain of the ladybug charm into the stiff soil to keep it secure.

It looked really pretty there.

Slowly he walked away. I didn't want him to leave, and I stayed by my grave for a while rewinding his visit over and over. I didn't want our moment to pass me by.

Holding onto the moment, I leaned against my grave. The only sound was a few cars driving by. I had the whole afternoon to relish the warm and treasured feeling from his visit; I was truly at peace, until a car parked alongside the cemetery gate.

Immediately I recognized it—it was Sonia's car. Jett had bashed her side mirrors, but those were easy to replace, a lot easier to fix than Gwen's car.

It made me nervous when Sonia and Gwen got out of the car—and Heidi too.

A frigid surge of air came right at me.

Gwen held a bouquet of flowers in her hand, but they weren't for me. They weren't here to see me.

I could hear Heidi asking Gwen in utter amazement, "You seriously sliced her face?"

"Sliced is a nice way to put it," Sonia said, laughing and bumping against Gwen's elbow like the two of them had formed an even tighter bond since the fight.

"She sliced my car, that's what she gets." Gwen was confident that Jett had gotten what she deserved.

"I heard her face is totally distorted," Sonia said with some astonishment in her tone.

"Oh well." Gwen said, smirking like she was proud to have ruined Jett's face.

"That's insane!" Heidi's crackle, as she imagined Gwen holding a high heel in her hand and whacking it across Jett's face, made me wish I had power to make the pine tree they were walking by just happen to break and land on them all.

They made their way through the cemetery, their snickering filling the air. I could tell Sonia was especially uncomfortable walking among the graves, and she kept warning, "Careful, don't step on anyone!" She was a snot, joking around saying, "Watch out! You just stepped on someone!"

Someday I would show them. I'd make sure they realized how careless and heartless they were.

Heidi was also looking around in a cautious way, as if she was a little scared to be here in the cemetery among the graves, and asked, "Can we make this fast?"

I kept my distance as they went to see Gwen's grandmother, who was buried nearby.

I was sure it crossed Heidi's mind that my body was in this cemetery too. She had to have read the newspaper about the funeral and burial details or been told I was buried here.

The way her freshly trimmed bangs made her long eyelashes stand out, how her newly cut and styled dark blond hair swung back and forth so freely and the sunlight kissed her face like she was a goddess irritated me. I hated that she looked so polished.

She had no right to be here.

They had no respect for the dead with their loud mouths, acting as if they were on some historical adventure while looking at how old or young the graves were around them.

I stiffened when Sonia said, "Look at this one," and they all looked at a grave of a girl who died when she was only three years old.

Their oohing and aahing over the old graves in the cemetery upset me. This wasn't a place to poke fun at the graves that were so old the date of death was hardly legible, or stand over the dead and gawk at their resting place.

Their presence disrupted the peace. I wished they'd leave.

While Gwen placed her flowers at her grandmother's grave, Heidi's eyes panned across the cemetery. We were soon staring at each other, her eyes fixed on my grave, maybe because the mound in front of it looked fresher than the other graves around it.

I tensed up when she told Sonia and Gwen she would be right back, and started to walk in my direction. She was drawing closer and closer to me and my grave.

Only a few feet away from my grave, she ran her hands through her hair and twirled the ends in a nervous way. I was happy that the sight of my grave made her uncomfortable. I knew Heidi hadn't planned to visit my grave this weekend. She thought it was rude of Sonia and Gwen to make her trek through the cemetery to see Gwen's grandmother, when she would have rather spent her time away from the correctional institute surrounded by the luxuries of manicures, facials, and a steak dinner—not death.

But here she was. Right in front of my grave, staring at my name and the day I died.

I wanted to tell her that one day she would die. She would be under the earth, unable to move. One day it could be all over for her too, and who knew where she'd end up afterward.

It would have been great to tell her that she ruined my life, and show her each detail of my broken body. Maybe she would fall to the ground and say she was sorry over and over but I doubted it. I studied her loathing expression as she looked down at my name, her eyes holding nothing but disdain for me. But I wasn't the one who put her in the correctional institute—she shouldn't blame me.

There were no words between us at all. Standing in front of me, she didn't say anything about the beautiful gravestone picked out by my parents, or that she was sorry I had died, or that she couldn't believe I was under the ground below her. I wanted her to go away, go back to her beautifying, and long life.

"Looks like someone recently put those there." Sonia was standing next to us now and pointed to Phoenix's daffodils. I wanted to tell Sonia, "Yeah, I get visitors all the time, and you have no right to be here." When she stepped closer to my flowers, I helped flick her gaze away when the wind brushed against her eyes.

Gwen was finishing up kneeling by her Grandmother's grave and was about to join them, to see what they were looking at.

Heidi stood there beside the mound above my casket, with her arms wrapped around herself, like she was cold. Maybe she was imagining what it would be like to feel even colder while lying buried in a dark casket and decaying under the ground, but probably not.

She never could handle it. I wanted to tell her she had no idea the type of strength it took to be dead and how well I was taking it, but it would be a lie. I wished my frightening face and peeling skin could rise up from my grave and scare the shit out of her.

When Gwen came over she looked surprised and said quietly, "Oh, Is that her?"

Heidi and Sonia nodded their heads slowly.

Gwen stood between them and put her arms across both of their shoulders. From a distance it might have looked like my friends were visiting me and having a deep moment together, only it was the opposite. Heidi, Gwen, and Sonia didn't look miserable enough, their energy wasn't heartfelt enough—they were like three weeds ruining my beautiful plot.

Heidi shook off Gwen's arm after a moment, stepping back away from me and my grave like she was ready to leave.

Maybe the truth of things was hitting the small voice in her heart, and it was telling her all the things I wanted to say. Well, I hoped so anyway.

I wanted just one tear to roll down Heidi's cheek for me, just one.

Every time she took a step away I took a step toward her, until I was right in Heidi's face and went over her facial features with the cold wind. I wanted her soul to know that one day she'd realize she had been the lucky one. One day she'd feel bad and do something to let my friends and family know she was sorry.

I told her to get out of here and never come back, not until she had something sincere to say.

Maybe they could all feel my presence, because Sonia reached for Heidi and Gwen, saying, "Let's get out of here. Cemeteries freak me out. Come on, we're going to be late!"

Sonia and Gwen had set up a manicure and pedicure session for them all to enjoy before Heidi met Jackson for dinner. They couldn't even leave in peace—on the way out Sonia dared Heidi to hurdle an old grave. I felt horrible when she cleared it and their laughing rolled over the whole cemetery again.

Heidi did look back toward my grave once, but I didn't believe that meant she was sorry. Sonia and Gwen always would be there to remind Heidi that it wasn't her fault. In their minds, Heidi didn't need to blame herself or carry around a guilt trip, because it had been my fault for driving foolishly and killing myself. But I hoped in time she would be deeply changed by seeing where my body was now.

All she was thinking about was probably steak. Jackson had made a reservation for the two of them at The Harkrider, one of the most expensive steakhouses in town. It was to be a grand hullabaloo weekend for her, full of good food and pampering.

I would do my best to avoid them all.

I hopped up to the tallest grave in the cemetery, which was over one hundred and fifty years old, and pushed off of it with the sharp chill of March cooing at my back. I traveled with the roaring wind, letting it take me wherever.

It pulled me toward downtown Syracuse.

I peeked into a counseling session. My mother and father were sitting with a grief counselor, and my mother was telling them about our drive around the lake. My father was looking at my mother with lost puppy dog eyes; it was the first time he had heard about this, but I was glad he knew about our secret drive.

Around my mother's neck was my "e" charm necklace. After our drive around the lake she wore it often, rubbing the charm between her fingers to calm her nerves. I knew she didn't want to be telling a stranger about her anger and pain.

I was proud of her for wearing some color today. She had done her hair too, and I slid down the curls of her reddish hair and the gray strands that now looked like silver. I wanted to let her know I was there. When she ran her hands through the strands I had touched and shared with my father and the counselor the hope she felt by wearing my necklace, it was like she could feel me nearby.

I felt a sense of peace being there, watching her speak. I knew it was hard for her to say out loud that she had been struggling. I was proud of my father too, for admitting he had been drinking a lot more than usual lately and that he often felt the urge to smoke a cigarette.

I only stayed for a little while longer and then went to see what Evan was up to.

He wasn't at his place near the Le Moyne College campus, and I could feel his energy somewhere in the neighborhood but decided to just spread my hello all over his room.

On his desk was a notepad with the words Sprint-A-Thon on it, so I knew my mother had told him about it and was glad he knew.

Like hands, I cupped myself around the dark knight chess pieces on his dresser and said into them what I wanted to say to Evan. "I know, and I don't care who you choose to love or be with. It's okay with me, just as long as you have someone who is true."

～

That evening, secretly and behind Zara's back, Eva was getting dolled up to meet Caleb; his parents were at the Turning Stone Casino for the night and there was plenty of alcohol at his house to drink. After drinking it they'd probably cuddle in his basement until after midnight. I didn't plan on witnessing it.

When Zara said she was tired and not in the mood to go out, Brett texted back that he wasn't feeling good either. It was only eight p.m., and they said goodnight with many *xoxoxos*.

Something made me feel skeptical about Brett's text message. He didn't have any symptoms of a cold or flu to be sick all of a sudden. Zara had been too tired to question him about why he didn't feel well, and I wanted to believe him. He had always been a good guy to her, and I went through my memories of him and the vibes I felt while going to check on Jett.

She was standing over her stove burner. The flame was on and she was burning a page of a fashion magazine. A stack of magazines with beautiful women on the covers sat on the counter. She burned glossy page after glossy page, then stacked the burnt pages on top of each other in another pile. She liked watching the pages get crisp and hot, and would blow out the flame or let the sink water extinguish it. When she was finished she took them outside, dug a hole, and buried them.

She looked really happy and relieved when she was finished with her therapy project. Without her mother at home tonight to yell at her or call her stupid and ugly, she'd enjoy the night watching romantic movies. I could tell she wasn't in the mood to be around anyone, and maybe she just wanted to be alone. I sat with her for a little while, wanting to help her when she started to peel off the bandages from her face, to let her face get some air.

I had let Heidi's presence slip out of my worries and I went to find Phoenix at the arcade.

He had a gun in his hand and was playing some hunting game. The thought of dead animals made me cringe, even if it was just a game, but he looked cute standing there, so cute in his shooting stance, and I went over to him.

When Phoenix's arcade card loaded a grand amount of winning points, I wanted to squeeze him tight. He was going to play again. Maybe I would have actually asked to try to shoot one if I had been alive, and maybe he would have been impressed with how well I could hit a target.

We were heading over to the prize counter; I had just looped myself through Phoenix's arm, when a gust of deceitful energy overshadowed the air around us.

I wished it wasn't true. Brett's arm was wrapped around that chick. I had seen her in the halls—she was some sophomore foreign exchange student, from Russia, I think.

That little brat was pleading with Brett to let her have the huge white fluffy bunny that hung behind the prize counter. I shook myself. He was unbelievable.

When Phoenix saw them together a troubled feeling washed over him. We both knew it wasn't right.

That night I didn't follow Brett and the girl, not wanting to know where they were going after the arcade. I wanted to believe they were just friends and it was innocent, but I felt desperate to call Zara.

I wanted to run to her and was starting to leave when I was jerked back by a burst of deadly cold air colliding into me. It knocked me down like a hard punch to the face.

Heidi had just walked into the arcade.

Like they were walking the red carpet, waving hello to everyone, Jackson presented Heidi on his arm as if she was a famous celebrity, and she was spreading hugs around the arcade.

I stayed low to the ground, looking up at her malicious smile.

She never got to hug Phoenix, thank God.

Being at my grave that afternoon made it extremely awkward for him to see Heidi now. I'm glad he realized it was best to not stay at the arcade. I wanted him to leave and was relieved when he put on his coat and snuck out the back exit before Jackson and Heidi could notice him.

Although Phoenix didn't know Heidi and her friends had also been at my grave that afternoon, I wished the last person to visit me today had been him. I hated knowing Heidi and her stupid friends had stood in front of my grave after him and taken over the air he had stood within. They ruined the peaceful moment he had left there for me. I had to get out of the arcade.

In a few minutes Sonia and Gwen would show up, and Jackson and Heidi would be laughing with them. But all I could hear was a dog howling for help and the rattling of a chain. I wondered why these awful sounds were coming at me.

I followed the trail from the howls to see what was going on.

In the cold night air, I approached a dog.

The dog had gotten loose, but the chain was still around his neck while he ran wildly toward the thruway. Just minutes ago, he had been pounding the pavement and breathing happily, but now his free-spirited run came to a sudden stop. It wasn't just the whack to the ribs and the crunch to his legs, or the car smacking against the dog's nose—his death came in a more gruesome way.

The chain around the dog's neck got caught in the car's tires. The dog was dragged for about mile, thumping along the thruway, the chain choking him until it broke and he was flung into a ditch beside the road. The careless driver didn't even stop to see if the dog was okay.

Heidi loved that dog. It was like a member of her family, and she hated to leave him behind while she spent time at the correctional institute.

Her parents knew she hadn't been out with Jackson and her friends in a while and didn't want to dampen her fun night by texting her that the dog got loose. So they waited, figuring the dog would come home soon.

The dog was still lying there in the ditch. Cars were whisking by, and every time one passed, the glow from its headlights would shine on the dog's body.

I knelt down beside him and quickly realized his soul had escaped. He was gone.

Heidi would be incredibly heartbroken.

I should have loved that she could feel the pain from something so horrible and brutal, but I didn't feel anything good about it.

On Sunday morning, while Heidi discovered her dog was dead, and her parents collected the dog's remains and prepared to bury it in their backyard by a lilac tree, I focused on the tattoo needles going in and out of Zara's skin.

The illustration of the shoe and angel wing was taped to the wall. Eva and Jett were waiting their turn and admiring how beautiful the angel wing already looked on Zara's lower back. The artist was doing a great job with the shading, highlighting, and detail—the angel wing appeared so soft and delicate, and the shoe looked exactly like a pair of my running shoes.

Our everlasting friendship was marked when my initials E.M.M were etched into their skin.

It did look painful, and it took a lot of patience to stay still, so they held each other's hands through it and sang songs.

It took all day. They had lied to their parents, saying they were going to get an early brunch together, see a movie, do some shopping, and visit my grave.

Once their lower backs were imprinted with my memory in the same way, they did go visit me at my grave. I beat them to it, of course.

The sun was shining again, and I leaned against the side of my gravestone while waiting on them, just letting the warmth of the day embrace me.

Eva led the way on her crutches, while Jett pushed Zara in her wheelchair up the slight hill toward my grave. They had brought me fresh flowers, which they placed next to Phoenix's daffodils.

They didn't say much, but they didn't have to. I knew they hadn't healed, not from my death or the fight, but I was confident that one day things would get better.

As they held hands and smiled at me, I smiled back at each of them. As long as we had each other we would be fine.

Jett helped Zara stand up. It was cute when they lifted up their coats and sweaters to show me their fresh tattoos. I admired them so much. I had the strongest friends in the world—and the most beautiful. It had nothing to do with their faces, or how skinny they were, or how much money they had. They helped me pull through, and being with them made it easier to handle my feeling of displacement in this new state of existence. I didn't feel so alone.

That evening I went to Willow Lake before sundown to be close to nature. I loved to be around the wind, the air, the landscape of this earth; I'd collect the energies from them all and wonder about the purpose of things.

After a while the moon was out, so round and large and bright, shining on Willow Lake. I stopped by Maple Point and climbed up to the top of my favorite maple tree to feel the largeness of the full moon staring right back at me. But after a while I felt too lively to stay still. There'd be other full moons to appreciate.

I traveled through the neighborhoods of my hometown and stopped at my best friends' houses. I didn't always say goodnight to my friends, but I had an impulse tonight.

Zara was sound asleep and must have been too tired to take off her makeup; smudges of lipstick were on her pillow. Like a comforting massage I rubbed softly along her sore back, shoulder blades, and skull, knowing she'd be inspired to put her marketing skills to use again soon—and she'd do better than she expected on the SAT too. Even when she found out the truth about Brett, the pain from that heartbreak would later lead her to something true and long-lasting.

I took my short cut through the ghetto part of Willow Ridge to Eva's. The diet pills were still hidden in her dresser drawer, but her face didn't look as pale. I kissed her forehead, hoping she'd finally realize she didn't need them anymore, or Caleb. I wanted her to know that when she was true to herself, she would become such a positive influence for others.

Jett's bandaged face was fully hidden under her covers. I glided under her bandages, passed over the cuts on her face, and spread my care into her wounds. She'd find her confidence again. I knew she would find a reason to love herself again. Under and around her skin her soul was waiting. It just wanted the chance.

I hopped out Jett's window and soared toward home.

My parents were already tucked in bed and just about to drift to sleep. Pressed against my mother's heart, I told her everything would be okay, and she reached for my father's hand. I gave my father a hug and whispered that I wanted to run with him again, and wanted him to make some time for us soon.

As I snuggled up against Phoenix, another day came to an end, and everything felt like it was right where it should be. Of course, I dwelled that if I didn't spend those extra minutes to buy that strapless padded bra I might still be alive. I still regretted buying it, but I settled into a calm, comfortable position and prepared to make some peace with myself.

I hadn't been ready to die. Death snuck in and grabbed me, and it had happened too fast for me to do all the things I wanted to do. But it wasn't too late for me to share myself now in these new ways. I just had to accept it, because there would be more memories for us. There would always be a brand-new moment to share with my friends and family—we still had a lot time, a lot of time to spend together.

Tomorrow was a new Monday.
I'd been dead for a month.

I couldn't stop time from moving forward. Time moves unstoppably, and each day would take me further away from the day I had died and what could have been. But I could still be here, along for the ride.

Phoenix had decided not to play lacrosse this season and barely noticed the first practice passing him by. He didn't seem to miss it or his teammates, because he had a new group, his friends from architecture class. But I really missed running.

At the first outdoor track practice Coach Berlet chose one of the slowest runners on the team, a girl who never, ever won a race, to take my place as the captain. He knew being the captain had meant a lot to me, and the whole thing frustrated me at first. I couldn't believe I could be replaced so quickly. It was hard to deal with how my death could help others advance. Many of my teammates who had been in my shadow would now get their chance to shine on the track. I wanted to be big enough to be happy for them, but I hated it. It would hurt for a while, but like many things, I would learn to accept it.

This month was full of surprises, full of great changes, and there was another unexpected surprise about to show up. I could feel its shivering cold energy and knew the direction it was coming from.

It was in the form of a letter. It was being sent to Eva's house right now and would arrive soon. I wasn't sure why Heidi would even dare write a letter to one of my friends, but I could hope perhaps the words inside expressed the remorse I wanted to hear from her. Maybe losing something that she had loved reminded her of how quickly it could all be taken away. Just maybe she realized what she took away from me.

# Acknowledgements

While writing this book I was going through my own deep grief and couldn't settle on the end of life being the end-all. My father believed there was more out there, and I started thinking a lot about that and what happens to the soul when we die and how the energy and love within a person and all living things doesn't just fade. There have been many signs of my father since he passed and I can tell his spirit lives on. Losing him has been the greatest heartache of my life, but I have a belief that goodbye doesn't have to be goodbye, it's just a different type of hello. I want to thank my father for his words of wisdom that are always on my mind.

Very warm thanks go to my mother Isabel White and sister Lauren Carpenter for their support and constant care.

I also want to thank Jennifer DeMeritt, Stephanie Nikolopoulos and Kerry Cohen.

A special and loving thanks goes to my husband Todd Harkrider, my best friend, whose love and belief in me inspires me.

Isobella Jade was raised in the Syracuse, NY area, where she went to high school and was a competitive track runner. She now lives in New York City with her husband. Isobella is known as one of the shortest models out there and also is the author of her modeling memoir titled *Almost 5'4", Short Stuff: on the job with an x-small model,* a collection of short stories with tips and advice for height challenged models, and a graphic novel *Model Life.*

The *Careful, Quiet, Invisible* series was partially inspired by her father's tragic sudden death in 2011. To learn more about the series stop by her website: www.isobelladreams.com

*Careful*

STOP BY WWW.ISOBELLADREAMS.COM FOR EXCLUSIVE *CAREFUL, QUIET, INVISIBLE* SERIES UPDATES AND SPECIAL PROMOTIONS.

CPSIA information can be obtained at www.ICGtesting.com
Printed in the USA
BVOW020916130712

294966BV00011B/1/P